CW01096073

A FRESH START AT WAGGING TAILS DOGS' HOME

SARAH HOPE

Boldwood

First published in Great Britain in 2024 by Boldwood Books Ltd.

Cover Design by Head Design Ltd

Cover Illustration: Shutterstock

A CIP catalogue record for this book is available from the British Library.

Paperback ISBN 978-1-80549-070-8

Large Print ISBN 978-1-80549-071-5

Hardback ISBN 978-1-80549-069-2

Ebook ISBN 978-1-80549-072-2

Kindle ISBN 978-1-80549-073-9

Audio CD ISBN 978-1-80549-064-7

MP3 CD ISBN 978-1-80549-065-4

Digital audio download ISBN 978-1-80549-068-5

Boldwood Books Ltd
23 Bowerdean Street
London SW6 3TN
www.boldwoodbooks.com

For my children. Let's change our stars.

xXx

1

Sally paused again, probably for the eighth time that morning, and waited for Puddles to stop lunging on his lead. Blowing her hair from her face, she looked across at Alex who had borrowed Dougal, Poppy's cockapoo, and pocketed the treat she'd been using in an attempt to distract the small dachshund.

'I think I'm going to have to start back at the beginning with his training. Sorry for wasting your time, Alex.'

'Hey, no problem. He's a real rascal, isn't he?' Alex began to walk Dougal towards the paddock gate.

Sally waited until Puddles had calmed down before following, keeping a few paces behind.

'See, this is fine. He's walking like an angel now.' She glanced down as Puddles' little legs ran to keep up with her and pulled a treat from her pocket. 'Good boy, Puddles.'

'You'll get there with him.' Alex slipped through the gate from the top paddock into the bottom paddock, leaving it unlatched for Sally. 'You always do. We don't call you the dog whisperer for nothing.'

'Ha ha, I think Puddles might actually make me hand that title back.' Sally pulled the gate open. 'That's the third time I think I've managed to train him not to lunge or bark at other dogs walking past, and the third time he's shown me up. Honestly, no one would believe I actually thought he was ready.'

'I believe you.' Alex glanced over his shoulder, looked at Puddles, and frowned. 'That's the problem when we don't have a dog's history – we have no idea what he's faced in his little life.'

'I know.' Sally swallowed. 'Flora thinks he may have been used as bait in a dog-fighting ring. The scars suggest it.' She bent down and traced her finger across the large crescent-shaped scar on his back leg before fussing him behind the ears. He could be a royal pain with other dogs, but he was the complete opposite with humans, trusting and loving – a small miracle if he had been mistreated.

'I've said it before and I'll say it again, I hate humans.' Alex shook his head before looking back at Sally and grinning. 'Apart from my Wagging Tails family, of course.'

'Of course!' Sally laughed. 'I know what you mean though – some people just don't deserve the love of an animal.'

'Nope.' Alex pointed ahead towards the courtyard. 'Looks as though we've got company. What do you think? Prospective adopter or someone looking to surrender their pup?'

'Umm…' Sally peered ahead, squinting her eyes to make out the man's head. 'Neither. He doesn't look like a dog person. Besides, I shouldn't think he could kneel and pet a dog in that suit. My guess is a salesperson.'

Alex nodded. 'Good spot.'

'Years of working in law will give you that.'

Maybe the years she'd spent training to be a solicitor hadn't gone to waste after all. She paused to let Alex through the gate into the courtyard before following with Puddles. She shook her head. That felt like a lifetime ago now.

'I guess we'll soon find out.' Alex kicked the gate wide, so it stayed open for Sally.

'I'm sure we will. In fact, I'll leave Puddles in here for a run around whilst we go speak to him.'

Bending down, Sally unclasped the bright green lead from Puddles' collar and distracted him by throwing a ball as she slipped through the gate.

'You don't fancy testing Puddles' social skills on a stranger?'

'Not on one who looks as though he'd be happy to sue us if Puddles so much as stares at him.' Sally laughed as she watched the man hovering at the gate leading to the lane outside Wagging Tails. There was something about him that made her feel uneasy – she'd never been a fan of goatees on a man, but it wasn't that, it was something else. Something about his presence.

'Fair point.' Alex paused as Sally jogged to catch him and Dougal up.

As they neared the gate, Sally pushed her shoulders back and plastered what she hoped was a welcoming grin on her face.

'Hi, how can we help you today?'

The man turned sharply and looked her up and down. 'Are you the owner of this place?'

'No, no, I'm not, but we both work here, so I'm sure we can help if you have a query.' Sally pushed her hands into her pockets and held his gaze. Over the years of training and studying law, she'd learned not to show people if she felt intimidated.

'Is she available to speak to me?'

'I'm afraid she isn't at the moment.'

And she wasn't. Flora had left for the suppliers a couple of hours ago. With anyone else, Sally would probably have offered to make them a cuppa and let them wait – Flora would be back any minute now – but not him, though. The sooner he left, the better.

'In that case, can I ask you to go to the trouble of ensuring she receives a letter?' The man leaned his briefcase on the top of the gate and clicked it open.

Sally glanced down at Dougal, who had positioned himself behind Alex's legs, his head leaning against the back of his knees.

'Of course,' she said.

'Thank you.' The man thrust a white envelope towards her before clicking shut his briefcase and turning away.

'Well, he was jolly nice.' Alex scowled as he watched the man step into his BMW and drive away.

'I'm glad it wasn't just me who felt something was off with him. Did you see the way Dougal reacted?'

Kneeling down, she fussed over the small cockapoo.

'I felt it. I have a nice warm patch behind my knees now.' Alex chuckled. 'Never mind, I'm sure that'll be the last we see of him. He didn't particularly seem a dog person – and that's an understatement – so I can't imagine he wanted to enquire about adoption.' Alex turned. 'I'll pop the kettle on while you put Puddles back into his kennel. Tea or coffee?'

'Coffee please. Strong with—'

'Two sugars because even though you're sweet enough as you are, there's always room for improvement.' Alex jumped back to avoid the empty poop bag Sally threw at him. 'Hey, I was being nice!'

'Ha ha, I'd hate to hear you say something horrible then!' Sally laughed and held out her hand. 'Can I have that poop bag back, please? It's my last one.'

Alex scrunched up his face and held the small bag in the air before passing it to her. 'Go on then, even if only to prove to you how nice I am.'

'Thanks.' She took the bag and held her hand up as she turned away. 'See you in a min.'

As she walked back towards the bottom paddock, Sally glanced towards the gate out onto the lane and shuddered. She'd got such a funny feeling from that man, and she just couldn't shake off a sense of unease. She looked down at the envelope in her hand. Apart from 'The Owner' typed in Times Roman in black ink, the envelope gave nothing away – no watermark or return address – nothing.

Sally pocketed the poop bag and tucked the envelope under her arm before opening the gate into the bottom paddock.

'Puddles, over here.' Sally knelt down as Puddles trotted over, waiting until he'd sat next to her before clipping his lead to his collar. 'You're such a little mystery, aren't you? You can't stand other dogs but you're so well trained in all other aspects and I think possibly even the most well-behaved pup we've had at Wagging Tails. Come on, let's get you back in the warmth of your kennel.'

She began walking towards the gate and looked down at him. She smiled as his little legs sped along at a million miles per hour just to keep up with her slow walk. He must have an owner out there somewhere, a loving family who were missing him. It was the only explanation she and Flora could think of. He must have been stolen before he'd been abandoned on the streets.

She sighed. Darryl had plastered his photo throughout the *Trestow Telegraph* for weeks now, and Sally had posted information in numerous local and not-so-local social media groups, including his picture. All they could do now was cross their fingers and wait. Someone would be missing him. Sally was sure of that. They just had to hope that someone came forward soon.

'Let's get you inside.'

She pushed open the door to the reception area. As she slipped through to the kennels, she could hear Alex and Ginny talking in the kitchen. Alex was likely telling Ginny all about their encounter with the stranger by the gate. Flora would be back soon enough, and they could find out what was inside the mysterious envelope.

Sally wrapped the lead around her wrist to shorten it, readying herself for the inevitable. Yep, sure enough, as soon as they walked past the first kennel, Puddles began pulling on the lead and barking. She quickened her pace, making the journey to the very last kennel as fast as possible.

The tiny dachshund had barely been at Wagging Tails an hour before Flora had made the decision to move him into the kennel at the far end. Yes, it meant he had to be walked past the other dogs on his way in and out, but it was better than him becoming distressed every time another dog was walked past his kennel. At least this way he could hopefully relax once he was safely inside his temporary home.

'Here we go, home sweet home for now, little Puddles.'

Sally unclipped Puddles' collar and closed the kennel door before standing and watching him. They all knew they were kidding themselves – he never relaxed, not fully. He was always on guard, waiting to be forced to choose between flight or fight.

Taking a treat from her pocket, Sally bent down and slipped it through the metal bars.

'Whatever has happened to you, you're safe here, Puddles. I just wish you could understand that.'

With a sigh, she made her way back into the reception area. She let the door swing quietly shut behind her and looked out across the courtyard. The van was parked outside now. Flora was back.

As she pushed the kitchen door open, Alex looked towards her.

'Here she is.' Alex held out a mug to her. 'I was just telling Flora and Ginny about the encounter we had with the strange man hovering by the gate.'

'The strange man hovering by the gate.' Ginny laughed. 'It sounds like the title to a thriller or something.'

'Oh, it could have been. He was really off, wasn't he, Sally?' Alex leaned against the counter, his hands wrapped around his mug.

'I don't think he was here to adopt, he didn't seem at all interested in Dougal, who we had with us at the time, and normally potential adopters at least greet the dogs.' As Sally placed her mug on the table, she pulled the envelope from her pocket. 'Here you go, Flora. He gave us strict instructions to pass this on to you.'

Flora turned the envelope over and rolled her eyes. 'I bet I know who this is from.'

'Who?' Ginny asked as she reached into the biscuit tin.

'A man called Lyle.'

Flora tore the envelope in two before scrunching it in the palm of her hand.

'Lyle? I don't think I've heard you talk about a Lyle before.' Ginny bit into her biscuit, and then quickly wiped away the crumbs from her top.

'Ooh, the mystery deepens. Who is he?' Alex hitched his mouth into a playful grin. 'An ex-lover's son who, after hunting you down for years, is after vengeance on behalf of his father after you ran off with his inheritance?'

'Ha ha, nothing so innocent, I'm afraid.' Flora chuckled. 'No, he works for a property developer who is trying to buy this place. He's rung me at least five times over the past month.'

'A property developer?' Sally raised her eyebrows.

'Yep, apparently his company bought the fields behind and has now decided they want to expand to include Wagging Tails.' Flora threw the scrunched-up pieces of envelope in the bin. 'Of course, it goes without saying that I won't be selling, and I'll be standing against planning permission being granted.'

'Too right. We don't want a huge housing estate behind us.' Alex shook his head.

'And think of the noise,' Ginny added.

'How much land have they bought?' Sally wrapped her hands around her mug.

'I'm not completely sure, but from the short conversation I had with him on the phone last week, it sounds like a lot. I'm assuming it's all of Mary and Giles's old place.'

'The whole farm? I thought they were selling it to another farmer?'

Sally took a sip of her tea. They'd known the farm was up for sale. After Mary had passed away last year, Giles had told them he would be putting the farm on the market. His children had no interest in continuing the family business and he'd decided to move to Wales to be nearer his daughter.

'I'm guessing so, yes. I assumed the same.'

'So what do they want with Wagging Tails?' Sally frowned. 'They'll have more than enough land to build on and make their millions, surely?'

Flora shrugged. 'Greed, I suppose.'

'Maybe. Still, if he's already contacted you, then it seems odd that he won't accept your decision.' Ginny pulled another Jammie Dodger from the tin. 'I could see if Darryl will ask around. I know he has a couple of contacts in the council. They might have heard something about this man's plans.'

'Oh yes please, if you wouldn't mind, Ginny, lovely.' Flora smiled. 'I'm not going to give it another thought, but it would be interesting if Darryl could find anything out.'

2

'I'm so glad you talked me into this.' Sally grinned and held up her bag of chips before flicking her hair from her eyes.

Ginny shifted position and stretched her legs out in front of her on the sand. 'Yes, well, you really do need to start taking proper lunch breaks.'

'Umm.' Sally looked out across the ocean. The day was warm, uncharacteristically so for this time of the year, but with it being term-time and out of season for tourists, they had the whole cove to themselves. Not that it got busy during the tourist season. Or Sally didn't think it did, anyway. She'd only arrived down here in West Par last summer, but it hadn't seemed as though their small village was a holiday hotspot or anything. Probably thanks to the village being small and positioned away from any main roads.

'You know I'm right and, besides, I have orders from Flora to try to encourage you not to work through your breaks.'

'You're a fine one to talk.' Sally laughed as she popped a chip into her mouth.

Ginny looked down at her feet and circled her ankles. 'Well, maybe, but we can't have you getting burned out, not with the likes of little Puddles relying on you. And besides, I don't have a second job – you do.'

'Yes, but the training sessions I do in the evening don't really feel like a job. I enjoy them.' Sally tucked a loose strand of hair behind her ears. 'A bit like working at Wagging Tails, really. That doesn't even feel remotely like work.'

'Ha ha, I know what you mean.' Ginny turned towards her. 'You haven't told me how your date went last night.'

'Oh, so that's the real reason you dragged me to the beach then – to quiz me about my love life?' Sally laughed as she watched a squabble of seagulls dip and dive over the water. 'Honestly, I've told him I don't see a future between us.'

'What?' Tucking her legs up beneath her, Ginny turned to face Sally. 'You only said yesterday that he's everything you look for in a guy.'

'I know. He is. He's kind, funny, and he wants the same things as me, but...' She shrugged.

'But what?'

'I don't know. He... I guess I just don't feel that spark.' She closed her eyes against the low spring sun.

'You literally said he was perfect.' Ginny scrunched up her forehead.

'And he is. On paper.' Even in real life, he'd been pretty perfect. Last night had been their second date, and they'd chatted into the small hours, taking their conversation to the all-night café in Trestow when the pub had closed.

'Umm... this is about your ex again, isn't it? You always do this. You meet these wonderful guys, but you always hold them up against him.'

'Huh, you remember me talking about Andy?'

'Of course I do. Especially being as the last time you spoke about him was before you went on the first date with this guy.'

'Oh.' Sally bit another chip in half, letting the salt linger on her tongue before it dissolved. She turned towards Ginny. 'Do I really talk about him that much?'

'Only when comparing the men on the dating sites to him. It's Andy this, Andy that.'

'Oi.' Sally threw a chip at Ginny. 'I'm not that bad.'

Ginny watched the chip land on top of her chip wrappers. 'Thanks very much.'

Smiling, Sally shook her head before frowning. 'Andy isn't even my ex. He's my ex, ex, ex...'

She counted it out on her fingers. It wasn't that she'd had lots of relationships since Andy. Quite the opposite. It was just that she hadn't let anyone get close to her the way she had with him and so all the relationships since had been fleeting – some would probably argue not even fully fledged relationships. Ginny was right. She compared every man she met to Andy. Which was daft. She knew it was. It had been seven years since they'd gone their separate ways. Seven years of building walls around her heart. Seven years of not giving any other man a chance.

'You're right, though. It is because of him, but what do I do about it? I can't help the way I feel. I mean felt.'

'I don't know. I've never had that problem. My ex, Jason, was the complete opposite.' Ginny shivered. 'He wasn't a very nice person at all.'

'See, that's my problem. It's because Andy was nice. He was kind, caring, funny... He was everything I look for in a guy.'

'I suppose you just need to remember why you split up.' Ginny pointed a chip at her. 'That should help you remove the rose-tinted glasses.'

Sally swallowed. 'That's why it's so difficult. It wasn't as though we split up because something went wrong in our relationship. We hardly even argued. It was quite the opposite, really. I had to move back to my hometown.' She placed her chip wrappers on her knees. 'No, that's not actually true. I felt like I should move back, to finish my training at my parents' law firm.'

'Why didn't he move back with you?'

Sally picked up a chip before placing it back down. 'He wanted to follow his dreams. Once we'd finished uni, we travelled for four years, working along the way. When we came back to England for one summer, my parents made it no secret they thought I should put my law degree to good use and finish my training.'

'But he wanted to carry on travelling?'

Sally nodded slowly. 'He said he didn't, that he'd move back with me, but I knew he didn't want to. Settling down in one place was the complete opposite of what we'd spoken about, so I broke up with him.'

'You broke up with him?' Ginny said, pointing.

'I did. It was for the best. I didn't want him regretting his decision and holding it against me.'

'Wow. I didn't see that coming. I assumed he'd broken up with you.'

'Oh, thanks.'

'No, no. Just because of the way you speak about him. The way you compare any man you try to date to him. I assumed the break-up hadn't been your choice.'

Sally nodded sadly. Yes, it had been her choice, but she really hadn't thought there was an alternative. She'd thought she'd done the right thing, letting him live the life he wanted.

'I sometimes wonder how things would have turned out if I hadn't broken up with him.'

'I bet. Sorry...' Ginny tailed off.

'It's okay. It's true. And now I don't even use that precious law degree my parents were so desperate for me to have. I didn't even finish my last year of training.' Sally snorted.

'Do you regret that?'

'What? No chance. I was never interested in becoming a solicitor. It was what was expected of me, to follow in my parents' – and then my sister's – footsteps. To work at the family law firm. Me though? It was never my passion. Working with the dogs is my passion.'

She grinned as she thought about the dogs in their care – Ralph, Puddles, and the newbies who had arrived more recently. Each and every one of them was why she did what she did.

Ginny shook her head. 'I can't imagine you as a solicitor.'

'Not serious enough?' Sally raised an eyebrow.

'Not that. Just that I guess I'd always thought of you as someone who preferred the company of animals to humans.'

'Umm... I guess you're right.' Sally threw her last chip in her mouth and scrunched her chip wrappers up. 'Talking of which, we'd better get back.'

'Hold on, we've not finished talking about date guy yet. Gary was it? Or Gavin?'

'Gary. There's nothing else to say. I messaged him this morning and told him I'm not ready for a relationship.'

Standing up, Sally held out her hand for Ginny's chip wrappers.

'Thanks.' Ginny passed her the wrappers and stood up, too. 'Are you really not ready for a relationship yet? After seven years? Or is it that you're comparing everyone you meet to Andy?'

Sally shrugged. 'I don't have time for anyone. What between working here and evening training classes twice a week, I've not even mowed the lawn in weeks.'

'Oh, I bet your neighbour loves that.' Ginny laughed.

'Ha ha, exactly. I've already had Mrs Moreton tell me to go careful in case I stumble over the flowerbeds.' Sally grinned. 'It's not even that long.'

'You mean it's less than a metre tall?'

'Exactly.' Sally laughed, joining Ginny, and threw the chip wrappers in the bin at the top of the beach.

* * *

'Who are you taking out for training?' Ginny asked once they'd got back to Wagging Tails. 'I'll go and walk someone else.' She held the gate to the courtyard open.

'Thanks. I'm going to take Luke out and do some socialisation skills with him,' Sally said as she slipped through.

'Oh, I love Luke. He's such a sweet little thing.' Ginny closed the gate behind them. 'Or should I say a sweet *big* thing? I think he's one of the tallest greyhounds we've ever had!'

'He's such a sweetie. And with a bit of socialisation and training, he's going to make a wonderful companion for someone.'

'He sure will. Plus, he's such a bright boy. I think he'll adjust to home life after being on the racetracks quite quickly.'

'Yes, I think you're right.' Sally held the door to the reception area open and paused. Great, that man was back. Glancing back at Ginny, Sally grimaced before clearing her throat and stepping inside. Lyle, the suited man who had given her and Alex the envelope, was standing in front of the counter and, judging by Flora's expression, he wasn't quite getting the hint that he wasn't welcome.

'Hello, lovelies.' Flora's face relaxed as Sally and Ginny stepped inside.

'Afternoon.' Sally walked behind the counter and positioned herself next to Flora.

Lyle glanced at her for a moment, a look of irritation flashing across his face, before turning his attention back to Flora.

'As I said, I think you'll find our offer is more than satisfactory.'

Flora crossed her arms. 'And as I've said to you, I'm not interested and nor will I ever be.'

'I think you'll find the offer life-changing, Mrs Matthews.' He pushed a cheque, face down, across the counter.

'I don't think you understand,' Ginny cut in. 'She said she's not interested.'

Reaching across the counter, she pushed the cheque back.

Ignoring both Ginny and Sally, Lyle pushed it back towards Flora.

'Take a look, but, if you insist, I shall have a word with my partner and see if we can come up with a more enticing offer.'

And with that, Lyle stalked out of the room, the door swinging shut behind him as he crossed the courtyard.

Sally frowned. 'I didn't see his car in the lay-by.' Yesterday, he'd just pulled up outside the gate.

'No, he parked up in the car park this time.' Flora sighed. 'Who does he think he is? Coming in here and trying to negotiate with me… I've told him time and time again I'm not interested in selling.'

Ginny picked up the cheque. 'It'll be interesting to see how much he's offering, though. It'll tell us how desperate his company is.'

'No, that's what he wants – for us to look.' Flora took the cheque and tore it into a million pieces before throwing it in the bin below the counter. 'That's where it belongs.'

3

Sally took the final bite of her cheese toastie before pushing the empty plate aside and pulling the pet shop catalogue from the bag at her feet. After picking up her mug, she leaned back in her chair and looked around the small café. This was one of her favourite escapes, situated in a small courtyard off a side road in Trestow, the closest town to West Par. She watched as Harold, the owner, bustled about serving cakes and tea to the customers. She took another mouthful of coffee and held it in her mouth, letting the bittersweet taste linger. She'd not found another coffee place good enough to compete with Harold's yet.

She placed her mug down and focused on the task in hand – choosing new equipment. She flicked through the thin catalogue and there it was – the page with the agility equipment. Some of this would be the perfect addition to what they already had and would be fantastic for Nala, the very energetic one-year-old Flora had taken on from the pound last week. As a collie-cross, Nala was bright and needed something that would get her thinking alongside running off some of the energy she had.

Sally pulled the order form from the back of the catalogue and scribbled down the items she wanted – a see-saw and a new A-frame. Those, in addition to the wobble balls, new frisbees and tennis balls she had in a bag at her feet, would keep the Wagging Tails' dogs occupied for a while.

'Do you want a top-up, Sally, dear?'

Sally looked up and shook her head as Harold indicated her almost empty mug. 'No, thank you. As much as I'd love one, I really must get back to work.'

'Of course.' Harold smiled, the laughter lines around his eyes deepening. 'You get back to those lovely little pups of yours.'

She watched as Harold bustled back behind the counter before picking up her mug and taking another sip. She really did need to get back, and she was excited to see how Ralph would react to one of the wobble balls she'd bought.

Sally sighed. Ralph had people who loved and cared for him, and that was more than many. He was happy at the home; she knew he was, but...

She slipped the catalogue inside her bags which she rested on her knees, keeping the order form out. She'd pop that back to the pet shop on her way to her car. Hopefully they wouldn't have to wait too long for the delivery.

Sally paused, her bag handles looped over her wrists, and picked up her mug again, taking a big gulp and draining the remaining coffee. The café was getting busier now. The lunchtime rush beginning. She looked across to a mum with a pram and toddler in tow and nodded towards her table.

'I'm just leaving if you want this one?'

'Thank you, that would be lovely.' The mum turned to her young son. 'George, go and sit over there and we'll get your new colouring book out.'

Sally balanced her empty mug on her plate and picked it up. The least she could do was to take it to the counter and save Harold a job. With only him working here today, she knew he was about to get rushed off his feet.

As she walked the short distance between the table and the counter, she lifted her plate up as another toddler ran towards her.

'Sorry.' A woman apologised as she chased her young girl towards the back of the café.

'No worries.' Sally smiled. The toddler group held in the community hall must have just finished.

She turned towards the counter and froze. It couldn't be.

'Great, thanks, Harold. You're a star.'

It was. She knew that voice. She knew that face. Those eyes. He even sported the same haircut – the slightly too long surfer style. The stubble, though, that was new. She shook her head. New? What was she thinking? She hadn't set eyes on him in seven years. But it was him. Wasn't it?

She watched as he turned and leaned against the counter, pulling his mobile from the back pocket of his jeans and scrolling down the screen as he waited for Harold to make up his order. He hadn't seen her. That was probably a good thing. He wouldn't remember her, anyway. Not after all this time.

Her mouth suddenly dry, she swallowed. She needed to get out of here, and quickly. She held her breath as she lowered the plate and mug to the counter, the mug wobbling and clattering against the plate.

'Do you need some help with...?' He turned and the colour drained from his face as he spotted her.

Too late. She quickly picked up the mug, setting it back on top of the plate. She could feel her cheeks burning as she met his gaze.

'Andy.'

He rubbed the palm of his hand across his face and blinked. 'Sally? It is you, isn't it?'

Sally glanced towards the door and bit down on her bottom lip. She'd daydreamed about this moment for years – randomly meeting him – and yet now it was happening, it was all she could do to stop herself from running at breakneck speed out of the door and into the street.

'Yes, yes, it is.' She shook her head, forcing herself to meet his gaze again. 'How... how are you?'

'Good, thanks. You?'

'Yep, great, thanks.' She nodded. What was she supposed to say?

What was either of them supposed to say after seven years of not seeing each other?

'Here's your coffee, Andy, mate,' Harold said, interrupting the awkward silence hanging in the air as he placed a cardboard takeaway cup on the counter.

Tearing his eyes from her, Andy picked up the cup. 'Thanks.'

'Anyway, I'd better...' Sally pointed towards the door.

'Yes, yes, of course. I'll walk with you.' Andy held his hand out, signalling her to go ahead.

She nodded. Why did he want to walk with her? What was she supposed to say? What did he want her to say? She couldn't very well blurt out how much she missed him and tell him she regretted her decision to end things, following the expectations her family had put upon her.

Andy pulled the door open and held it for her. 'Maybe we could—'

'Andy, mate, you've forgotten your toastie.' Harold's voice rose above the hubbub in the café. 'It'll be ready in a moment.'

Andy raised his coffee cup to him before turning back to Sally. 'Maybe we can meet for a drink? A coffee? Or dinner?'

Had that been a look of disappointment that had flashed across his face when Harold had called him back?

Sally swapped her shopping bags into the other hand and held her hand against the door. 'Coffee would be nice.'

'Fantastic. Great, great. I'll message you.' He smiled. 'Have you still got the same number?'

Sally nodded. She did. She'd never changed it. Just in case.

'Yes. I'd best...' She nodded towards the street as she stepped outside.

'Yes, of course. It's been lovely running into you again.'

'You too.'

Turning, she let the door fall closed behind her. As she crossed the road, she glanced back briefly. He was still there, on the other side of the door, watching her. It was him. Andy. She'd only been speaking to Ginny about him the other day and now, what? He was here in Trestow? Did he live here? Had he moved down to Cornwall? Or was he just passing through? But Harold had known his name, and had even called him 'mate', he couldn't just be passing through. Harold knew him.

At the car park, she pulled her keys from her pocket, hearing the familiar little 'click' as she unlocked her trusty old Focus, her hands shaking. She threw her bags on the passenger seat, sat down and stared at the wall in front of her car.

Would Andy really message her and arrange a catch-up, or was he just being polite? He was probably just being polite. It was what people said to each other when they ran into one another unexpectedly. He wouldn't really message. Why would he want to? She'd been the one to finish with him.

She shook her head and laughed at herself. Who did she think she was? Just because she'd pined after him, just because she'd regretted her decision all those years ago, it didn't mean he had. He'd probably had a long string of relationships since her.

Or else he was married. Happily settled down. Yes, he probably had his own little family now, wife, kids, probably a Labrador or two thrown in. She was lucky he had even recognised her.

She slapped the steering wheel. Enough. That was enough. She was not going to go down the road of daydreaming. No. She was going to go back to Wagging Tails, give Ralph his wobble ball and forget all about this chance encounter with the man she loved. She shook her head. Used to love. She would forget the chance encounter with the man she used to love. A long time ago. Years ago.

4

After stepping through the door into the reception area, Sally lowered her bags onto the counter and sighed.

'Are you okay? You look as though you've seen a ghost.' Ginny frowned, looking up from her clipboard.

'I have.' Sally slipped onto the stool behind the counter and held out her hands. She was still shaking.

Ginny hung the clipboard back up. 'What on earth has happened?'

'This will make you laugh. You know we were talking about my ex, Andy, the other day?'

'Yes?'

'Well…' Sally took a deep breath. 'I've just run into him at the café.'

'What? Seriously?' Ginny planted the palms of her hands flat against the surface of the counter.

'Yes, seriously.'

'So? What happened? Did you speak to him?'

'Yes. I was just leaving and he looked around, saw me – he actually recognised me – and asked how I was.' Sally pinched the bridge of her nose. 'Or at least I think he did. Or asked something anyway. It was all a bit of a blur to be honest, but he did say he was going to message me to arrange meeting for a coffee and a catch-up.'

'Ooh, when are you meeting?'

'We're not. He won't really message.'

'Why don't you think he will?'

'I don't know. Why would he? I'm nothing to him now. Just the woman who broke his heart seven years ago. He's probably settled down. Happy. He looked happy.'

Had he had a ring on his finger? She hadn't noticed one, but she hadn't looked either. She shook her head. It didn't matter. The absence of a ring didn't mean he was single.

'He might,' Ginny said. 'If he said he would message, then I'm sure he will. Have you checked your phone?' She indicated to Sally.

Sally pulled her mobile from her back pocket. 'No, there's no point, though.'

With her thumb hovering over the screen, she frowned.

'Give him a bit of time. You've only just got back. He's probably still out.'

'It's not that. He's already messaged.' She blinked. Yep, he definitely had.

'Then what are you waiting for? What does it say?' Ginny leaned her elbows on the counter and cupped her chin in her hands, watching Sally intently.

'I...' Taking a deep breath, Sally opened the message.

Sally? I hope this is you, anyway! Lovely to run in to you earlier. Would be fantastic to catch up over coffee. You free this evening? 6 p.m.? The Unicorn? Andy x

She shifted the stool closer to the counter and showed the screen to Ginny.

'He put a kiss.' Ginny pointed.

'He always used to put a kiss to everyone. That means nothing.' A smile flickered across Sally's lips before she frowned again. The kiss meant nothing. More than nothing. 'What shall I say?'

'Yes? You've not got a training session tonight, have you? Please say you haven't?'

'No, that's tomorrow.' She joined Ginny in resting her elbows on the counter. 'What do I say? How do I reply?'

Ginny laughed. 'You say yes. You say that you'd love to meet for a catch up and you'll see him at the pub tonight.'

'I can't.'

'Why?' Ginny sighed. 'You've not got a training session, and you were literally talking about him the other day. Why on earth wouldn't you want to meet him?'

'I do. I want to... I just...' Sally shrugged. She couldn't explain it. 'I don't want to find out he has a partner, a wife, kids. I know he probably does, but I don't know if I'm ready to find out.' She shook her head. 'That doesn't even make sense.'

'Hey, yes it does.' Ginny reached across the counter and cupped Sally's hands, so they were both cradling the mobile. 'But even if he does have a family, at least you'll know.'

Sally took a deep breath and straightened her back. 'You're right. It's best to know. At least I can have closure after all of this time and move on.'

Ginny nodded before grinning. 'That or something else entirely.'

Sally tapped her mobile against her chin. She knew Ginny was just trying to be nice, to tell her something she wanted to hear, but she didn't want to hear it. It was her own fault she and Andy had split up and she wanted him to have had a nice life. That's why she'd broken their relationship off – for him – and if he was still single, then that would make her feel worse.

'Go on then.' Ginny indicated the phone. 'Reply.'

'Yes. Okay. It would be nice to hear how he's been. The adventures he's been up to.' Sally began typing. 'Done. I'm meeting him tonight.' She swallowed as her stomach lurched. Was she really going to have coffee and a catch-up with the man who she'd quite possibly made the biggest mistake of her life for?

'Good. I'm sure you'll have a great time.' Ginny picked up the clipboard again.

'Maybe. I guess if anything it will be interesting to hear all about the places he's visited. The places I could have visited if I'd followed my own path in life.'

'You'll have only regretted not going if you'd ignored his text or turned him down.'

'I know. You're right.'

And Ginny was. Sally was glad she'd agreed to meet him. She was. It was just nerves, that's all. And regret.

'Right,' Ginny said, turning and hanging the clipboard up once more. 'I'm going to go and take Ralph out into the top paddock.' She picked up his lead.

'Oh, I bought him a wobble ball. I thought he might like the interaction.' Sally rummaged through the bags before pulling out the bright green ball.

'That looks good. I'm sure he will.' Ginny took the ball and turned towards the door. 'See you later.'

Raising her hand in a reply, Sally looked down to her bags just as the tring-tring of the landline filled the room.

'Afternoon, Wagging Tails Dogs' Home. How can I help you?'

'Hello, I think you have my dog. The small dachshund.'

* * *

'Imagine that, Puddles, your family are coming to take you home.' Sally fussed over the dog sitting next to her on the sand. Flora had been right – Puddles did have a home. She traced the small black marking by his tail – a little heart.

She watched as he stretched his front paws out, yawned and turned around before settling back down.

'I bet you're tired out after terrorising poor Mr Euston and his little dog, Gray. There really was no need for you to be quite so vocal when you saw them coming.'

She blushed as she remembered poor Gray almost pulling Mr Euston over when they'd come round the corner and Puddles had begun to pull on his lead and yap continuously. Hopefully, when his family came to pick him up tomorrow, they'd shed some light on how he'd got into this habit. She wondered whether he'd always been grumpy towards other dogs or if something had happened to him before coming into their care. Whatever the answer, she was determined to help his family and had been scouring the internet for trainers close to them in St Ives, who would be able to carry on with the training she'd begun.

Sally turned her face towards the sun. It was warm today. Again. The fresh warmth the promise of spring brought with it and the hope of summer on the cusp of the horizon. It was strange to think that in a few months she'd have been down here for a year.

So much had changed in such a short space of time. She'd be forever grateful for her nan for making her take the leap to leave her training and the city. *Be true to yourself* – those four small words, that short sentence, had transformed her life. It had given her the push to take a long, hard look at her life and the path her future was taking. Yes, it had been difficult admitting to her parents – and to herself – that she wasn't happy. That she wasn't happy being on the career path she was, living in the city, everything.

Next to her, Puddles' ears shot up, the fur on his neck bristling.

She turned to look and, sure enough, a couple had stepped onto the beach, walking their West Highland. Sally looked down at Puddles and wrapped his lead tighter around her wrist.

'Time to leave, hey? Let's get you back to your kennel. You must be tired after training and now a walk.'

The beach, although not far for most, must have seemed like a marathon for Puddles on his small legs. Sally began standing up, glad of the excuse to leave her thoughts behind.

Just as Sally was standing up, Puddles shot forward, tugging on his lead, heading towards the unsuspecting dog. His lead quickly pulled taut as he bared his teeth and began barking, the noise echoing around the cove.

It was in the moment between sitting and standing that Sally realised the small West Highland wasn't on a lead.

Quickly scrambling to her feet, she called across to the couple: 'Put your dog on a lead, please.'

The man looked at her and smiled. 'Don't worry, she's friendly.'

With Puddles' lead now as short as she could get it without dragging the poor pup up her leg, Sally indicated to him as the West Highland, seemingly as oblivious to the fact that the tone of Puddles' barks didn't suggest he wanted to play, continued to trot towards them.

'Yours might be, but mine's not. He will attack your dog. Please get her away.'

Sally watched as realisation dawned on the couple and the woman began to sprint towards her dog. 'Sophie, Sophie, come.'

As the dog continued to approach them, Sally stepped in front of Puddles and braced herself. There wasn't much else she could do. If she dragged Puddles up the beach, the other dog would only follow, excited now to see what the commotion was about.

With the dog now in lunging distance, Sally watched as, at the last moment, the woman swooped the small dog into her arms and took a few short, quick steps back.

'You really shouldn't be walking him here if he's that unfriendly.' The woman nodded towards Puddles, who was still barking and trying his best to tug on his lead and reach the other dog.

Sally opened and closed her mouth, shocked at the woman's retort. 'He's on a lead and has a yellow lead cover warning he is a nervous dog. Roaming dogs should be put on a lead when approaching another dog on a lead.'

The man walked across and stood at his partner's side. 'Well, that's just not right. Our dog is perfectly friendly. Why shouldn't she be allowed to be off-lead?'

Seriously? Had these people never heard of the etiquette of walking a dog, or were they just completely devoid of any common sense?

'I didn't say you weren't able to walk her off-lead. It's great that she can be, but not all dogs can. They all have the right to go for a walk too and if people just follow the rules, everyone can be kept safe and happy. If you spot the yellow lead cover, hopefully you'll now realise that means the dog is nervous and to keep yours away.'

Sally bit down on her bottom lip. There was so much more she wanted to say, so much more she wanted to shout at them, but it wasn't worth it. But if this encounter today had just taught them to look out for the yellow lead covers and to even just be a little more wary of letting their dog bounce up to one on a lead, then it might save some heartache in the future.

The man tutted, took his dog and turned around, shortly followed by his partner.

'Come on, Puddles, let's get you home.'

Sally was surprised to hear her voice shaking. She hated encounters like this. It wasn't Puddles' fault he'd been mistreated and had developed a deep-rooted fear of other dogs. It was the fault of the humans who had mistreated him. And yet people like that couple felt it was their given right to let their dog roam everywhere regardless as to whether it was putting their dog or another at risk or not.

Turning and leading him up the beach, Sally looked down at Puddles, who was still tugging on the lead, desperate to get back down to the other dog.

Sally glanced behind her. Yep, the dog was still off-lead, although luckily it was more interested in the ball its owners were throwing than in Puddles now.

5

With Puddles safely in his kennel, Sally walked down the corridor and paused outside the door to Ralph's. Kneeling down, she slipped her hands through the bars of his door and fussed him behind the ears, the gorgeous Staffie looking up at her with his deep dark eyes.

'It's such an unfair world sometimes, isn't it, sweetheart?'

Sally pushed the door open to the reception area. Flora was perched on the stool behind the counter, and rain was now beating against the window, a fine sheen of water glistening against the slabs of the courtyard.

Pausing with her pen in hand, Flora looked at her and frowned. 'Sally, are you okay, lovely?'

Sally shrugged. 'Yes. I just had an encounter with a couple on the beach who let their off-lead dog wander towards Puddles.'

'Oh dear.' Flora placed the pen down and closed her notebook. 'Did Puddles attack the other dog?'

'No, the couple eventually realised that I wasn't lying when I said Puddles would attack their dog and took him away.'

Flora tutted. 'Did they not see the bright yellow lead covering?'

'I don't know, but they assured me their dog was friendly.'

'Oh, for goodness' sake. When will people begin to realise that it doesn't matter if their precious dog is friendly? If they're approaching a dog who isn't, they're putting their dog at risk as well as causing unnecessary suffering to the reactive dog.'

'I know. I don't understand people sometimes.' Sally pinched the bridge of her nose. She was getting a headache now.

'And they'd be the first to complain if one of our dogs went for theirs, even if it was their fault as the owners.'

'Exactly. And it doesn't cross their mind that if one of our dogs did hurt theirs, they could never be rehomed.' Sally swallowed. 'Or worse.'

'You're right, lovely. Some people just don't think.' Flora patted her on the forearm. 'I bet they were tourists. The locals are all very good at knowing when they need to keep their distance.'

'Probably.'

'Now, why don't you come on through to the kitchen and I'll pop the kettle on?'

Sally looked down at her schedule. She should be taking Nemo, one of three puppies a farmer had found in his field last week, out for training.

'Come on. That can wait. I need to pick your brains about Puddles' family, anyway.'

'Okay.'

Relieved of the distraction, Sally pinned her schedule back up on the pinboard and followed Flora through to the kitchen.

'It was a woman who rung up,' Sally continued. 'She said she'd seen Puddles' photo in the *Trestow Telegraph*. She sounded nice. Quite emotional that she may have found her missing dog.'

'Oh, that does sound hopeful. And she knows what to bring with her?' Flora clicked the kettle on.

'Yes, I told her we'd need photographs of her with Puddles and anything else she can use as evidence to show ownership of him.'

'Good, good. It sounds as though you've covered all bases, then.' Flora placed two mugs in front of the kettle. 'Did she say what his name was?'

'Yes. Benny. I tried calling him by that name, but he didn't seem to recognise it, not responding at all.' Sally pulled the biscuit tin towards her.

'That's strange. Although he may have been missing a while. But you'd expect there to be a flicker of recognition at least. Did she say how long he's been missing?'

'Three weeks. Apparently, he got out of their garden after their fence was blown down in that storm we had.'

'I guess tomorrow will tell if he's who she thinks he is.' Flora took a biscuit from the tin and passed it back to Sally.

'Yes.' Sally nodded as she took her mug, wrapping her hands around the warm ceramic. Three weeks wasn't long. And depending on where Puddles had spent his time away from his family, it might not be long enough to explain his temperament towards other dogs. Maybe he had always been the way he was and it had nothing to do with his disappearance after all.

* * *

'I'm sorry, you're doing what?' Andy leaned his elbows on the table, his full attention on Sally.

She laughed. She knew he'd heard her the first time. 'I said I'm working as a dog trainer at a local dogs' home and I also run evening classes for the locals.'

Leaning back in his chair, Andy grinned, the small dimple forming in his left cheek. 'That's what I thought you'd said. Wow, I bet that pleases your parents.'

She circled the glass in her hand before wiping off a dribble of orange juice from the rim.

'I think you can imagine the response I got when I told them I'd decided to give up training to be a solicitor with only one year to go.'

Andy raised his eyebrows. 'One year left. You got further than I thought you would.'

'Oi, what do you mean by that?' She picked up the cardboard beer mat and threw it at him frisbee style. 'I had a very promising career ahead of me, actually.'

'Hey, no, I didn't mean you weren't capable of becoming a solicitor.' He held his hands up, palms forward. 'You're the smartest woman I know. What I meant is I'm surprised you stayed living in the city that long. And stomached the life I'm assuming your parents involved you in – black tie events, charity balls, evenings at the theatre...'

'There's nothing wrong with the theatre,' she said sulkily.

He was right, though. Why had she stayed so long? Of course she knew. She'd tried her best to carry on with her studies, to let her parents and sister immerse her into the life they so loved – she'd needed to, she'd needed to make a new life. It hadn't worked. She'd failed. And she'd eventually realised that she was building the wrong kind of life: she needed her own and not to live hers to the expectations of others.

'You've got guts, sticking up to them, your parents.'

'They were okay.' She shrugged.

Yes, it had been hard. She'd been terrified of disappointing them, which was probably why she'd stuck at her training for so long, but her parents had been okay. They hadn't pretended to understand her decision to move hundreds of miles away – and to a place she barely knew after only visiting the area on a girlie holiday – but they'd eventually accepted her decision.

'Anyway, how about you? Still travelling? Tell me about all the wonderful places you've been to. Did you make it to the Galapagos in the end?'

Andy smiled. 'I remember that conversation. We were on that beach in Ibiza, the one with the fire-eaters and the huge campfires.'

'That's right.' Sally grinned. 'So, tell me all about it. What was it like? Did you see the giant tortoises and the iguanas? I missed out, so I need to live it through you.'

'Ha.' Andy glanced towards the door before looking back at her. 'My life took a different path, too.'

She frowned. He'd met someone. That made sense. They'd probably met shortly after she and Andy had split. He'd chosen settled domestic life over travelling. She looked down at her hands, twisting the silver rope bracelet her nan had given her the Christmas before she'd passed away.

'Wife? Children? Labrador?'

'Ha ha, nothing as romantic as that, I'm afraid.' He leaned forward and rubbed the back of his neck. 'No, my dad got sick, and I took over the family business.'

'I'm sorry to hear that.'

She'd always looked to Larry as a second dad. Growing up, Andy's dad had been there for her far more often than her own. He'd been the one who had driven them to prom, taken her out in his car when she was learning to drive. He'd even been the one who had sat outside the doctor's surgery waiting patiently when, at seventeen, she and Andy had thought she was pregnant. She grimaced. She certainly would never have told her own dad about that, but Larry, he never judged. Him or Andy's mum. They'd been there for both of them.

'Is he all right now?' she asked.

Andy looked down at the table, lost in his thoughts for a moment, before meeting her eyes. 'He... umm... He passed away.'

'Oh.' She clasped her hands around her glass, her knuckles white. 'I'm so sorry. When?'

Andy cleared his throat. 'A year and three months after we went our separate ways.'

She nodded slowly. She should have been there. Supported him.

'I know you two were close. Are you okay?' He touched her briefly, the pads of his fingers resting against the back of her hand.

'Yes, sorry. It should be me comforting you.' She smiled weakly, swiping the back of her hand across her eyes. 'I'm so sorry I wasn't there for you.'

'It's not your fault. I should have contacted you and let you know, but at the time everything was just such a blur.' He downed the dregs of his drink and held his glass up. 'The same?'

'Um... yes, please.' She passed him her empty glass and he walked up to the bar.

Twisting in her chair, she watched him go. His shoulders were slumped. He still missed his dad. She rolled her eyes at herself. Of course he did. Larry had been one of the good guys. One of those lovely people who would do anything for anyone else, no questions asked. A bit like Flora, really. She was one of those people, too.

She turned back to the table and retrieved the beer mat she'd thrown at him, turning and tapping its edge against the wooden tabletop. She'd ended their relationship thinking she was giving Andy the freedom he deserved, only to have abandoned him in his hour of need.

'You look deep in thought.' Andy placed a fresh glass of orange juice on the table in front of her.

She smiled as he slipped into the chair opposite. 'Thanks.'

'You're welcome.' He took a sip of his – a lager shandy – before breaking into a grin. 'So why Trestow? Why Cornwall? I know it's an absolutely stunning place, but what brought you here? The job?'

'No, I actually didn't have a job when I moved. I'd been here – well, not here, to Looe – with my sister and a couple of friends and I fell in love with the area.'

'So you came here without a job lined up? Just because you liked the place?' Andy grinned, a glint forming in his eyes. 'There's still the adventurer in you then. Your parents didn't educate it out of you.'

'Ha ha, no. Although I think they tried their best to mould me into who they wanted me to be.' She shrugged. 'My nan left me a bit of money. Enough to rent a place for a few months. I'd already finished my training to be a dog trainer. I researched villages in Cornwall, knew I wanted to stay relatively near to Looe and stumbled across West Par. The rest is history, as they say.'

'And you now have the two jobs?'

'Yes. Although I only train privately three times a week.'

She smiled. He was right. Moving down here on a whim had been something she would have done years ago, before she'd begun training to be a solicitor, and the change had made her feel a little more like her old self again.

'How about you?' she asked. 'What brings you to Trestow then?'

Sighing, Andy interlocked his fingers, cracking his knuckles. 'In short, business.'

'You're still running your dad's company? Buying and renovating houses? Selling them on? It's a long way to travel.'

'You know me, I like to travel and nowadays I go where there's money to be made.'

She looked into his eyes. Dare she ask?

'No wife? Or kids?' She cleared her throat as she felt the searing heat of a blush flashing across her face. 'What I mean is, you're happy to be away from home for periods of time?'

The telltale signs of a grin danced at the corners of Andy's mouth. 'No wife. No kids. I was married for a short time. A couple of years. Until we realised we both wanted different things and just weren't as in love as we thought we were.'

Sally nodded slowly. He had been married. Wow.

'Sorry to hear about your divorce.'

'Don't be. It was for the best. For both of us.' He shrugged. 'She's remarried. Has a little family now.'

'Right.' She took a sip of her orange juice. He didn't sound particularly upset. Had the break-up really been that amicable? But then she stopped the thought as it was forming: it was none of her business.

* * *

'This is me.' Sally clicked her keys and her car lights flashed in response. 'Thank you for walking me to my car, although as you can see there really was no need.'

She laughed and looked around the well-lit, empty car park.

Andy grinned at her. 'It's been amazing to catch up with you. Maybe we could meet up another time?'

'Yes, that would be nice.'

It had shocked them both when the pub landlord had shouted last orders. The evening had flown by in such a flash. It had felt just like old times, passing the evening away chatting and laughing, reminiscing.

'Great. I'll message you.' Stepping forward, Andy hugged her.

Sally stood awkwardly. Was this a quick, friendly hug or something more? She didn't move for a moment before, eventually, placing her arms around him – but just as she made contact, he stepped back.

She turned towards her car quickly, trying to hide her embarrassment.

'See you,' she said.

'Bye.' He waved.

After opening the door and slipping into the driver's seat, Sally watched in the rear-view mirror as he walked away. Why had she done that? Why hadn't she just hugged him back? They'd always hugged. Proper long hugs, not polite ones. Hugs which were all-encompassing. They'd even hugged when she'd ended the relationship.

She clicked her seat belt in. There wasn't any point overthinking it now. It was done. She just hoped her reaction wouldn't put him off hugging her next time. If they did actually meet up again. She could do with one of his hugs. She'd missed them.

Turning the radio on, she twisted the volume control until the cheesy tunes of the late-night show drowned out her thoughts.

6

Sally looked from the photos on the table in the kitchen to Flora. This wasn't Puddles. The dog in the picture looked similar, uncannily similar, in fact, but it wasn't him. There was a slight difference in the facial markings on the fur. She straightened her back and looked across at Laura, the woman she'd spoken to on the phone.

'Is it him? Please tell me it's him. I'm going out of my mind with worry. I've been scouring the town every night calling his name, putting posters up in any and every shop that will allow me and posting every day in the local groups. Please tell me it's him,' she begged, twisting the strap of her handbag in her hands.

Flora walked around the table towards her. 'I'm not sure it is, lovely. I'm so sorry.'

'Oh, really?' Laura's shoulders shook.

'Here, if you look at these markings around his eyes...' Flora picked up one of the photos and pointed. 'The dog we have doesn't have these.'

'But that's the only difference? Maybe his fur has grown and obscured them?'

'Sally, why don't you go and bring him out and we'll double-check, but I'm afraid I don't want you to get your hopes up.' Flora laid the photograph back on the table and patted the woman's arm.

'Okay. I won't.' Laura nodded, her hair flicking into her eyes.

Walking out of the kitchen, Sally sighed. It wasn't him. Both she and Flora knew that, but she understood why Flora had asked her to fetch Puddles. It would at least lay to rest any doubts the woman was having.

She opened Puddles' kennel door, being careful to grab his collar and secure a lead to him before he could run down the corridor and terrorise the other dogs in their care.

'Come on, Puddles.'

She pushed the kitchen door open and watched as Laura dropped the tissue she was using to wipe her eyes and lowered herself to her knees, her arms outstretched.

'Benny? Benny, is that you?'

Letting the door swing shut behind her, Sally unclipped the lead and watched as Puddles circled the room, sniffing the floor, oblivious of the woman who hoped he would be her beloved dog.

Laura sat back on her haunches. 'It isn't him, is it?'

'I'm afraid it's not, lovely.' Flora patted her gently on the back. 'Why don't I have a word with Darryl at the *Trestow Telegraph* and ask him to put a photo of Benny and some information about him in the next edition?'

'You'd do that?'

'Yes, of course. Let's see if we can't shed some light on where your boy has gone.'

'Okay, thank you. That would be great. Thank you.' Standing up, Laura scooped the photos from the table. She held them out to Flora. 'You really don't think he'll mind?'

'I'm sure he won't.' Flora indicated the door. 'Come on through to the reception area and I'll jot down your details. I can ask Darryl to give you a call and he can collect some more information from you. How does that sound?'

'Thank you.' Laura wiped her eyes and followed Flora out of the kitchen, stopping briefly to glance back at Puddles before closing the door behind her.

Sally patted her lap and picked Puddles up as he ventured towards her. 'Sorry, Puddles. But we won't give up hope. Your family could still be looking for you.'

She fussed behind his ears as he settled on her lap before pulling her mobile from her pocket. Andy hadn't messaged again. Not since they'd arranged last night's catch-up. He'd said he'd be in touch to arrange another meet-up before he went home. She put her phone down on the table. He'd probably just said that to be polite or else the awkward hug/non-hug at the end of the evening had put him off.

Tilting her head, she listened out for any sounds from reception.

'It sounds as though Flora is showing the poor lady out to her car,' she said to Puddles. 'Come on, let's get you back to your kennel. I need to take Dory out for her on-lead training before I go home.'

She popped Puddles onto the floor and walked towards the door, opening it slightly to check Flora really had shown Laura out. The last thing she wanted was to walk Puddles through and cause her more upset if she was still here.

Yep, the reception area was quiet.

She walked through just at the same time as Flora returned, and this time, there was someone else behind her. Sally set her jaw. It was that man Lyle, the property developer. Again.

As he stepped through the door, Puddles lunged at his ankles, barking. Sally had to cover her mouth to smother a laugh. She guided Puddles past him and through the door towards the kennels.

'You're not normally like that with people, hey, Puddles,' she said as she led him down the corridor. 'Did you just not like him?' She lowered her voice as she unclipped his lead. 'I don't blame you. I don't much either. You're a good judge of character.'

She watched as he slunk reluctantly into his kennel, his ears pricked up on high alert by the sounds of the other dogs and his encounter with Lyle.

Heading back to reception, Sally stopped before she stepped back inside. With her hand on the door, she listened. She could hear Flora and Lyle speaking – or more accurately, Lyle talking at Flora. He just wasn't getting the message that Flora wasn't going to change her mind about selling Wagging Tails, was he?

Sally pushed the door open, trying to hide the scowl on her face with a fake smile.

'Hello again. Lyle, isn't it?'

Lyle stopped mid-sentence to Flora and gave her the slightest nod in acknowledgement before turning back.

'I'm Sally. I work here,' she continued. 'I'm pretty sure Flora has made her decision quite clear to you.' She joined Flora behind the counter and laid her hands, palms down, on the countertop.

'That's right. I have.' Flora looked him in the eye. 'I don't think I need to keep repeating myself. Wagging Tails and its land is not for sale and never will be.'

'I understand your decision,' he said, 'but I'd hate for the little dogs in your care to be traumatised by the building work that will be going on just beyond your boundary line. Surely, as the owner, your priority is to them and their well-being. Of course, we'll do all we can to endeavour to keep any disruption to a minimum, but I can imagine the strange noises and sights as the builders move in and commence work will have a detrimental effect on their lives. On all your lives.'

'I have made my position clear.' Flora shifted on her feet, straightening her back a little. 'I will not be changing my mind.'

'Understood.' Lyle stepped back from the counter, his hands in the air.

'Thank you.' Flora relaxed her shoulders as he made his way to the door.

With his hand on the door handle, Lyle turned around. 'It pains me to think how our building work may disrupt and unsettle your little dogs' home,' he said, his free hand against his chest, 'but you know best.'

Sally crossed her arms and glared at him. 'I think you've said enough.'

Nodding slowly, Lyle removed his hand from his chest. 'You're right. Let's just hope the council don't shut you down when your hundreds of new neighbours begin to complain about the noise when they move into their new homes. I can only imagine how noisy your little kennels can be.' He glanced towards the door leading to the kennels and, as if on cue, a raucous barking commenced.

Sally moved around from the other side of the counter and shut the door firmly behind him.

'Oh dear. What are we going to do?' Flora sank her head into her hands.

'Nothing. It's all talk, that's all. When they try to get planning consent, we'll object. I can't imagine very many locals in West Par will be happy with a few hundred new homes being built. Can you imagine the impact the builders' traffic alone will have on the narrow roads around here?'

'Yes, you're right. The council won't grant them planning permission.' Straightening her back again, Flora nodded. 'He does sound very confident, though. Almost as though he thinks he'll get the go-ahead.'

'He does, but that's just part of the scare tactics. He's got to come across as confident or no one would take him seriously.' Sally smiled. 'Just imagine his face when his plans are turned down.'

'Oh, I'd like to be a fly on the wall in that room, I would.' Flora chuckled just as Percy walked through the door. She held her hand up in greeting.

'Was that who I think it was?' He indicated behind him.

'Lyle, yes, I'm afraid so.'

'What does he want now?' Pulling off the flat cap he'd been wearing since Christmas, when he'd received it as a gift, he shook his head.

'Trying to scare us by threatening to get the council on us about the noise the dogs will make when the houses have been built.' Flora shook her head. 'But I'm not going to give him or his construction work another thought. As Sally reminded me, it's extremely unlikely he'll even be granted planning permission and if he is, then the whole of West Par is likely to appeal against it.'

'That's right.' Percy nodded. 'Good thinking.'

'Hopefully, he won't be bothering us again, and if he does, we can just tell him a few home truths about his precious development.' Flora shook her head. 'How dare he threaten our dogs?'

'Yes, I agree. We need to try not to let him bother us.' Sally picked up Dory's lead. 'Right, I'm off to take Dory out.'

'Okay, lovely. Good luck and thank you for support earlier.' Flora smiled at her before turning back to Percy.

'No worries.'

Pushing the door to the kennels open, Sally waited for the excited barking to subside before making her way to Dory's kennel. At least Flora was feeling more positive now.

7

Sally placed the last chair down along the edge of the community hall before looking around the large room and smiling. She'd built her evening training business up from nothing in just a few short months and it still shocked her how popular they had become. Hearing the groan of the door swinging open, she straightened her back and grinned as a mum and two teenagers entered, an excitable young springer spaniel pup by their heels.

'Evening, Eve. Hi, kids. How's this little one doing with her commands?'

Eve looked towards her eldest son. 'You've pretty much got her doing exactly what you want her to, haven't you, Joel?'

Joel shrugged. 'I just do what you showed me to.'

'That's good. Well done. It sounds as though Betty here is making good progress.' Sally knelt down and fussed the dog behind the ears, her whole body swinging from side to side in appreciation.

'Well, that's Joel. Joel has her under control. Me and Daniel however...' Eve looked at her youngest son, who pulled a cap lower over his head at the mention of his name. '...It's as though she uses all her attention for Joel and forgets about us two, isn't it?'

Eve laughed and looked across at Daniel, who nodded.

'Ah, are you being selective who you listen to?' Sally stroked Betty again before standing up. 'If she's acting on command with Joel, then she can do it. I'd suggest today that, Joel, maybe you could help me out with a few things around the class and your mum and Daniel can focus on getting the practice in. What do you say?'

'Good idea.' Eve nodded.

'Okay, great. Take a seat and get yourselves a drink if you want one and we'll make a start as soon as everyone's arrived.' Sally grinned as the family made their way towards the chairs.

'Sally?'

Sally beamed before dropping to her knees and beckoning over the Lhasa apso and Pomeranian-cross coming through the door. 'Alfie, Oscar! What are you two doing here?'

'Hi. I'm sorry to just drop by like this.' The woman who had walked in with Alfie and Oscar smiled.

Sally stood up and held her hand out to the woman at the other end of the leads. 'Stacey, I'm so sorry. I should be saying hello to you first. How have these little ones been?'

Sally had spent weeks training Oscar to walk on the lead when the pair had arrived at Wagging Tails after being surrendered by their owner, Mr Thomas, a local animal hoarder. She'd missed the pair when Stacey had rehomed them – Oscar with his cheeky little face and funny mannerisms and Alfie who just took everything in his stride, often giving Oscar little side-looks of embarrassment.

'They've been great, thanks. It feels as though they've always been a part of the family.' Bending down, Stacey fussed over them before straightening her back again and gesturing at Oscar. 'This one though, just recently, has started to be a royal pain on the lead again.'

'Oh, Oscar.' Sally looked down at him and shook her head.

'I know you said to expect some setbacks as he adjusts to life at home with us, but if I'm honest, I thought we'd been lucky and skipped that part as it's been a couple of months now and he's been an absolute joy up to a few days ago.' Stacey frowned and held out her hands, which Sally noted were covered in grazes. 'He had me over on this morning's walk.'

'Oh, Oscar. Up to your old tricks again?' Sally shook her head. 'I hope you're okay after your fall?'

'Oh, yes. Luckily, I was able to shoot my hands out and save myself. It's more my ego that's damaged rather than anything else.' Stacey laughed.

'Glad to hear you're okay, but you've come to the right place. He's trainable. We know that as he's been walking fine with you all this time. I think we'll probably just need to refresh his walking skills a little.'

'Are you sure you don't mind us joining? I know it's smack bang in the middle of your class term,' she said sheepishly. 'After this morning's disaster, I just remember you saying to pop by if there were any issues.' She looked towards the door as two other families walked in with their dogs.

'Of course not. I always have room for my Wagging Tails dogs.' Sally beamed. It was a shame Oscar was playing up, but it was always a pleasure to meet one of the rehomed dogs again. 'Come on in and find a chair.'

'Thank you.' Stacey reached down and fussed Oscar and Alfie. 'I really appreciate this.'

'You're welcome. Hopefully, we can get Oscar's little problem ironed out soon enough.' Sally watched Stacey walk them across to a chair before turning to the two families who had just arrived. 'Evening, all. Come on in.'

After checking all of her students were inside, Sally shut the door before turning to the group of people in front of her.

* * *

A quiet round of applause sounded through the hall as a large lurcher, Bob, sat patiently at the other end of the hall to his owner, David. Bob was the last of the dogs in the class to master the skill of 'Stay' and the whole class had been rooting for him.

Sally looked around the group of people, who were all smiling, happy for David and Bob. This was why she didn't think she'd travel again. This was the reason she'd decided to lay down her roots here, in

West Par and with Trestow on her doorstep – because of the community. She'd found communities like this before, on her travels with Andy – definitely not while in the city – and she'd always said to herself that one day, when she was ready to settle down, she'd find a place where she felt as though she belonged. And she had.

Standing up, Sally grinned. She finished clapping before turning to David and Bob. 'Well done. You are both a fantastic example of perseverance. David, at any moment during the last few weeks you could have walked out of this door and told yourself it wasn't working for you, but you didn't. You kept your faith in the beautiful Bob here and you carried on and just look at your reward.'

'Thank you.' David fussed over the lurcher. 'I'm so proud of him.'

Sally wiped a tear from her eye. 'You should be proud of yourself too. I know we all are.'

'Absolutely. Well done, David,' Dee, a woman with a small terrier, called out from the group.

'You've all been fantastic tonight, both humans and dogs.' Sally grinned. 'Thank you for coming and I look forward to next week's lesson.'

Once everyone had left, Sally closed the door behind them and turned to survey the hall. Clearing up was always the challenging bit. After a day at Wagging Tails and then teaching two back-to-back training sessions, by the time she had said goodbye to the last of her students she was ready to flop into bed.

She shook herself. She could stand here thinking about what she had to do or she could just get on with it and get it done. As she made her way around the hall picking up stray cups and stacking any remaining chairs away, she began planning her next session in her head. Now Stacey had joined them, she needed to add in a little more lead training, which would be good for all of them anyway, especially Eve's excitable spaniel. Yes, she'd tweak the timetable a little.

She washed and dried the last of the cups and returned them to the cupboard before putting the large bucket beneath the tap and watching it fill. All that was needed now was to mop the floor and she could be on her way home.

She yawned as she watched the water foam and fill the bucket. Then, after turning the tap off, she hefted the bucket from the sink and turned around, almost dropping the bucket as she spotted Andy standing in the kitchen doorway.

'Andy! You almost gave me a heart attack!'

'Sorry, I did knock and call.' He grinned and held up two takeaway cups.

'I had the tap on. Didn't hear you.' She placed the bucket on the floor and reached for the mop to wipe up the splodges that had spilled. 'How did you know I'd be here?'

'Oh, it was quite easy. You said you were teaching tonight and I remembered seeing a poster in the supermarket advertising dog training.' He shrugged.

'Right.' She looked down at the bucket and felt a blush creep across her face. She really thought she'd pushed him away after that awkward hug. 'What can I do for you? I'm afraid the session has just finished if you were wanting to join?' She paused. 'Have you even got a dog?'

'Ha, no I haven't – you've got me. I came to see you and bring you hot chocolate from Harold's.'

'Seriously? Harold's? How did you manage that? His café's not open at this time and, trust me, I've checked.' She raised an eyebrow.

'Ah, well, when you're lodging upstairs, he's quite happy to make a hot chocolate.'

'You're lodging with him? You never said.'

But why would he? She hadn't asked where he was living.

'Yes, for the time being anyway. I'm waiting for a few things to be tied up for my next project.'

'Ah, okay. I'd always assumed you lived on site. You know, maybe in a caravan in the garden or a tent in the middle of the chaos of the renovations or something.' Leaning the mop against the doorway, Sally accepted the offered takeaway cup and took a sip, savouring the velvety chocolate liquid before swallowing. 'Thank you. You don't know how much I love these.'

'No, but I do remember how much you love hot chocolate and who doesn't love Harold's Café so it was a win-win.'

'Well, thank you.' She smiled.

'How did tonight's session go?' He glanced around the hall.

'Really well, I think. I had a visit from a couple of dogs I'd worked with at the dogs' home, which was a treat. I always love running into dogs we've rehomed.'

'I can imagine that must be rewarding.' Andy leaned against the wall, his trainer against the wood.

'It is.'

Andy looked slowly around the room again, deep creases appearing on his forehead. 'I'm so glad you stood up to your parents and followed your dream.'

'Me too.' She shuddered. 'When I think back to all those years I wasted trying to do the "right thing"...' with her free hand, she made speech marks in the air '...and please other people...'

'But you took the leap.' He glanced down at the floor before meeting her eyes. 'You should be proud of yourself. Not many people are brave enough to change tracks like you have.'

She shrugged. 'I wasn't brave, I just knew I needed to do something else, follow my heart.'

'That is brave. Standing up for what you want to do, for what you believe is right, is brave.'

Andy looked beyond her, his eyes focusing on the wall behind and knitted his eyebrows together, a deep expression flushing across his face.

'Are you okay?'

He looked at her, forcing a smile. 'Of course.'

'Umm...'

He wasn't. She'd always been able to tell when something wasn't right with him. She'd known him long enough and well enough to be able to see through the mask he portrayed to the world.

'I'm okay, Sally.'

She raised her eyebrows. 'Okay.'

Shaking his head, the frown now completely gone, he grinned. 'Who wouldn't be okay when holding a cup of Harold's finest hot chocolate?'

Sally laughed. He'd tell her when and if he wanted to.

'That's very true,' she said.

'Anyway, I'd better get going.' He nodded towards the door. 'Will you be okay here?'

'Of course.'

Stepping forward, he wrapped his arms around her, his cardboard takeaway cup resting on her shoulder blade.

This time Sally sunk into his embrace, and relaxed, her breathing slowly matching his as had always happened. She took a deep breath. Was he wearing the same aftershave? No, he couldn't be. Not after all this time.

As he retreated, she called out, 'Hey, Andy.'

'Yes?' He turned around, his hand on the door handle.

'Are you sure you're all right?'

He nodded slowly. 'Catch you another time.'

Sally watched as he disappeared, and the door clicked gently shut behind him. There was definitely something on his mind. And why had he sought her out and waited around until the end of class if he wasn't going to talk to her about whatever it was?

She downed the rest of her hot chocolate. Maybe he was just still in shock at them having run into each other, or maybe the renovation project he was working on had fallen through.

She picked up the mop again. There was no point stewing and trying to second guess; he was a totally different person to the one she'd left seven years ago.

8

'Hurry up, Sally.' Alex swung the gate into the courtyard open as Sally walked through. 'How long does it take to get back from the beach? We've been waiting.'

'Sorry, I ran into Mr Euston and he was asking about the agility class I'm starting up.' Sally quickened her step to match Alex's, young Dory running to keep up with them. 'What's the emergency, anyway? You didn't say in your text, just that I had to come back.'

'We're holding a staff meeting. Everyone else is in the kitchen.'

'A staff meeting? But we're not scheduled one and isn't Flora still out at the vet's with Nemo?' Flora was usually in charge of the staff meetings.

'Yes, yes. She's out, but that's why we've got to hurry.'

'Okay...' She frowned. Alex wasn't making any sense.

At the door into the reception area, Alex paused and looked back at her. 'We're trying to organise a surprise for Flora's birthday, so we need to get the meeting wrapped up before she comes back. I don't want her suspecting a thing.'

'Oh right. That makes sense. Okay, I'll just pop Dory back in her kennel and be in with you.' She headed towards the kennels.

'There you go, Dory,' she said, giving the dog a treat. 'Good girl.'

As she closed her kennel door, one of Dory's brothers, the third of the *Finding Nemo* pups, Marlin, nudged his nose against the bars.

'You want one too, Marlin? Here you go.' She fussed him behind the ears before turning and walking back towards the kitchen.

Sally slipped through the door Alex was holding open for her and sat at the table. Everyone but Flora was there: Susan, Percy, Ginny and Tim, all seemingly waiting for her to arrive.

'Sorry.'

'No need to apologise, Sally.' Susan chuckled. 'Alex, here, is quite the fan of organising things last minute.' She nodded towards Alex as she placed a mug of freshly made coffee in front of Sally.

'No, I'm not,' Alex said. 'That's the whole point. We need to start organising Flora's birthday surprise so we don't leave it until the last minute.' He peered out of the kitchen door and, deeming it safe to continue the meeting, slipped into the chair at the head of the table.

'I know. I know. But a little bit of warning wouldn't have gone amiss.' Susan smiled and shook her head.

'Well, yes, admittedly this was quite last minute,' Alex continued, 'but I had to wait until Flora was out.' He pulled a wedge of papers towards him. 'Right, now that we all know why we're here. Let's get some ideas flowing. It's Flora's big birthday – sixty-five – so we need to do something fitting.'

'How about a big dog walk? We could invite all the old Wagging Tails dogs and go to the woods or somewhere?' Ginny looked around the group.

'Ooh, or how about a trip to the beach? One of the big beaches?' Susan took a sip from her mug.

Percy cleared his throat. 'Why not a traditional party? The weather should be good, and we could hold it in the top paddock. There are the gazebos we bought last year for the summer fayre in the shed. I could put those up just in case.'

'I like that idea.' Alex pointed his pen at Percy. 'Like you say, it's traditional, but if we go big, it could be spectacular!'

'Yes, we could definitely invite our old dogs.' Ginny rubbed her hands together.

'Is that so you can see them or for Flora?' Susan laughed.

'Flora, of course.' Ginny grinned.

'How about we have a photographer take portraits of the dogs and their families? We could charge and raise a bit of cash for the home at the same time?' Sally wrapped her hands around her mug.

'Now, that is a good idea.' Percy stroked his beard. 'Flora would appreciate some money being raised. We could even see if we could get some photographs taken to update the website and social media?'

Ginny pulled her mobile from her pocket. 'I could ask Darryl if he knows anyone from the paper who would be willing to volunteer their time. I'll message him now. There's no time like the present.'

'Good thinking.' Alex scribbled on the paper.

'What about a cake?' Susan asked. 'I'd love to bake her one, but I don't think my nerves would take it knowing that so many people will be seeing it.'

'Your cakes are amazing, Susan, but if you don't want to bake one, we could ask Elsie and Wendy at The Cornish Bay Bakery. They'd obviously be invited, anyway,' Alex said.

'Good thinking.' Susan pulled a plate of biscuits towards her, took one, and passed them around.

'There's someone on my course in college who makes wicked balloon animals. I could ask her to come?' Tim said. 'We'd have to provide the balloons, but...'

'Yes! That would be perfect.' Alex nodded. 'Do you think she'd come?'

'I don't see why not. She does them for parties and birthdays in her spare time so it would be free advertising for her too.'

'I used to have a friend who made balloon animals. Huge balloon arches too,' Percy said.

'So that's decided, then.' Alex stood up and peered around the kitchen door. 'We'll have a huge party for Flora's birthday. Flora's just got back – so quick, who's doing what?'

'You've got good hearing, lad.' Percy raised his eyebrows.

'What can I say?' Alex smiled before slipping back into his chair, his pen poised over the paper.

'I'm happy to ring around some of our old rescue dogs,' Ginny said.

'I thought you would be.' Susan laughed. 'I'll help.'

'I'll get the paddocks in shipshape for the big day.' Percy reached across and took another biscuit.

'I can pop into Elsie's and order the cake, if you like?' Sally said, pulling her mobile out, ready to type any information she needed to remember in the notes section. 'What style are we going for?'

'Something fun, I think. With dogs on.'

'And big. Everyone will want a slice.' Percy pointed to Sally's phone. 'I need to get myself one of those things. I don't think I have that option on my brick.' He tapped his large mobile, which was sitting on the table.

Sally could hear the door to Wagging Tails opening and shutting. They had about another two minutes whilst Flora returned Nemo to his kennel before they'd have to wind the meeting down.

Alex, too, kept his eyes on the kitchen door. 'Percy, can you write a list of people Flora might like to invite, please? Besides the dogs and their adopters, I mean.'

'I will, yes. I'll ask Poppy to help too. She might know of any family Flora would want to invite.'

'Great.' Alex turned his papers over and nodded towards the door as it opened.

Flora walked through and sat down in a chair, her shoulders slumping.

'Is everything okay?' Ginny asked. 'What did Mack say about Nemo's paw? Does he need treatment?'

'Oh, he's fine, love. It was a grass seed, and we caught it early, so little Nemo will be as right as rain.'

'Then what's the matter?' Susan leaned across the table. 'You look as though something's happened?'

'I'll put a brew on, love.' Percy patted Flora's shoulder as he walked past.

'Thanks, I could do with one.' Flora smiled at him. 'I've had Sylvia on the phone.'

'From the pound?'

'That's right. She's got this gorgeous greyhound and we're her last hope.' Flora pinched the bridge of her nose. 'She's rung everyone, all the local rescues as well as the national greyhound rescue centres, but no one's able or willing to take her on.'

'Oh, bless her, and we all know how notoriously difficult greyhounds are to rehome.' Susan sighed. 'Is she an ex-racer?'

'Exactly. A lot of people think they need long walks and lots of exercise. They don't realise they only actually need short walks and are happiest lounging around all day. Sylvia didn't mention if she was an ex-racer or not.' Flora took her drink from Percy. 'Thanks. Besides, we don't have any room. Our kennels are full already.'

'There's that couple who are coming tomorrow to see Peony, the young Staffie.' Ginny pulled her mug towards her and nodded her thanks to Percy. 'The home visit has been done, so if the meet goes well and she gets on with their other dog, her kennel could be free in a couple of days.'

'Oh, that's right.' Flora's face lit up. 'Of course, I'd forgotten we were so far along in the rehoming process for her. I'll go and give Sylvia another call and see if there's any chance she can hold on to her for a few days.'

'And then there're the puppies. We've already had some interest in them,' Susan said.

'Yes, and they're bound to be snapped up being as they're young pups. We should definitely be able to have her then,' Flora said, standing. 'Sylvia said the poor thing suffers from separation anxiety, so with that and her being a greyhound, I know she'll definitely be a tricky one to rehome, but to think of the alternative...'

Sally nodded. 'You never know, we might just find the perfect person.'

'Yes, yes. Let's think positively. I'll call her now.' Flora put her empty mug into the dishwasher and left the room.

'Right, I'm going to work with Annie.' Sally stood up and took her mug to the sink.

Annie was an elderly golden retriever and Sally knew she'd make a perfect companion for someone – if only Sally could just stop her from getting spooked by every passing car. And that would be another kennel free when she was rehomed.

9

Remember to get us some cheese & onion pasties. Ginny x

Sally grinned as she texted a quick reply and pushed open the door to The Cornish Bay Bakery, a small bell above the door tinkling to announce her arrival. Both Ginny and Alex must have reminded her at least six times to pick them up some pasties since she'd said she was going to pop to Elsie's bakery to order Flora's cake this morning. She might just get one for herself too, see what all the fuss was about.

'Hello, Sally, love. Nice to see you in the bay,' Elsie called across from where she was sliding two trays full of freshly baked cakes behind the glass of the bakery counter. 'What can we get you?'

'I'm actually here to have a quick word with you about ordering a cake for Flora's birthday.'

'Ah, yes, Flora's birthday. Come on through to the kitchen and we'll have a chat.' Elsie picked up two empty trays from the top of the counter and led the way through into the kitchen.

'Thanks.' Sally looked around the huge stainless-steel kitchen. It certainly wasn't what she'd been expecting it to look like.

'Coffee?' Elsie filled a mug from a cafetiere and passed it to Sally.

'Thank you.' Sally took a sip. It was good.

Elsie washed her hands before drying them on a tea towel which she then flung over her shoulder. 'So, tell me, what sort of cake were you thinking?'

'I'm not really sure. Alex suggested something fun. And with dogs on.'

'Yes, of course.' Elsie nodded. 'One moment and I'll see if Wendy is free. She's the one that usually decorates the cakes.'

'Okay.' Sally watched as Elsie disappeared back into the bakery, returning a few moments later with Wendy.

'Hi, Sally. Elsie said you wanted a cake for Flora's birthday.' Wendy placed a large sketchbook on the stainless-steel tabletop and pulled a stool from beneath the table, indicating Sally to do the same.

'How big do you need it?' Elsie asked. 'Is it for everyone at Wagging Tails?' She plunged her hands into a bowl and pulled out a large lump of bread dough.

'We've decided to organise a surprise party and invite Flora's friends, as well as some previous adopters. We're at the very beginning of the planning. We only really decided on a party a couple of days ago, so we don't have any numbers yet.'

'Ooh, sounds fun.' Elsie began to knead the dough. 'Don't worry too much about numbers. We can work with what you've told us so far. If need be, I can always bake an extra cake just for serving up.'

'Yes, that's a good idea.' Wendy scribbled at the top of her sketchbook. 'We can concentrate on the display cake now, if you want to call it that, and then decide on how many serving cakes we'll need when you've got a clearer idea of the number of guests. So, are you thinking a tiered cake or a large flat one, perhaps square?'

'A larger flat one, I think.' Sally took another sip of her coffee. She hadn't really discussed much about the cake with the Wagging Tails team; they'd all just seemed to trust her with the decision.

'Great. I think that will be better. I can make some little dog figures out of icing to go on top.' Wendy shook her head. 'No, I know! Maybe we could have a couple of dog heads here and here…' She quickly sketched a cake before adding the detail. 'And some balloons... she's going to be sixty-five, isn't she?'

'Yes. That's right, which is why we want to throw her a party, mark her special day.'

'Perfect.' Wendy continued to draw, a look of concentration on her face. 'What do you think? Obviously it's a super quick sketch and I'll do a more detailed version later, but what do you think of what we've got so far?'

Sally peered at the drawing. 'Wow, it looks amazing.'

If that was what Wendy could draw in the short few minutes they'd been sitting there, she was looking forward to seeing the finished design.

Wendy shrugged. 'Thanks, it's just super quick. Oh, can you get any photographs of some of your dogs, the ones you have at the home at the moment or ones you've already rehomed? Then I can incorporate them into the finished design.'

Sally grinned and pulled her mobile from her pocket. 'That's a great idea. I can send a couple over now, but I'll have to ask Susan or Ginny for some of the older dogs.'

'Brilliant.' Wendy glanced at the clock on the back wall. 'I'd better run as I have a meeting with a client any time now, but I'm super excited to make a start on this.'

'Thank you.' Sally drank the rest of her drink. 'I'd better get going too.'

'Do you want to take anything back to the team?' Elsie wiped her hands on her apron. 'On the house, of course.'

'Well, I'm under super strict instructions to buy some of your cheese and onion pasties.' Sally grinned. 'I don't think Ginny or Alex will let me back in if I don't return with some.'

'Cheese and onion pasties it is then.' Elsie chuckled. 'In fact, I have some coming out of the oven in just a second.'

'Perfect.'

* * *

Walking towards the reception area, Sally pocketed her car keys before pulling her canvas bag up higher on her shoulder. Those pasties smelled delicious.

She stopped for a moment, hearing a noise. What was that? Well, it was a dog, obviously, but not one she recognised. It was a high-pitched, sad whine.

She pushed the door open, just in time to see Ginny racing from the toilet towards the door to the kennels.

What was going on?

Sally followed her, making her way down the corridor. 'Ginny?'

'I'm in here.'

Sally paused outside the third kennel down. Ginny was sitting on a duvet, a beautiful, mottled greyhound leaning up against her. The whining had stopped now, and the other dogs were settling down again.

'Oh, is this our new one from the pound?'

'Yes, meet Cindy.' Ginny smiled and wrapped her arm around the greyhound. 'And in the hour and a half since she's been here, we've learned very quickly that she doesn't like being left alone. At all.'

'Ah, I wondered what the whining was about.' Sally joined Ginny on the duvet and fussed Cindy behind the ears. 'You're a beauty, aren't you?'

'She is, but that commotion was because I needed the loo, and I was only gone about thirty seconds.' Ginny grimaced. 'I think we might have our work cut out with this one.'

'Aw, bless her. Do you know her history?'

'Only bits and pieces. Apparently, her previous owner bought her off a website a few months ago and couldn't cope with her whining. The pound picked her up as a stray, but a neighbour of the owner recognised her, came forward and explained.'

'But the owner didn't want to take her back even though she'd been found?'

'Nope. Sylvia said the owner was more than likely the one to have kicked her out in the first place.'

'Aw, that's not very nice, is it, Cindy?' Sally smiled. 'Well, you've come to the right place now.'

'Yes, she has.' Ginny rubbed her hand up and down the dog's side.

'We're going to have to have a bit of a shuffle around in here, though. Flora's suggested we move the three puppies from the first kennel into the one next to this and then Luke into this one because, as you can hear, every time Cindy starts whining she sets off Puddles barking and with the puppies so young, they'll probably do the same.'

'Good idea. We don't want the pups near Puddles.'

'Anyway, Flora had to run out to grab some grain-free food, as that's what Cindy is on, so when she's back, we'll start playing musical kennels.'

'Aw, she really is lovely.' Sally looked down at Cindy. 'She's almost smiling being cuddled by you.'

Ginny nodded. 'She certainly is and to think what would have happened to her if Flora hadn't taken her in.'

Sally shuddered. She'd never get used to the fact that so many dogs were put to sleep for no other reason than they'd been given up by their owners and the rescue centres were full.

'Changing the subject as it'll just upset the both of us: have you seen Andy since your catch-up the other evening?'

Ginny shifted on the duvet to face her, Cindy quickly repositioning herself so as much of her body was still against Ginny's as possible.

'I have.' Sally nodded, an involuntary smile lifting the corners of her lips.

'Go on then...'

'Well, there's not much to tell, but he popped into the community hall in Trestow after my class.'

'Really? Just like that? He just turned up? You hadn't invited him?'

'Nope. He brought me hot chocolate from Harold's Café.'

'Aw, I love Harold's hot choccie!'

'Same here.' Sally shifted position on the duvet as Cindy stretched out.

'That can't be it, though? He couldn't have just brought you a drink? Tell me more.'

'Honestly, there's isn't much more to say. It was a bit strange, if I'm honest. He came, gave me the drink and left.' She frowned. 'He mentioned that he thought it was great I'd moved down here and changed careers, but that really was about it.'

'Huh?' Ginny frowned.

'Exactly. That was my thought too. He looked a bit... sad, I guess. And I'm not sure if he wanted to talk to me, but then changed his mind.' Sally stared at the wall opposite. She still hadn't worked out why he had sought her out after her class.

'Have you spoken to him since? Or messaged him?'

'No, maybe I should. I mean, message him – shouldn't I? Make sure everything's okay?'

Should she? If he'd wanted to talk about anything, he would have.

'Yes, definitely,' Ginny said. 'He might just need that push from you. That's odd though. You said he seemed really happy when you went out for that drink.'

'He did.' Sally shook her head. 'I know he's down here on business, so it's probably something to do with that. He's probably absolutely fine now.'

Still, she thought, she'd drop him a text, check in on him.

'Ginny, I'm back. Are you ready to help me move the dogs around, lovely?' Flora's voice wafted down the corridor.

Sally stood up. 'I'll go and help make a start shifting their things if you want to stay with Cindy for a while.'

'Thanks. It's probably for the best. As soon as she starts whining again, she'll have everyone joining in with her and the moving around will be even more stressful.' Ginny grimaced.

Sally pulled Cindy's kennel door closed behind her and went to tell Flora what they'd just discussed.

'Oh, thanks, lovely. Sylvia did warn me about the separation anxiety Cindy had, but, boy, I didn't think she'd begin as soon as we stepped foot outside.' Flora opened the door to the puppies' kennel. 'Are you all right helping me take these three into the kitchen and sitting with them there? Then I'll bring Luke and move the others around. It'll be easier with one free kennel to play with, but I hate to think what these three will get up to in the kitchen alone.'

'Ha ha, yes, they'll definitely scoff the biscuits, for starters!' Sally clipped leads to Dory, Nemo and Marlin. 'Come on, you three. It's a change of scenery for you.'

'Thanks,' Flora said. 'I'll call you if I need any more help or if not when I'm finished here.' She rolled her sleeves up and began to drag the puppies' beds into a pile in the corridor.

Sally looked down at the pups by her feet. 'Come on, you three. Let's go and explore the kitchen.'

10

Sally looked around the small café. Her stomach rumbled as the telltale aroma of a cooked breakfast wafted through from the kitchen. Harold was busy serving behind the counter, attending to people dropping by to collect coffees in takeaway cups or breakfast rolls. Apart from a couple sitting on a table by the window, the tables were empty, but soon it would be busy, when the office workers came in or parents on their way back from the school run.

Sally looked at her phone again. Andy had definitely said he could meet for breakfast. She'd taken Ginny's advice and messaged him once she'd got home yesterday. So where was he? She glanced at the door behind the counter that led to the flat upstairs. It wasn't as though he had far to travel – one staircase. He shouldn't be late, let alone by twenty minutes.

Unless he hadn't wanted to meet and just said he would? But why though? Because it was the easiest thing to do? She picked up a sachet of sugar from a small pot in the middle of the table and shook it, the small granules shifting down to one end. No, if he wasn't going to turn up, he wouldn't have arranged to meet here, where he was staying.

She checked her watch. She needed to be at work in just under an hour. She'd grab something for breakfast and eat it at work. There wasn't any point in waiting any longer.

Standing up, she slipped her mobile into her pocket and picked up her bag.

'Sally, sorry.' Andy appeared then, slipping into the chair opposite where Sally had been sitting.

'Where did you just come from? I'd given up waiting.' Letting her bag drop back to the floor, Sally sat down again.

'I just had a quick meeting. Sorry, I thought I'd be back before you got here, but it went on longer than I thought.'

Sally frowned. 'You had a meeting at eight in the morning?'

'Well, not a meeting as such. More like a quick catch-up with a colleague.' Andy nodded as Harold refilled Sally's mug and poured him a coffee. 'Thanks, mate.'

Sally said her thanks too and pulled her steaming mug towards her, looking at Andy. He seemed a bit happier today, at least.

'So what did you want to talk about?' Andy asked.

'Umm...' Should she bring up the fact he'd looked so down the other night? He seemed a lot happier now, should she just leave it? No, she'd mention it. It would at least give him the opportunity to talk if he wanted to. 'Nothing really. You seemed quite deflated when I saw you last, after my training class, so I wanted to see if everything was all right.'

Andy smiled, his dimple reappearing by the corner of his lips. 'You were worried about me.'

'No.' Sally shifted position in her seat. 'Yes, I guess I was. I hadn't seen you for ages and when I first saw you again you seemed so happy and yet the other night, you just seemed a bit... well, sad.'

'Aw, thank you.' He reached out and touched her hand.

'Don't say it like that.' She flared her nostrils.

'Like what?'

'Like I'm being daft to worry.' She laughed.

'I didn't mean it like that. I'm touched. It means a lot that you still worry about me, even if...' He frowned as a heavy silence descended.

Sally looked down into her mug. Was he really referring to their break-up?

'That was years ago,' she muttered.

'I know. Still, it hurt.' He shrugged off his coat. 'It hurt at the time.'

'Right.' She frowned and picked up the sachet of sugar again. They didn't need to have this conversation. It was in the past. 'Have you done much sightseeing since you've been here?'

Andy took a long sip of his coffee before answering. 'I haven't. I haven't really had time but...'

'Wait.' Andy was right. They should talk about the break-up and clear the air. She held her hand up, a fierce heat creeping up her neck. If they didn't speak about what happened, it would only raise its head again, or worse, he'd disappear, and she'd never have the opportunity to explain herself properly.

'What?' He glanced behind him as if expecting an interruption.

'Sorry, but you're right, we should talk about it. About why I broke things off with you.'

'You don't need to explain yourself. It was over seven years ago now.'

'I do and the comment you made just then proves that I do, that you hold it against me.'

'Okay, fine. Explain.' He leaned back in the chair and rubbed his face with his hand.

Leaning forward, Sally folded the top of the sugar down, squashing the granules to the bottom. There was so much to say, so why was she struggling to find the words?

'I wanted to explain at the time but knew if I did, you wouldn't have walked away.'

'What do you mean?'

'I wanted you to carry on travelling,' she said, still struggling to find the words. 'There were so many places you'd planned to go, to experience.'

Straightening his back, Andy frowned, a deep crease returning between his eyes. 'You told me you didn't think we'd work. You made me believe you didn't love me any more.'

Sally rolled the sugar sachet from both ends, squishing the sugar in the middle. 'You wanted to travel. You'd always wanted to travel.'

'I wanted you.' His voice was quiet, coarse. 'It should have been my decision to make.'

'I couldn't be the one to stop you from following your dream.' She looked down at the sachet between her fingers.

'It was our dream. Both of ours.'

What was he saying?

'I—'

'But look how well that turned out.' He slumped back in his chair.

'What do you mean?' She looked up at him, locking eyes.

'I came back to England, anyway, didn't I?' Pushing his chair back, he paused, his eyes fixed on hers, a million words hanging in the silence. After what felt like ten minutes but which was probably only seconds, he stood up. 'I have to go.'

'But...'

It was too late; he'd already reached the door. Sally looked down as the sachet burst in her hands, sugar granules cascading across her finger and thumb and onto the tabletop.

* * *

Sally closed her car door quietly and made her way across the courtyard towards Wagging Tails. She felt sick. Was Andy seriously suggesting that he wouldn't have resented her if she'd asked him to stay? She'd thought she was doing the right thing. The right thing for him.

She picked out a granule of sugar that was caught beneath her nail. He'd ended up settling down in England anyway, moving back home, taking over his dad's renovation business. What would have happened if she hadn't broken up with him? He was right. She'd made the decision for him.

She pushed the door to reception open and slipped out of her coat.

'Hey, Sally. You're early,' Ginny said as she walked through the kitchen door carrying a mug. 'The kettle's just boiled if you want a coffee?'

'I'm okay, thanks.' The two mugs she'd drank at Harold's would be enough for her for the time being.

'Okay. I'm just taking this through to Flora. Goodness knows she needs it, and then I'll be back out.'

Sally nodded, hanging up her coat before following Ginny through to the kennels.

'Morning, Sally.' Flora stood up when she saw them both coming in.

'Is everything okay? Have you slept in the kennels?' Sally looked from Flora, still in her pyjamas and her hair dishevelled, to the blanket strewn across the floor of Cindy's kennel, the large dog still curled up on her duvet bed.

'Yes, most of the night anyway. Haven't I, Cindy?' Flora glanced at the dog before turning back to them, leaning against the door of the kennel. 'She had everyone barking with her whining. I could hear it from the cottage. You should have heard little Puddles down the end. It's shocking how loud his bark is for such a little dog.'

Sally grimaced. 'You could hear them from the cottage?'

Flora nodded. 'I know we've had dogs suffering from separation anxiety before, but normally they just destroy their beds or mess their kennels.' She yawned for a moment before carrying on. 'They normally settle after a while. But not Cindy, here. Not until I came over.'

'Why don't you go back to the cottage for a nap and we'll try to come up with a solution?' Ginny passed Flora the mug of steaming coffee.

'Aw, thanks, love. I won't sleep though but I will go and freshen up, if you're both sure you don't mind?' Flora picked up the blanket from the floor with her free hand and hooked it over the crook of her arm.

'Yes, of course.' Sally stepped aside as Flora passed them.

'Right, now, Cindy, what are we going to do about you?' Ginny placed her hands on her hips and looked down at the sleeping dog.

'Yes, we can't have her disturbing the other dogs all the time.' Sally glanced down the end of the corridor towards Puddles' kennel.

'No, we really can't. And we can't have Flora sleeping in the kennels every night.'

Biting down on her lip, Sally had an idea. She pushed open the door into the reception area. 'I won't be a minute. I've just thought of something.'

Whether it would actually be a convenient solution or indeed feasible at all, she wasn't sure. Yet. And it wouldn't solve the night-time issue but might just help during the day.

She moved towards the other end of the reception area and tugged open the door to the storage cupboard. Would this work? Would they be able to transform this into a temporary kennel for Cindy? It would mean she'd be able to either see or at least hear people the majority of the time, and it was a decent size. More the size of an understairs cupboard than anything else. Bigger even.

Stepping inside, Sally looked at the large shelving unit filling one end. They'd need to find a new home for that and the huge storage boxes it was housing. And the spare duvets and dog beds piled up on the floor.

'What's your idea?' Ginny called out, holding the door to the kennels open so Cindy knew they was still there.

'This. If we convert it into a temporary kennel, Cindy wouldn't be alone. Not during the day, anyway.' She looked at the door. 'We'd need to swap the door for something she could see through, though.'

'Umm.' Ginny glanced down and pinched the bridge of her nose. 'I was going to say a dog gate, you know the ones that are like baby gates but taller, but being a greyhound, she'd likely be able to jump it.'

'It's not a bad idea, to begin with, at least. If one of us is always in here she might not feel the need to try to escape, and when we're not, we lock the front door so she's safe if she does jump it.'

'That's true. We can speak to Susan when she gets in. She's great with all that stuff, and Percy might be able to think of a solution too.'

Sally nodded. 'I'll start shifting a few things around. Do you think it'll be okay to put the shelving unit against the back wall in the kitchen? I know it'll get in the way, but I'm not sure where else it can go.'

'It'll be better than having all the dogs barking all day.' Ginny grimaced.

'That's very true.' Sally laughed. 'I'll make a start now then.'

'Great. I'm just going to take Ralph out quickly while it's still quiet, and then I'll come and help you.'

As soon as the door clicked shut behind Ginny and Ralph, Cindy began whining again. Sally hurried towards her kennel, dropping the box she was holding to the floor, before Cindy had the chance to set the other dogs off.

'Come on, Cindy. Why don't you come out here with me for a while?'

Bending over the greyhound, Sally clipped a lead to her collar and led her out into the reception area. After securing the lead to the cupboard door, she carried on with her task, shifting boxes from the huge shelving unit.

'What do you think of this place? Do you think we'll be able to turn it into a cosy kennel for you?'

Sally smiled as Cindy yawned and stretched, arching her back as she stuck out her long front legs.

'I think we can. That way, you'll be near us.' She frowned. It still wouldn't solve the problem of the night times. 'During the day, anyway.'

11

'Just listen to that.' Flora paused and tilted her head, her hand on the kitchen door handle.

'What? I can't hear anything?' Sally opened her sandwich box.

'Exactly. Peace.' Flora propped the kitchen door open. 'You're a total genius coming up with the idea to turn the storage cupboard into a temporary kennel.'

'Ah, no. Far from it.' Sally laughed.

'Ha ha, you are, Sally,' Alex said. 'Just say, yes, I know I am! Own it.'

Sally grinned before picking up her sandwich.

'Anyone else?' Flora indicated the kettle before getting more mugs from the cupboard. 'So the day times are sorted now. We just need to think about what we do when we go home of an evening.'

'I don't mind sleeping over,' Ginny said.

'Don't you dare, young lady.' Flora set Ginny's mug down on the table.

'I really don't mind.' She picked out an olive from her couscous salad, a disgusted look crossing her face. 'It's these olives I do mind. Why do they have to put them in all the time?'

'Well, I mind.' Flora wagged her finger at her. 'No, if anyone is going to sleep over, it'll be me. I'd have her over at the cottage, but we need to dog test her first because of little Dougal.'

'I'd offer, but what with my training sessions, she'd be on her own some of the time.' Sally peeled the crust from her sandwich. She really should start cutting them off when she made them.

'No, we'll work something out,' Flora said. 'I can always keep her and Dougal in separate rooms back at the cottage until they've got to know each other.' She set the last of the mugs on the table and sat down. 'But it's such a relief knowing she's safe and happier now.'

'Yes. We just need to find someone who wants to adopt a greyhound – someone who literally doesn't go out of the house apart from walks.' Ginny sighed.

'I'll spend some time training her although it's going to take a while being as her separation anxiety is so severe.' Sally took a bite of her sandwich and swallowed. 'It's not impossible, though.'

'No, nothing's impossible.' Flora sank back in her chair, holding her mug to her chest. 'I'm just glad she's with us, and now we have that extra kennel made up we still have an empty space for an emergency or someone from the pound.'

'And the puppies are going tomorrow,' Alex added.

'Yes, of course. Good, that's what I like. I like to have space just in case.' Flora stood up. 'Right, I'm going to see how Percy and Susan are getting on sorting out that shed.'

Sally stood too. 'I'll come and help.'

'No, you have your lunch, love. You've done enough today, shifting stuff around. They'll be fine. Percy and Susan have had this on their to-do list for months now and I know Percy will be glad to have a reason to get it crossed off. And once we shift some of this stuff out there, we'll have a bit more room in here again too.' Flora nodded towards the shelving unit that Sally had dragged through from the cupboard.

'Okay, thanks.' Shifting in her chair, Sally pulled her mobile from the back pocket of her jeans. Nothing. Andy hadn't messaged or tried to ring.

'Are you all right, Sally?' Ginny looked across at her, another olive halfway to the small pile she'd made next to her bowl.

'Yes, I'm fine.' Sally smiled as she turned her mobile over and placed it down with the screen flat against the table.

Ginny leaned across and gestured to it. 'Did you...?'

'Ginny? Flora? Is anyone about?' A voice filtered through from the reception area.

'Oh, that's Darryl.' Ginny twisted in her chair. 'In here, Darryl.'

Stepping through the open door, Darryl held up his hand in a greeting before glancing back towards reception. 'What's going on with the extra kennel you've made up? And who's the beautiful greyhound?'

'Ah, that's Cindy. She suffers from separation anxiety. This way, even when we're in here, she can hear us and seems content.' Ginny hugged him before nodding towards the kettle. 'Do you want a drink? I didn't know you were coming for lunch?'

'I'm not. Sorry, I can't stay.' He looked down at Ginny's lunch and laughed. 'You found olives.'

'Ha, yes. Do you want them?'

Darryl scrunched up his nose. 'No, thanks.'

'Fair enough. What's up then if you've not come to spend lunch with us?'

'Is Flora about?' Darryl glanced back out towards the reception area.

Ginny slipped back into her chair. 'She's sorting the storage shed out with Percy and Susan.'

'Oh, I didn't see them.'

'They might have popped over to the cottage then.' Alex took a long sip from his mug. 'Have you got some news for us? Please don't tell us you're having to stop the adoption articles in the paper?'

Darryl frowned. 'No, I wish it were that simple.'

'What do you mean?' Turning in her chair, Ginny took his hand in hers. 'What's happened?'

'I guess I might as well tell you before going to find Flora.' Darryl rubbed his free hand over his face. 'You're going to find out, anyway.'

'Now you're worrying me.' Ginny pulled out the chair next to her and indicated he sit down.

Slumping heavily into the chair, Darryl clasped his hands on the top of the table. 'It's about the trouble you've been having with that new developer.'

'Trouble? I thought that had all blown over?' Ginny rubbed his arm. 'That Lyle guy was just trying his luck. There's no way he'd ever get planning permission to build a new estate behind Wagging Tails. There's not adequate access to the land.'

'That's what the conclusion would normally be.' He ran the palm of his hand across his face again.

'What do you mean, "normally"?' Sally laid her half-eaten sandwich back in its plastic container. 'What's different about this time?'

'Trevor Watson, that's who. He's the difference.'

'I've heard of him.' Alex crossed his legs. 'He's one of the councillors, isn't he? One of the top bosses.'

'Yes. Or he was. Up until this morning. He's just been fired. Well, suspended following an enquiry, I should say.'

'Then what's he got to do with the planning application that Lyle guy is submitting?' Ginny asked.

Darryl met her gaze.

'Because the planning has already been accepted, that's what.'

Alex whistled. 'What? How?'

'I imagine a fair amount of money exchanged hands between Trevor Watson and the developers.' The ping of a message sounded, and Darryl pulled his mobile from his pocket. He glanced at it quickly before laying it on the table and tapping his fingers against it. 'I've got a couple of the team looking into the circumstances at the moment, trying to dig something up.'

'So, what can we do?' Sally asked. 'Is there anything we can do now planning permission has been granted?' She clicked the lid shut on her sandwich box. She suddenly didn't feel very hungry.

'Hounding the local MP, protests to attract news coverage. There's a fair bit that can be organised but, ultimately, it depends on whether the council are able to, or willing, to revoke the permission now it's already been given.'

'I can't imagine the majority of the council want all these hundreds of houses built. Imagine the strain it will put on the infrastructure, the doctors' surgeries, dentists, schools.' Sally shook her head.

'Not to mention what a nightmare the journey into West Par will become. The roads are so narrow anyway, if there're potentially hundreds or a thousand more cars using them…' Alex raised his eyebrows.

'And that's why Lyle is so intent on pressurising Flora to sell up. He knows he'll need at least two access points onto the development because the road leading to the land behind is even narrower than the road leading to our lane.' Ginny squashed the pile of olives with her fork, spraying a tiny amount of juice across the table.

'Exactly. Unfortunately, this all means that his company is unlikely to give in to any outside pressure. They'll be thinking that the sooner they make a start on the development, the harder it will be to have the permission revoked.'

Darryl stood up.

'But if it was given illegally, then surely Lyle won't have a leg to stand on if it's revoked?' Ginny passed him his mobile.

'That's if any illegal activity can be proven. It's just a rumour at the moment.' Darryl took his phone.

Alex uncrossed his legs. 'And I bet the last thing the council wants is for this to become public knowledge. They won't want it known that they have a corrupt system even if they've suspended the employee in question.'

'Exactly.' Darryl moved to the doorway. 'Right, I'd better go and let Flora know. It'll be worth trying to organise a community meeting in West Par as soon as possible.' He turned back to them. 'Oh, and we've no actual evidence that Trevor Watson has acted illegally – yet, anyway – so make sure to keep his name out of anything or we're all likely to be charged with slander.'

'Understood.' Alex held his forefinger and thumb to his mouth, making a zipping action across his lips. 'What's the name of the property developers Lyle owns? I'm assuming he's not a one-man band.'

'No. It's Fresh Image Developments, a relatively new company.'

'Huh, that name isn't very fitting for a corrupt company.' Alex stood up and placed his mug in the dishwasher. 'I'll draw up some posters and organise a meeting.'

'Good idea,' Ginny said, and stood up to say bye to Darryl. 'When we've organised it with Flora, I'll take Dory for a walk around the village and spread the word.'

Sally looked out of the window. Would this company really get away with building all of those new houses? And if they did, what would it mean for their idyllic sanctuary?

Whatever happened, she was sure of one thing – that they wouldn't be closed down and they wouldn't allow this development to disrupt their community. None of West Par would.

12

With a pang of guilt, Sally shut the door to Cindy's new kennel and stroked the greyhound's nose through the bars. Susan had worked her magic in record time to get this constructed and the makeshift kennel secure.

'Sorry, miss, you're not going to be happy, but we've all got to go to this meeting this evening.'

The greyhound lifted her paw, squeezing it through the bars and placing it on Sally's hand.

Smiling, Sally shook her head. 'As much as you plead, I'm sorry, but we've got to go. We've got to do our best to stop this development. For you, for all of the dogs we rescue, now and in the future.'

'Are you coming, Sally?' Alex pushed open the door to the courtyard and peered through.

'Yes, one second.'

'Is she okay, lovely?' Flora asked as Sally joined Alex, Flora, Percy, Ginny, Susan, Poppy and Darryl out in the courtyard.

'I guess we'll find out when we get back. I've put the radio on so if anything, hopefully it will distract the other dogs from her cries.'

'Fingers crossed.' She held her hand up, crossing her fingers.

'Right, let's do this.' Flora checked the door was locked before turning and leading the way across the courtyard.

'Is everyone ready for this?' Percy fell into step beside Flora.

'Oh yes. I'm ready for a fight.' Flora curled her hand into a fist and grinned. 'No one messes with our dogs.'

'No, you're right there, Flora.' Ginny linked arms with Darryl.

'I can't imagine anyone in West Par or the other local villages feel any different,' Susan said, waving as her partner, Malcolm pulled his car up outside the gate. He jumped out and held the gate open for everyone to pass through.

'Exactly. The whole community will be on our side,' Poppy said, shutting the gate behind them.

'I hope you're right.' Flora glanced back at Wagging Tails. 'Just to even imagine...'

'Don't, love,' Percy said. 'It's not worth the time wasted nor the tears. Nothing's changing.'

'Yes, you're right.' Flora nodded, her frown dispersing.

'Besides, if the story about Trevor Watson or whoever, comes out, no one's...' Sally paused, distracted by the sound of her mobile ringing. She pulled it from her pocket and frowned. It was Andy. 'Sorry, I best take this.'

She took a deep breath before answering, not sure she was ready to face the emotions Andy had brought out in her last time they'd met.

'Hey, Sally. It's Andy.'

Why did people always feel they had to introduce themselves even though they knew their name would be displayed? Force of habit, probably.

'Hi, Andy.'

'I just wondered if you were free to meet?'

'When?'

'Now? Later? I don't mind. The sooner the better.'

'Right.' Sally looked ahead as the others passed through the signs welcoming visitors to West Par and turned up the lane towards the small community hall. 'I can't. Not now, I mean. I'm busy. How about later?' She checked her watch. It was almost six o'clock. 'About eight, maybe?'

'Yes, eight would be good. I'll see you at Harold's.'

'Okay.' She ended the call and slipped her phone back into her pocket.

What did he want to talk about? Did he want to give her another hard time about not letting him choose whether to carry on travelling or stay behind with her? She swallowed. She supposed she had it coming.

* * *

'...not to mention the effect the new housing development will have on the roads.'

Flora finished her speech before sitting down at the long table at the front of West Par community hall.

Sally watched as looks were exchanged along the length of the table. Olive, who at seventy-two had lived all her life in West Par and been informally elected as spokeswoman for the village, sat in the middle, Flora on one side of her and the headmaster of the tiny primary school on the other. The other two seats at the table were taken by two local shopkeepers.

'But what about our children?' A woman sitting in the back row stood up. 'This development might be a good thing. A proportion of the houses built will have to be affordable housing. That's right, isn't it?'

'And it will be good for business.' The owner of the local corner shop, David, spoke up.

An elderly man sitting in the front row held his hand up. 'It might line your pockets, but if we can't access our doctor, our health will suffer.'

'And we all know how difficult it is to get an appointment already,' a woman standing at the back, rocking a baby to and fro, called out.

'I agree. There's so much pressure on local services already without more people coming into the area.' The other shopkeeper, Primrose, who owned an ice cream parlour at the edge of the beach, leaned forward and looked down the table at David. 'And don't you think the development will drive away the tourists we get? The people who buy the houses will just drive to the supermarket anyway. They won't be popping to your shop to buy things.'

David shrugged. 'Maybe.'

'I can promise you one thing.' The headteacher shifted his position. 'We won't be able to cope with an influx of pupils. Our classes are full as it is since that development went up outside East Par. We just don't have the space.'

A man stood up from one of the middle rows of chairs facing the table. 'I moved here because I liked the peace and quiet not...'

Sally's mobile shivered to life. Was it Andy again? She pulled it from her pocket and frowned. It was her sister, Linda. She never rang her. She stood up and made her way to the end of the row of chairs. 'Sorry.'

'All right?' Susan mouthed.

Sally nodded.

She stepped outside the hall, letting the door close quietly behind her before answering. 'Hi, Linda. Lovely to hear from you. How are things going?'

'Sally, have you got time to talk?' Her sister's tone was serious, urgent.

'Umm...' Sally glanced back at the door and sighed. 'Yes, is everything okay?'

'Not really, no it's not.'

'Why?' Sally walked down the lane towards the cobbled street leading down to the beach. She didn't think she'd ever heard Linda sound so unsure. She'd always been the confident one, the strong one, the one who never, ever asked for help. Not that Linda would ever ask Sally for help even if she needed it. That wasn't the type of relationship they had. No, they were more the sort of sisters who sent Christmas and birthday cards and spent the rest of the year trying to avoid any contact with one another. Sally sighed. She'd always wanted to be close to her. She'd always been envious of her friends' relationships with their siblings, but however hard she'd tried she and Linda were never going to see eye to eye or be close.

'I'm pregnant.' Linda's voice was quiet, subdued.

'Oh wow, congratulations! I didn't know you and Pearce were even trying!' Sally grinned. She was going to be an aunty! It had never crossed her mind that Linda would have kids. Not in a million years. She'd always been the career woman.

'Thank you. And no, we weren't.'

'Oh.' Sally stepped onto the beach, feeling the sand shift beneath her trainers. 'Are you happy?'

'Yes, I am. Pearce too. It's taken us a few months to get our heads around the upheaval and the change this little one will bring, but, yes, we're happy.'

'I'm thrilled for you then.' Sally looked towards the ocean. She'd always assumed she'd be the one of the two of them to have children. Linda and Pearce had been together for what? Fifteen years or something. And neither of them had ever given any indication that starting a family would be on the cards.

'Thanks.'

An awkward silence hung between them.

Sally stopped at the edge of the ocean, the water inching towards her with the tide. There was something else. Breaking the news that she was going to be an aunty wasn't the only reason Linda had rung her. Linda had said something was wrong, and judging by the tone of her voice, Sally had a feeling it was serious. 'Wait. You said it has taken you and Pearce months to get used to the idea of being parents. How far gone are you? When's the baby due?'

'In four months.'

'You're five months pregnant already! And you're only just telling me!' She swallowed. They'd never been close but not to tell her something this big? Until now?

'Yes, well, I've not long told Mum and Dad.'

'Really?' Sally kicked at the sand. 'But you work with them. How did you get away with hiding your bump?'

'That's the reason I'm ringing you.'

'Because you didn't tell our parents straight away? Did they not guess? I mean, you do work together all day, every day. You share the same office space.' Sally lowered herself to the sand. She could feel a chill through her jeans.

'No they didn't. Until a couple of weeks ago, I hid my pregnancy because of the way things are at the office.'

'You're completely confusing me now. What do you mean?' She'd hid her pregnancy from their parents? Why? And what was going on at the office?

'Mum and Dad haven't been in the office much recently.'

Sally raised her eyebrows. 'Really? They've always been workaholics.'

'Not recently. Not for the last six months or so. Mum has...' The phone line fell quiet.

'Mum's what?' Sally traced a line in the sand with her fingertips. She'd not heard from either of her parents in a while. She hadn't really thought anything of it, though. She knew they weren't particularly that happy with her decision to move down here, and if she was honest with herself, she'd been quite happy to live in her little bubble in West Par and shield herself from the guilt.

'She's been a bit under the weather.'

'For six months?' Sally gripped the phone to her ear. 'Linda, what's going on? What aren't I being told?'

Linda's sigh was audible through the phone. 'She had a heart attack.'

'A heart attack? What? When?'

'Six months ago. She's been taking it easy since then and, of course, you know what Dad is like. He's hardly been away from her side for...'

Linda's voice grew muffled as Sally lowered the phone. A heart attack? Six months ago? And no one had thought to tell her?

'Sally? Sally, are you still there?'

Sally held her phone next to her ear again and spoke, her voice barely above a whisper. 'Is she okay now?'

'Yes, she's fine. She's made a full recovery, and I kept expecting them to return to work, you know, so I've been holding down the fort, which is why I've only recently told them about my pregnancy.'

'Right. And she's definitely okay? And Dad is too?'

'Yes, yes, they are. They've been holidaying, gallivanting around without a care in the world for the past three months. I assumed they'd just decided to take a break, to make certain Mum had fully recovered before returning to the office.'

'Why didn't they tell me? Why didn't you? I should have been there for Mum. For Dad. For the both of them.' She dug her fingers into the sand, scooping it up into her palm.

'They didn't want me to. They didn't want you to worry.'

'But you're telling me now.'

Something that big, that important, and she was the last to know. She might as well have moved to the other side of the world.

'Exactly. I'm telling you now.'

'Huh, yes, it's a bit late, though, isn't it? It's not as though I can help with anything now.' Lifting her hand, she watched as the sand dribbled through the gaps in her fingers.

'Actually, that's why I'm ringing. You can.'

'What can I do? You just said Mum is better.' Her voice caught. No one had rung and told her, not Mum, Dad, Linda. She hadn't been given the chance to even visit her in the hospital. What if the worst had happened, and she hadn't been given the opportunity to say goodbye? 'You should have told me.'

'That's what I said. I told Dad you'd want to know, but every time I brought it up, he said there was no point in worrying you because there was nothing you could have done from down there. I understand his thinking in a way.' Linda paused. 'Anyway, there is something you can do. Mum wants to take early retirement and, obviously, Dad just wants whatever she does. And then I'll be going on maternity leave and I've been thinking about maybe going back part-time.'

'Oh.' Linda had always loved work, put her everything into her career. It had never crossed Sally's mind that she would want to go part-time. Sally shrugged, but then she'd never thought Linda would want children either. Maybe she just didn't know her as well as she thought she did.

'Yes, I think so. I know this will be our only child and I might want to cut my hours at the office. I want to be able to make that choice, anyway.'

Sally dug her hand beneath the surface of the sand again. 'I still don't understand how I can help.'

'Come home. We can run the law firm together. Or at least you can be the ears while I'm on maternity.'

'Come home?' Sally blinked. 'This is my home now.'

'Really?' Linda's curt tone did little to mask her surprise.

'Yes, really. I haven't finished my training, anyway. I wouldn't be able to even work as a qualified solicitor, let alone become a partner.'

'You've almost finished your training.'

'Hardly.' Sally clenched her hand around her phone. She hadn't finished her training. Yes, she only had a year to go but it was still a year and she'd been out of the business for so long now. Besides, she'd left for a reason. Linda couldn't ask her to go back. She couldn't.

'Even so, you'll be there. You'll be able to see what's going on, keep an eye on everything. This is our future. The firm. Mum and Dad built it up from scratch and now it's our turn to do our bit.'

What?

'No, no it's not. I left the city, I left the firm. I left my training for a reason. It wasn't for me. It wasn't the dream I wanted to follow.'

'Sally, I've done my bit, more than my bit. All I'm asking of you is to do yours.'

Sally held the phone in front of her and stared at the small screen. 'You stayed because you followed your passion. You wanted to take over the firm. I didn't, so you haven't done "your bit". You've done exactly what you wanted to.'

Linda sighed. 'You're impossible sometimes, Sally, but fine. Don't become a partner, but please just help with this transition. Dominic's still working for us. You know he's always had his eye on running the place. He's itching to jump into Mum and Dad's shoes, and I won't be there to stop him muscling his way in when I'm on maternity leave, but you could come back and just keep an eye on things, let him know that one of our family is there. Just for a few months if you really can't spare any more time. We just need someone around to keep a check on everything, to keep things in order.'

'Linda, you know I can't. West Par is where my life is now.' She watched as the sand cascaded through the spaces between her fingers again. Linda couldn't ask her to do this. Give her life up. It wasn't fair.

'Great. Thanks for nothing. And you wonder why no one told you when Mum was poorly.'

And that was it. The call had ended. The silence of the night enveloped her.

13

Stepping through the cottage doorway, Sally threw her keys into the small wicker basket on the windowsill of the porch. She slipped her trainers off and kicked them across the small hallway, watching as they landed in a heap against the opposite wall.

In the living room, she threw herself onto the sofa, her coat crumpling against the back cushions. Had Linda really just rung and asked – no, tried to guilt-trip – her into returning home?

She didn't owe her sister anything. Linda hadn't particularly been supportive when she'd taken the leap to move down here. In fact, she hadn't even been there for her when she'd split up with the love of her life. If anything, she'd made life more difficult than it had had to be, teasing her for missing Andy, piling admin jobs on her to 'help' her keep busy.

No, Sally really didn't owe her anything. She'd tried to follow her family's expectations. She'd tried. Besides, Linda had wanted to go into the family business. That had always been her dream. Not Sally's.

A loud tring rang through the silent living room and Sally rummaged in her coat pocket for her mobile, holding it to her ear before she'd even glanced at the name.

'Linda, I can't do it. I just can't. It's—'

'It's Andy. Not Linda. Sorry to disappoint you.'

Sally sat forward. 'Andy?' Her eyes automatically flickered to the mantelpiece and the small carriage clock her parents had given her when she'd moved into her first apartment in the city. It was half past eight. She'd meant to have been meeting Andy at eight. 'Andy. I'm so sorry, I—'

'Hey, don't worry. It sounds as though you've got other things on your mind. We can reschedule.'

'No, no, that's fine.' The last thing she wanted to do was to reschedule. Right now, if there was one thing in this world she could do with, which could make her feel better, it was one of his hugs. 'I'll come now.'

'Are you at home? Let me come to you. What's your address?'

'Are you sure?'

'Of course I'm sure.'

Sally gave him her address before slumping back against the cushions and closing her eyes. She tried – and failed – to clear her mind. To just have a few moments of silence before she had to try to figure everything out. She didn't know what to think any more. She'd messed up big time with Andy, ruined both their lives by breaking up with him to try to please her parents, her family. And now, after all this time, she'd met up with him again, and Linda was trying to get her to return to London.

She swiped the back of her hand across her face. She was crying. She hadn't even realised she was. Blinking, she looked around the room, looked at the pile of clean washing stacked precariously on the small dining table by the window, the pile of notebooks and pens scattered on the coffee table, the vacuum standing redundant in front of the television, its cable snaking across the floor to the plug socket on the other side of the room.

She jumped up from her seat and hurried around, tidying up. Andy knew she wasn't a particularly tidy person. It had always been him tidying their room, whether they'd been staying at a hotel, hostel or in a campervan. Or a tent, for that matter. He'd always kept everything in its place. Luckily, by the very nature of backpacking, there hadn't been that much mess she could make simply because they hadn't had much. But this… this wasn't the impression she wanted to give him.

She was scooping the clean washing in her arms just as the doorbell rang. Drat. Shifting the clothes into one arm, she pulled open the front door.

'Do you need a hand?' Andy closed the door with one hand whilst shooting his other out to catch a T-shirt that was starting to fall from her arms.

'Thanks.'

'Where do you want it?'

Walking back into the living room, Sally shrugged before emptying the contents of her arms back onto the table. He'd seen it now.

'Here will be fine. I'll put it away later.'

Or tomorrow. Or more likely at the weekend.

'There you go.' Andy folded the T-shirt and carefully laid it on top of the crumpled pile.

'I'm sorry I didn't meet you at Harold's. Do you want a drink? I'm afraid I haven't got any hot chocolate – not that I could make it like he does anyway, but I've got tea, coffee…' In the kitchen, which led off from the living room, she pulled open the cupboard above the kettle. 'Or green tea.'

'Normal tea's good, thanks. And don't apologise about forgetting to meet. It looks as though you've been on the go all day.'

'What do you mean?'

She had, but how did he know?

Chuckling, he gestured towards her. 'You've still got your coat on.'

'Oh.' She could feel the heat of embarrassment flicker across her face as she shrugged out of her coat, looking for somewhere to place it. 'No wonder I felt warm in here.'

'Anyway, thanks for agreeing to meet. I won't keep you long. I just wanted to clear the air from this morning.' He held out his hand for her coat, took it and hooked it over the door handle.

'Right.' She took two cups from the drying rack beside the sink and swilled them under the tap, the crockery clinking together as she did so.

What did he want her to say? She swallowed, a lump forming in her throat. She wasn't going to cry. She wasn't. Not in front of him.

'It didn't feel right just leaving it how it was…'

'No, I know.' She placed two tea bags in the cups, blinking back the tears stinging the backs of her eyes. She'd abandoned him to follow her parents' expectations of her, hurting him in the process and now... now, she'd upset Linda and let her and her parents down all over again by refusing to move back. She just couldn't do anything right. Not a thing. She'd even missed the end of the meeting about the development. Probably the most important part where everyone decided what action should be taken to save West Par, to save Wagging Tails.

'I want you to know—'

Taking a deep, shuddering breath, she spun around. 'I'm sorry. I'm so sorry. I didn't want to hurt you. I didn't mean to hurt you. I was just trying to do the right thing. The right thing by you. The right thing by my family and I messed it all up. I'm still messing it all up. I can't do anything right. I can't please everyone. Or anyone, it seems. I just can't.'

'Whoa.' Andy held his hands up, confusion etched across his face. 'What's going on, Sally?'

'I don't know any more.' She pressed the heels of her hands against her eyes, waiting for the inevitable stars to form in the darkness.

'It's okay.'

She could feel his warmth as he stepped towards her, his arms as he wrapped them around her body, pulling her close against him. With her eyes still tightly closed, she laid her forehead in the crook between his shoulder and neck and let the tears flow.

'Everything will be all right.'

Sally pulled away, wiping her eyes. 'I'm so sorry. I didn't mean to... you know.'

'Mean to what? Get upset?' Andy clasped her hands in his. 'This is me. You can talk to me.' He searched her face. 'What's going on?'

'Honestly, I feel as though I've walked into a parallel universe or something. Everything was fine, great. A week or so ago, everything was fine. I was happy – happy with my job, happy with my life down here and now everything's falling apart.'

'Look, I'm sorry if any of what you're feeling is anything to do with us running into each other. I know it's brought up feelings I'd buried long ago, but I don't want you to feel guilty. I don't want to dredge up anything.' He stepped back, running his fingers through his hair.

'No, it's not you. I mean, it's not not you. It is, but not all of it.' She shook her head. She wasn't making any sense. It was all she could do to think clearly, let alone articulate how she was feeling. Leaning against the work surface behind her, she faced Andy and steadied her breathing. 'It's been so lovely to meet up with you again. To run into you down here, of all places.'

'But it's made you question your decisions back then?'

'No.' She shook her head. That hadn't come out right. There was more. She hadn't explained herself.

'Oh, right.' He looked down at the floor, frowning.

'No, no, that's not how I meant it.' She closed her eyes for a moment. She hadn't meant it to sound so callous, so uncaring. She did care. She knew she'd hurt him. 'That's not what I meant. I was being honest the other day when I told you that I hadn't meant to hurt you, that I thought I was breaking up with you for the right reasons. For you. And I still think I made the right decision.'

She had, hadn't she?

Andy nodded slowly before shaking his head. 'Well, that's put me in my place then.'

'Andy, I was only trying to do the right thing. I felt I didn't have a choice but to move back to the city and restart my studies. The only choice I felt I had left was to try to do the right thing by you and at the time I was convinced the right thing was to let you do what you wanted; let you carry on travelling. I didn't know you were going to end up back in England a few months later.'

He nodded slowly.

How could she make him understand?

'You didn't reach out to me when you moved back.' She bit down on her bottom lip. That had sounded accusatory.

Andy laughed, a low, hollow noise that sounded anything but happy. 'Because you'd told me you didn't love me. Because you'd broken my heart.'

'I know. I...' She shouldn't have said that. A silence hung in the air, thick with unsaid words, as their eyes locked. 'I'm sorry.'

'No, I'm sorry. I shouldn't have brought it up.' He gave her a quick, short smile. 'Has something else happened? You said everything was falling apart?'

'I...' She gripped the work surface behind her. 'Linda rang. My mum had a heart attack.'

'Oh, Sally, I'm so sorry. Is she okay?' He drew her in for another hug.

'She's fine. It happened months ago.' Her voice was muffled against his jumper.

'Months ago? You didn't say when we met up the other day.' He stepped back.

'That's because I've only just found out. Linda rang to try to get me to go back and finish my training.' She turned and pulled the tea bags from the mugs. They'd been in there too long; a thin layer of scum had collected on the surface of the water.

'They didn't tell you at the time?'

Sally shook her head. 'Apparently they didn't want to worry me.'

Andy passed her the milk.

'Thanks. And now, by the sounds of it, my parents have all but retired and Linda is pregnant, so she wants me to go and keep an eye on the firm...' Placing the milk down, she stirred the tea. 'So, nobody tries to step in whilst she's on maternity leave.'

'She's asking you to give up your life here?' He placed the milk bottle back in the fridge.

Sally shrugged. That's what Linda had asked, hadn't she? 'Pretty much.'

'What are you going to do?' He picked up his mug and led the way through into the living room.

'I don't know. I told her I wouldn't, but now... I don't know. I feel guilty.' She sank into the sofa cushions, wrapping her hands around her mug.

'You're not really thinking about going back? Are you?'

'No.' She looked around the small living room. She loved it here. She was happy. Working at Wagging Tails was everything she'd dreamed of. She had friends, a life she loved. 'I don't know. You did, didn't you?'

On the sofa next to her, Andy placed his mug on his knee and looked into her eyes. 'Yes, I did, but it wasn't as simple as that. I'd just lost you and...'

She swallowed.

He held up his mug-free hand. 'Hear me out. I'm not saying that to try to make you feel bad. I'm trying to explain how things were different for me.'

'Okay.'

'When I got the call from my mum to say that my dad was sick, she wasn't asking me to come home. The opposite, in fact; she'd rung just to let me know and had said that my dad wanted me to carry on travelling, to live my life to the fullest.' He looked across at the fireplace opposite, seemingly lost in his own thoughts for a while, before shaking himself and looking back at her. 'But, the truth was, I wasn't really enjoying myself. I was going through the motions, going from place to place, doing all the off-the-beaten-track stuff we'd planned to do before you left, but it wasn't the same. Not without you.'

'Sorry.' Sally curled her legs up beneath her. She'd always assumed he'd been off having the time of his life. It hadn't occurred to her that travelling had been a 'them' thing rather than something they'd do on their own.

'No, don't please. What happened happened and you had your reasons. What I mean is, our situations were different. You're happy living down here. I wasn't happy.' He shrugged. 'It was a no-brainer me coming back.'

She understood, but he'd still taken over his dad's business. He'd still made the decision to stay, to do the right thing by his family. 'You still took over your dad's business, though. You followed in his footsteps. What your dad, your parents, wanted for you.'

'Nah, you remember my parents. As long as I was happy, they didn't care what it was I chose to do. My dad had no fixed views on me taking over his business.' He looked towards the fireplace again. 'I like to think he'd be proud of me and, yes, that's why I took over initially.' He frowned. 'That and I didn't have a clue what to do with myself.'

'And you stayed?'

'Yes. I get to travel still, mind, only in the UK, but I like it. I like discovering new places, getting to know new people, new communities. Plus, it's creative work, renovating old houses, breathing new life into them.'

'Yes, I guess it is. I can imagine you enjoying something like that.'

He shifted in his seat. 'The business has changed a bit now. I'm starting to take it in a different direction but, I don't know, I'll see if it's the right direction.'

'So, you think I should go back and carry on with my training? Help Linda with the business?' She frowned.

'No, the complete opposite. I was trying to explain how different our situations are. You've never been close to your parents, or Linda, for that matter.'

She nodded. However much his words stung, they both knew they were true. She'd have been envious of his relationship with his parents if they hadn't welcomed her into their family with open arms.

He shrugged. 'Sorry.'

'Don't be. It's the truth.' She sighed.

'There you go, then. And you've done it once before. You've tried to please them before by giving up travelling and returning to your studies. It's not as though you haven't tried to live the life they expected of you. Not that you should have ever been expected to in the first place.'

She gulped down the rest of her tea. 'Yes, you're right. I know you are. I just feel guilty.'

'Why don't you go and see them? Speak to your parents and Linda face to face. Explain your position.' He took her now empty mug and placed it on the coffee table alongside his and stood up. 'It's an idea. It might help make your mind up.'

She led him to the door.

'I'll think about it. Thanks for the chat.'

'You're welcome. Thanks for meeting.' He turned before stepping outside. 'Are you sure you're okay?'

'I will be.' She nodded and watched as he walked along the short path towards her gate. The light of the moon illuminated the cracked slabs, small yellow flowers having self-seeded sprung up through the cracks. That's what she'd first fallen in love with when she'd viewed the cottage – the tiny but wild garden. She waved as Andy held his hand up before closing the wrought-iron gate behind him.

14

Sally grinned as she watched Dory walking excitedly across the courtyard with her new family. This was by far the best part of working at Wagging Tails – connecting dogs with their second chance at life, with their forever homes.

'I hate this part.' Ginny closed the door and stood with her back against it.

'Aw, Ginny.' Sally drew her in for a quick hug. 'Dory is going to have a wonderful life with her new family. They've even booked a woodland lodge for a holiday in a couple of weeks. She's going to have the time of her life.'

'Oh, I know. And it's perfect, but I still find it difficult to say goodbye to them. Even after all these years working here.'

'What are you going to be like tomorrow?' Flora said, joining them, balancing a tray full of mugs in her hands. 'We have both Marlin and Nemo leaving us in the morning.' She slid the tray onto the counter and pulled a tissue from the box sitting on the shelf behind her. 'Here you go.'

'Huh, you can talk. I know that's why you went and made coffee, so we couldn't see your tears.' Ginny took the tissue and dabbed her eyes.

'I don't know what you're referring to. I was thirsty.' Flora winked before giving out the mugs.

Sally gratefully took the mug and gulped down the hot, bittersweet coffee.

'Hold on, let us finish ours before you ask for another.' Flora chuckled and picked up her mug. 'Are you okay today, Sally, lovely? I couldn't help but notice you left the meeting early last night and you don't look as though you've had much of a sleep.'

Sally lowered her mug. 'Oh, I'll be okay, thanks. Sorry for leaving the meeting. It was my sister on the phone, and she never rings me.'

'No need to apologise, lovely. I just wondered if you were okay, that's all.'

Sally shrugged. Was she okay? Her sister and parents hadn't told her about her mum being ill and then Linda had proceeded to try to guilt-trip her into returning to the city.

'I will be. Just family stuff.'

Flora nodded. 'You're welcome to take a day off if you need to sort anything out. You still haven't taken any holiday days since you started.'

Should she? Andy had said it might help to go and visit her parents. And Linda. Maybe she should take Flora up on the offer and go and face the music. She swallowed. It wasn't something she wanted to do. She'd rather clean out a thousand kennels than return to the city, even for just a day, but it might make things a little clearer for herself.

'Well, just give me a shout if you want to take some time.' Flora touched Sally's forearm. 'And I'm always here for a chat if you need it. I'm a good listener. Isn't that right, Ginny?'

'It sure is.' Ginny grinned. 'Oh, who's this?'

Sally looked up just as a woman rushed through the door. With her hair falling from a messy bun and her clothes crumpled, she looked as though she'd had less sleep than Sally herself.

'Is this Wagging Tails Dogs' Home?' The woman glanced around the reception area, pausing briefly as she looked at the sign behind the counter. 'Of course it is. I know it is. I saw the sign outside too.'

'Can we help you, lovely?' Flora placed her mug down and walked around the counter.

'Oh, I really hope so. I do.' She looked down at her creased shirt and jacket, smoothing the fabric with her hands. 'I must seem a complete state. I know I do, but I've travelled down from Yorkshire and I've only stopped once to get petrol and a quick coffee, and I'm really hoping I'm in the right place.'

'You've come from Yorkshire? That's a long way.' Flora glanced across at Ginny.

'I'll go and make you a coffee.' Acting on Flora's hint, Ginny disappeared into the kitchen.

'Yes, yes, it is.' The woman looked towards the door to the kennels as the dogs began to bark, spurred on by the woman's arrival. 'Is that where you keep the dogs?'

'Yes, it is.' Flora frowned. 'Can I ask why you've come all this way?'

'Yes, I saw him. On a post, a social media post.' The woman shook her head. 'No, that's not true. My friend saw him on a post and forwarded it to me.'

'Saw who, lovely?'

'My Eric. They saw my Eric. At least, I'm certain it's him. He has a tiny mark right above his tail which looks like a love heart. It's only tiny.' The woman held her thumb and forefinger a centimetre apart. 'But it was there, on the photo on social media.'

'Puddles. You're Puddles' owner, aren't you?' Sally pushed her mug away and smiled. Was this really his owner?

'Sorry... I...' The woman looked from Sally to Flora and back again. 'Eric is my dog, the little dachshund from the photo.' She pulled her mobile from her handbag and scrolled through before holding it up, a photo of Puddles looking back at them. 'This is Eric and I think you might have him.'

'We have a dachshund, yes.' Sally smiled. 'He didn't have a chip though, so we named him Puddles, just for the time being, but he does have the small heart shape on his fur.'

'He does. Do you think it's him then? Here, let me show you some more photos.' The woman swiped the screen on her mobile and held it up again. Another photograph of Puddles stared back at them; this time he was sitting in the woods, wearing a tiny yellow knitted coat, surrounded by other dogs.

Sally frowned. 'How long has he been missing?'

'A year and five months, three weeks and two days now.' The woman blinked. 'I know it's a long shot, a super long shot, but when my friend forwarded the post, I knew I had to come and check. Just for my peace of mind, if nothing else.'

'Here you go. I've popped a sugar in there too. I thought you might need it.' Ginny passed the woman a mug.

'Thank you. I must sound crazy, driving all the way from Yorkshire to Cornwall without so much as a phone call, but he's my world, my little Eric is, and ever since he's been gone I've spent every waking moment looking for him, searching through social media, ringing around dog homes.' She glanced down at her suit jacket. 'When I've not been at work, obviously.'

'Shall we go into the kitchen and Sally here can go and get him for you?' Flora held open the kitchen door. 'Miracles do happen. Not often, but sometimes, so let's not give up hope.'

'Yes, thank you.' The woman clasped the mug and followed Flora.

'What's your name, lovely?' Flora indicated a chair. 'I'm Flora and this is Ginny and Sally.'

'Helen. It's Helen.'

'Well, lovely to meet you, Helen.'

Sally pushed open the door towards the kennels. Flora was right, it would be a miracle if Puddles was Helen's dog, but stranger things had happened. Bending down at the door to Puddles' kennel, she clipped a lead to his collar.

'There's a lady here who's convinced she's your mummy,' she said to him. 'Shall we go and find her?'

She walked him past the other kennels as he pulled on his lead and yapped at them. A year and a half Helen had said her dog had been missing. And he'd gone missing in Yorkshire. Sally shook her head. He'd only been with them a month now and before that he'd spent seven days at the pound. Where he'd been and how he'd got all the way down here would likely be something they never found out.

Sally closed the door to the kennels behind her and paused in the reception area to give Puddles a moment to settle down.

'This is it. Let's go and see if you are who she's hoping you are.'

As soon as Sally pushed the kitchen door open, Helen turned around, abandoning her mug and dropped to the floor, her arms held out in front of her.

'Eric!'

The lead pulled taut as Puddles strained forward. Sally dropped it and watched as the small dog hurtled towards Helen, his tail circling around in his excitement.

'It's you. It's really you.' Helen wrapped her arms around him as Puddles clambered up to her knees. She glanced around the kitchen, tears streaming down her face. 'It's him. He's my Eric!'

'Oh, lovely, we can see that.' Flora knelt beside her and wrapped her arm around her shoulders. 'You've found your little one.'

'I have. I have. I really have.' Helen looked at Flora. 'This is real, isn't it? I've dreamed about this day for almost a year and a half now.'

'Yes, it's definitely real.' Sally kneeled on the floor next to Helen and Eric and stroked him before wiping her eyes on the sleeves of her cardigan. 'Flora, you're right. Miracles do happen.'

'That they do.' Flora rubbed Helen's shoulder. 'Can I ask what happened, lovely? How did he go missing?'

Burying her head in Eric's fur, Helen smothered him in kisses before looking at Flora. 'I let him off the lead in the fields behind my house. Just as I always did. We were going on the same walk we'd always gone on since he was a puppy. He knew the route; he knew the other dogs we'd meet. He should have known how to get back to me, how to get home even.' She kissed him again. 'But that day, he ran off chasing a bird and just never came back. I searched, the dog walkers we usually met searched. My brother even took a drone up over the fields, but there was no sign of him. Nothing at all. It was as though he'd just vanished into thin air.'

'Do you think he was stolen?' Ginny sat down, crossing her legs and leaning her back against the kitchen cupboard.

'After weeks of searching, I assumed he must have been, yes. I never gave up, though. I kept on ringing the rescue centres and posting his photograph everywhere.' She smiled as she looked into his eyes. 'I just never, ever imagined he'd have gotten down to Cornwall.'

'It's a long way.' Ginny nodded.

'Why didn't my number show up on his chip, though?'

'He doesn't have one.' Flora shook her head sadly. 'Unfortunately, a lot of these dog thieves take it out.'

'What do you think happened to him? Where do you think he's been all this time? I hoped he was at least sold to someone who cared for him and loved him as I do.' Helen ran her hand down Eric's back before looking back up at Flora. 'He has some scars. He didn't have any before.'

Sally exchanged looks with Flora and cleared her throat. Helen deserved to know the truth – what they assumed had happened to him, anyway. Helen needed to know so she could be prepared for any changes in behaviour.

'You said you used to meet other dogs on his walks?'

'Yes, that's right.' Helen shook her head and addressed Eric. 'I wonder what all your friends will think when we meet up with them again, hey? They'll be so shocked to see you.'

'We don't know for sure where he's been all this time. He came to us from the local pound, but there are some telltale signs that he may not have been in the best of hands.'

Helen looked back down at Eric before looking across at Sally. 'What do you mean? Has he been mistreated? The scars...'

'We believe so.' Flora laid her hand on Helen's forearm. 'As Sally says, there are a few things that suggest he has been. For example, he's quite terrified of other dogs now and lunges for them.'

'Oh, really?' Helen frowned before hugging Eric tightly against her. 'Oh, my poor baby, what has happened to you?'

'I can do some research and find some dog trainers local to you who can help you and Eric.' Sally shifted position, her legs going numb. 'And you may find things get a little better once he's home and feels secure again, but I'd definitely recommend you take him to a proper trainer who can help you both navigate his new behaviour and support you as he heals from his ordeal.'

'That would be amazing, please. Anything to help my Eric.' Helen looked around the room. 'Thank you all so much for taking good care of him.'

'You're very welcome, lovely. We love the dogs who come into our care like family. I'm just so glad Eric's story has such a happy ending.' Flora wiped her eyes.

Sally looked up as the kitchen door opened.

'Hey... Oh... That's not...' Alex paused, the door half open, his hand on the door handle, and pointed to Helen and Eric. 'You're not Puddles' owner, are you?'

Helen laughed as she cuddled Eric. 'Yes, this is Eric.'

'Eric is from Yorkshire.' Flora raised her eyebrows.

'Yorkshire?' Alex brought his hands to his cheeks. 'No way!'

'Yes, way.' Flora chuckled.

'Oh, wow! Wait, let me go and get Susan and Percy. They have to see this.' Alex turned on his heels and disappeared.

When Sally had watched Dory leave with her new family, she'd thought that was the best part of working here, but to literally be able to reunite people with their much loved and much missed dogs... Sally shook her head and smiled. Yes, that was the best part.

15

'Wow, that seriously happened? You're not making this up?'

'Ha ha, no I'm not. This woman, Helen, had literally seen Puddles', sorry, Eric's picture on social media, left work and travelled through the night all this way to see if it was him.'

Andy thanked the man behind the counter of the small rustic café at the nature reserve and passed Sally a takeaway mug. 'That's an amazing story. It's something you'd expect to read in a paper or in a magazine.'

'I know. I think Darryl, who is Ginny's partner, is going to run a story on it. He works at the *Trestow Telegraph*.'

'Ah yes. And this rescue centre you work at is in Trestow, right?'

'No, it's just outside West Par, not far from where I live.'

'Just outside West Par?'

'Yes.' Sally watched as a flicker of something washed over Andy's face. Recognition maybe? 'You know it?'

'Uh, no. I don't.'

'Right. Well, maybe you can pop by one day? I can introduce you to everyone, to the dogs.' She took a sip of her hot chocolate as they turned right down the gravel path in amongst the trees.

'Maybe.' Andy focused on the ground ahead.

Sally frowned. Had she said the wrong thing? Maybe she shouldn't have invited him over to Wagging Tails. It wasn't as though they were dating or anything. She closed her eyes for a moment. She'd been over-familiar with him. Seeing something that wasn't there. Any more.

She cleared her throat and watched as a pair of magpies swooped down and landed on the path ahead. 'It's beautiful, isn't it?'

Andy smiled, the tensions of the earlier conversation disappearing. 'Yes, it is.'

'I love it here, especially when the sun is setting. Shall we go into the meadow?' Sally passed him her cup before climbing up and swinging her leg over a stile. Once she'd jumped down the other side, she took both hers and his and waited for him to join her.

She looked across the meadow; the long grasses and wildflowers took her breath away. They did every time.

'Thanks.' Taking his cup in return, he followed her gaze and then took a sip. 'Have you given my suggestion of you visiting your parents any more thought?'

'I have.' Sally nodded and they made their way to a picnic bench at the edge of the meadow. 'I have some holiday days to take, so I'm thinking of going tomorrow.'

'I think that's a good idea.'

'Yes, or at least I'm hoping it is. I guess I'm worried that Linda, and my parents, are going to end up resenting me for not going back to keep an eye on things while Linda is off.'

'But your parents are still there, though, aren't they?' Andy sat down at the picnic bench.

'Yes.' Slipping onto the wooden bench opposite him, Sally wrapped her hands around her takeaway cup, the warmth from the hot liquid inside warming her hands. 'But I'm not sure how much they're actually in the office at the moment. Linda said something about them visiting places, probably making up for all of the holidays they never took.'

'Well, then, if they were worried, they'd be in the office more, surely?'

Sally shrugged. Linda hadn't made it sound as though they were in work very often at all.

'Unless my mum isn't as fully recovered as Linda made out.' She looked down at the lid of her cup. Would Linda have told her if she wasn't? No one had told her that her mum had even had a heart attack, so maybe they wouldn't. 'I guess I'll find out tomorrow.'

Reaching over, Andy touched the back of her hand. 'I'm sure it'll be fine and seeing how your mum is will help you feel more confident in your decision.'

'Maybe. Since Linda rang, I've been doubting my decision. You know, thinking maybe I was being selfish by telling her I wouldn't move back?'

'There's nothing selfish in wanting to lead your own life. She's living the life she wants to.'

'That's what I keep telling myself. And in truth, the way she spoke about me moving back, it was only to be a... I guess a caretaker for the firm. Just to check everything was ticking over until she was ready to work again after having the baby.' She ran the pad of her finger across a knot in the wood.

Andy scrunched up his face. 'She's only thinking of herself, then?'

'Unless I'm mistaken. Maybe I just didn't understand what she was asking of me.'

That was what Linda had implied, hadn't she? Not that she particularly wanted her to return because it was a family firm or anything, just to look after it, make sure no one else attempted a takeover while she was out of the picture.

'I must have got that wrong,' she said. 'I'll speak to her tomorrow. Check Mum and Dad are doing okay too.'

'Good idea. That's all you can do.'

Sally nodded and brought her cup to her lips again. The hot chocolate was anything but hot now. They must have been speaking longer than she'd realised. She looked across the meadow. The sun had finished setting and the moon now hung in the sky, a silver sliver surrounded by the dark of night penetrated by stars, looking like diamonds twinkling against the navy backdrop.

'This reminds me of our trip to Scotland.' Andy held his cup up to the sky, using it to indicate the stars.

'Oh yes! In Bertie, your dad's old campervan.'

'Ha ha, that's it.'

'It was green and white, wasn't it? The interior too. Your mum had even made curtains to match the paintwork.' Sally laughed. They'd loved that campervan, probably almost as much as his dad had, and they'd been overjoyed when his dad had entrusted his pride and joy into their care for the journey to the Scottish Highlands.

'That's right. And don't forget the rug. My mum had been so thrilled when she'd found the green and white striped thing at the car boot.'

'Yes, the rug. And the green crockery and white mugs.'

'That's right.' Twisting on the bench, he leaned his back against the tabletop and looked up into the night sky. 'We saw the Northern Lights, didn't we?'

'On our last night in the Highlands. I remember. We'd given up hope of seeing them, assuming we'd just gone at the wrong time of the year.' She smiled at the memory.

'And then we'd walked...'

'Stumbled.'

'Ha, yes, stumbled out of the pub and there they were, dancing away in the sky. Our own private showing.'

She nodded. 'I think of all the places we travelled to that was one of the highlights.' She rubbed her arms, the evening chill suddenly piercing her jumper.

'Are you cold?' Andy looked across at her. 'Do you want us to head back?'

'I'll be okay. I'd like to stay for a bit longer. Enjoy the view.' She smiled. After meeting up with Andy over the last few days, it almost felt as though nothing had ever come between them.

Standing up, Andy slipped off his jacket and then sat down next to her again, laying it over her shoulders.

'Now you'll get cold,' she said.

'No, I'm fine. You've always felt the cold more than me.'

Sally pulled the jacket tighter around herself and leaned against his shoulder. 'Thanks.'

'She's still going, you know.'

'Who?'

'Bertie.'

Sally widened her eyes. 'Seriously? That campervan was old when we drove it. It must be ancient now. Have you taken her on any more road trips?'

'Not for a long time. One day, maybe.'

Sally rested her head back against his shoulder.

'I can come with you tomorrow,' he said.

'To London?' She frowned.

'Yes, when you go to visit your parents.'

Sally shook her head. 'It's a long way. It'll take too much time away from your house renovations.'

She could feel Andy's shoulder move beneath her cheek as he shrugged. 'Nah, I need to speak to my bank manager, anyway.'

'Really? Surely it'll be easier to talk to them over the phone?' She straightened her back again and looked him in the eye.

He squirmed against her gaze. 'Maybe, but I could do with speaking to him in person. If you don't mind me tagging along, that is?'

'Of course not. A road trip to the city it will be then.' She grinned.

'Just like old times.'

She nodded. Although it wouldn't be, would it? They weren't together. They'd barely gotten to know one another again after running into each other the other day. And they weren't making the trip to sightsee or explore. No, it would be very different.

16

'Are you sure you'll be okay from here?' Andy looked at her.

'Yep. I'll be fine.' Sally nodded and looked down the leafy street towards her parents' large Victorian house before meeting his gaze and raising her eyebrows. 'Of course, you're more than welcome to come with me.'

'Well, umm...' He glanced down at the pavement before looking back at her and grimacing. 'There's nothing I'd love more than to have lunch and a catch-up with your parents, but I really should get along to that meeting with my bank manager.'

Sally shook her head and laughed. 'Ha, any excuse.' They both knew they were just teasing one another. She wouldn't put him through the ordeal of lunchtime with her parents, especially with Linda coming at some point, too.

'Well, yes. If I'm honest, it is.' He chuckled. 'I think I suffered enough when we were together.'

Sally smiled sadly. Now they weren't together, he didn't need to. That's what he was saying, wasn't it? She shook her head, pushing the thought away. Yes, they'd travelled up here as friends, but that was fine. It was more than she'd ever thought she'd get from him before they'd run into each other. She should be happy with being friends. She was happy.

'Just think of the lengths we went to avoid lunches, dinners and generally spending any time with my family.'

'Oh yes, I remember. I think the best one was when we hopped on that flight to Japan instead of returning to England to celebrate your mum's birthday.' He grinned.

Sally nodded. She felt terrible about that now. About avoiding them when she'd been younger. She should have made the effort and should have spent more time with them. Of course, she'd certainly made up for it when she'd returned to continue her training. She'd definitely spent time with them then. More than enough time.

'You'll be fine.' Andy took her by the shoulders and gently turned her to face their house. 'Go on.'

Sally took a deep breath and looked back at her parents' house, the front steps leading up to the shiny black door as imposing as it always had been. She felt Andy lift his hands from her shoulders. 'Okay. I've got this.'

Nothing. No answer from him? No mutterings of reassurance?

She looked back over her shoulder and pursed her lips. He was already about five metres away from her, walking in the other direction.

'That's it. You run and leave me to battle through lunch on my own.'

'Sorry.' Pausing, he turned back to her, holding his hands together, pleading.

'Great.' She shook her head and watched as he turned the corner out of sight. This was it. She was truly on her own now. She might as well go and face the music. Besides, if she turned up even five minutes late, that would be the topic of conversation for at least the next half-hour. If there was one thing her parents both hated...

Nope, she was doing it. She was. And she wasn't going to put it off any longer. Pulling her bag higher up onto her shoulder, she smoothed down her jumper and made her way towards the house. As she took one step at a time, she fought the urge to turn around, ring them, and make some excuse.

Reaching up, she rang the doorbell and stood back as she listened to its tune echo in the large hallway on the other side of the door. She was here for a reason. She was here to clear the air, to explain why she couldn't give up her life in West Par and, more importantly, to see how her mum was after her heart attack.

While she was waiting, she pulled out her phone and silenced it, jerking her head up as the door opened.

'Sally.' Her father's figure stood in the open doorway.

'Hi. Hi, Dad.' She quickly shoved her mobile into her back pocket and smiled at him. 'How have you been?'

'Good, good. Come on in.' Her dad moved aside, waiting for her to step inside before closing the door with a satisfying thud.

Standing in the middle of the hallway, she looked around. It looked as it always had. The same sideboard stood to the side, with the same statue of the lion, the same crystal vase held a similar bunch of lilies as it always had. She didn't know what she'd been expecting, but she'd been expecting to see something a little different. Anything. However small. Her mum had had a heart attack. Her parents had all but retired. And Sally had moved away, changed as a person.

'Your mum is waiting for us in the sitting room.' Her dad nodded towards a door leading off the large hallway and indicated for Sally to go through first.

Sally nodded and led the way. Pausing in the doorway, she watched as her mum unstacked a small tower of teacups from a tray and set them on the coffee table. She looked okay. Just like the house, the hallway, everything, she looked just as she had when Sally had seen her last almost a year ago.

'Mum?'

Her mum looked up from the teacups and straightened her back, smiling. 'Sally, darling. How wonderful to see you.'

'Hey, Mum.' Sally walked across to her and hugged her quickly around the shoulders, as they always did. She'd always deemed them a courtesy hug rather than a real one. It was probably why she'd always craved Andy's hugs so much.

'No, no. Give me a proper hug, Sally. I haven't seen you in such a long time.'

To her surprise, her mum wrapped her arms around her and pulled her closer. Slightly taken aback, Sally righted herself and hugged her back. They hadn't hugged like this – properly – since she was a child. 'Good to see you.'

'And you. Now let me take a good look at you.' Leaning back, her mum held her at arm's length, looking her up and down. 'You look well. The sea air must be treating you right.'

'Yes, yes, it is.' Stepping away, Sally perched on the edge of the sofa. 'But how about you? How have you been since your heart attack?'

'It was just a little health scare, that's all. Please don't fuss.' Sitting down, her mum clasped her hands in her lap.

'Oh, it wasn't a little health scare, as you well know, Patricia.' Her dad looked lovingly at his wife before turning back to Sally. 'But she's in tip-top health now.'

'Yes, well, enough of that. Let's have some tea before lunch.' Patricia glanced at the clock on the mantelpiece. 'You sister will be here soon.'

Sally shifted position on the floral sofa and looked across at her dad. 'I wish you'd told me. I wish you'd let me come and visit Mum in the hospital and help.'

'I was fine, Sally. Besides, I had your father there, Linda and Pearce too.'

Sally frowned and bit down on her bottom lip. That told her then. She hadn't been needed or wanted.

Her mum reached across and placed her hand over Sally's. 'Love, I'm glad your father didn't tell you. I'd have been so cross with him interrupting your adventure by the sea.'

'It's not an adventure, Mum. It's my life. I've made a life for myself down in West Par.'

'Are you still helping out with those animals? The dogs, isn't it?' Her father picked up the teapot and, holding the lid on, poured the tea.

And this was why she hadn't visited. 'It's my job. I actually have two jobs. I work at the dogs' home and have my own dog training business as well.'

'You have your own business?' Her dad raised his eyebrows.

'I do, yes.' She looked across at her dad. Was that a glint of pride flashing across his face? A super tiny glint, but a glint all the same? Pride or irritation. One of the two. Sally wasn't sure.

'Tell us more. Tell us where you live, who you work with.' Her mum held a plate of biscuits up and nodded towards them.

'Thanks.' Sally took a biscuit and placed it on the saucer, the heat from the tea warming it. 'It's beautiful. I live in a little cottage just a few minutes' walk from a beach. The dogs' home where I work is just outside the village I live in and it's amazing. The people I work with are amazing. The dogs we have coming through are amazing.' She cleared her throat. How many times was it socially acceptable to utter the word 'amazing' in one sentence? 'I really enjoy it.'

'It certainly sounds as if you do.' Her dad nodded.

'I do. I really do. I know it's not the career you wanted for me, and I know neither of you were happy about me moving away, but I feel at home there. I feel as though I belong.' She picked up her teacup and watched the swirls of tea calm as she held it still.

The soft thud of the front door closing interrupted them, followed by the click-click of shoes against the tiled floor of the hallway. Sally turned around as Linda appeared in the doorway to the sitting room. She was wearing her signature black skirt and jacket with a pale blue shirt. If it wasn't for the small mound of her tummy tugging against her jacket, Sally wouldn't have been able to tell she was pregnant.

'Linda, love, I thought you were coming for lunch? You're early.' Patricia stood up and hurried towards Linda, drawing her in for a hug.

Sally watched as her dad did the same. Maybe her mum's health scare, as she'd called it, had brought them closer together.

'I'm afraid something's come up. You know how it is, so I managed to get away now, but I won't be able to stay long.'

Sally placed her cup and saucer on the coffee table and stood up. 'Hi, Linda.'

'Sally.' Linda strutted towards her and perched on the sofa opposite. 'You came? I half expected you to cancel.'

Sally plastered a smile on her face. 'Congratulations. Again.' She indicated Linda's stomach.

'Thank you. Again.' Linda looked down at the tray on the coffee table.

'You have my teacup. I'll fetch another.' Her dad disappeared out of the room.

An awkward silence descended on the room and Sally shifted position before taking a sip of her tea, the scolding liquid burning the roof of her mouth. She should have put more milk in. 'Do you have a scan photo?'

'Sorry?' Linda picked up her cup and saucer.

'A scan photo? I just wondered if I could have a look at my niece or nephew.' Sally smiled.

'No, I don't. Not on me.'

'Right.' That answered that question then. Linda still didn't understand why Sally couldn't return to London.

'There we go.' Her dad sat back down and poured himself a tea before holding up the teapot. 'Would anyone care for a top-up?'

'No thanks,' Sally mumbled as she went to take another sip, pausing just before the teacup reached her mouth. Lowering it to the coffee table, she topped up with milk.

'I still can't understand why you can't come down to London temporarily and keep an eye on the office whilst I'm on maternity leave.' Setting her cup and saucer back on the coffee table with a clink, Linda leaned back against the sofa cushions and laid her hands over her stomach.

'I have a job.' Sally took a sip of her tea. Her throat suddenly felt very dry.

'Then take a sabbatical.'

Sally half coughed and half choked before forcing herself to swallow the tea in her mouth. 'I cannot put my life on hold. I work at a small dogs' home, and I run training classes. I can't take a sabbatical. I'd lose my livelihood, my cottage.'

'I'm sure someone with your expertise can get another job when you return.'

Sally opened and closed her mouth. Could Linda have sounded any more sarcastic? She didn't have the first clue what Sally's job involved, what training she'd put herself through in order to even get her job, in order to build her business. 'Linda, I have a life down in Cornwall. You cannot ask me to give it all up.'

Linda crossed her legs. 'You talk as though I have done nothing for this family. Nothing for the family firm.'

Was Linda really this entitled, or did she actually believe that Sally 'owed' her this?

'I wasn't told about Mum's heart attack. If you, or Dad, had told me I would have happily come and helped, done what I could. But now, you're asking me to give up everything I have worked so hard for and come and babysit the family firm, because we both know that's what it would be. I'm not trained. I wouldn't be any real help. I'd just be babysitting it, making sure nobody tried to elbow you out whilst you're on maternity leave.'

'I've dedicated my life to this firm. To Mum and Dad's firm.'

Sally put her cup and saucer down with a clatter against the wooden coffee table and stood up. She'd had enough. She couldn't deal with this. 'Yes, you've dedicated your life to it because it's your career. It's what you've always wanted to do. Ever since you were a child, you've known you wanted to go into the family firm. Well... guess what? I didn't.'

'Now, now, Sally, please sit back down.' Her mum stood up.

'No, I won't. I don't have to sit here and listen to this. I gave up my life once before to do what was expected of me. I tried to fit in, I tried to follow the career path I was expected to. I lost everything back then. Heck, I even finished with Andy, the love of my life. And now, you all expect me to do exactly the same.' She turned and strode to the door, letting the tears splash against her cheeks as she did so. She didn't care if they saw. She didn't care what they thought of her any more.

'Please wait, Sally, darling. Let's discuss this.' Her mum placed her hand on Sally's shoulder.

Sally turned around slowly. She swiped at her tears with the sleeve of her jumper. 'I'm sorry. I can't lose everything. Not again.'

'I know and we're not asking you to.'

Sally frowned. 'You are. Linda's literally just said what she expects me to do.'

'Yes, well, me and your father are not. Now, please, come and sit back down.'

Looking from her mum to Linda and back again, she slumped her shoulders. She was here now. She might as well listen to what her parents had to say on the matter. Following her mum back to the sofa, she sat back down.

Her dad cleared his throat. 'Linda is just concerned about the firm your mother and I have built up over the years. She wants to know it's in safe hands whilst she's absent.'

'I know. I know she does.' She pinched the bridge of her nose. She knew where Linda was coming from. She even kind of understood what she meant by implying that it was Sally's turn to step up, but Linda had chosen this life, this career. Why couldn't she accept that Sally hadn't?

'We'll sort something out.' Her dad looked at Sally before turning towards Linda. 'Your mum and I will hire someone in to keep an eye on things if needed. Sally has been telling us all about her new life in Cornwall and how she's settled. We'll sort something out here.'

Linda shrugged her shoulders. 'Fine.'

'That's decided then. Sally, you stay down in Cornwall, and we'll look into getting something in place when Linda goes on maternity leave.' Picking up the plate of biscuits, her dad passed them around. The conversation was over.

17

When they got to her front door, Sally turned around. 'Are you coming in?'

'If you're offering a takeaway, then yes, absolutely. I'm starving after all that travelling.' Andy rubbed his stomach as he stepped into the small hallway.

Sally laughed. 'Yes, I can order a takeaway.'

'Great. I'm in then.'

Slipping her shoes off, Sally walked into the living room and slumped on the sofa. She couldn't remember being quite as tired as she was right now. The train journey back from London hadn't been too bad – long, but at least they'd managed to find seats unlike the outbound journey which they'd spent half of squashed up between the toilets and the doors, holding on to anything they could to avoid falling into strangers as the train lurched to a stop at each station.

'Shall I start the fire?' Andy knelt down by the open fireplace and looked across at her.

'Oh yes, please. I'm freezing, which is probably just because I'm tired, but equally I'm too tired to move to start it.'

With the back of her head resting on the sofa cushions, she closed her eyes and listened as he piled logs and kindling into the open fire.

After the unmistakable 'swish' of a match, she could smell the all-encompassing charcoal smell of the kindling catching.

'Thank you for coming today.'

'No, thank you for letting me tag along.'

She could feel the cushion next to her dip as he sat down.

'How did the meeting with the bank manager go?' She hadn't been able to ask on the train. Although they'd managed to get seats, they hadn't been next to each other. In fact, she'd hardly spoken to him at all throughout the day. As soon as they'd arrived in Paddington, they'd gone straight to her parents' house and he'd left her to rush off to his meeting.

Feeling him shift next to her, she opened her eyes and watched as he leaned forward, looking down at the waxed wooden floorboards.

'You don't have to tell me...'

'No, it's not that. It went well. Better than I expected, in fact.' He looked at her out of the corner of his eye. 'I got the business loan I needed for the project.'

'That's great then. Congratulations.' She beamed. He deserved it. He hadn't spoken to her much about his business, but she knew it meant a lot to him. 'So, you'll be staying down here for a while, then?'

'Yes. Yes, I guess I will.' He knelt down next to the fire again and rearranged the logs.

'Don't sound so pleased, then!' She raised her eyebrows.

Maybe she'd misjudged him, misread his signals, but she'd begun to think he might want to rekindle things. She shook her head. No, she was being daft. The only thing he'd done to indicate such an idea was to spend time with her, which he would have done, anyway. And he would have made exactly the same effort if they'd simply been old friends, no romance involved.

Andy glanced back at her over his shoulder. 'I am pleased. I'm just not sure I'm doing the right thing.'

Leaning forward, she slipped out of her coat before standing up and flinging it over the dining chair. 'Fair enough.'

What else was she supposed to say? Did he mean that he wanted to rekindle things, but he was unsure? He was probably right to be. Look at how she'd ruined things last time. Besides, although they'd been inseparable seven years ago, a lot had happened between then and now. She'd moved down here and completely changed her life. He'd been married! It wouldn't be as simple as picking up from where they'd left off, and he'd know that. He'd always been the sensible one. The one to think actions through carefully before acting.

'I'll go and get the takeaway leaflets,' she said.

'Okay.' Andy looked back towards the fire as small flames began to flicker against the logs. 'Sally?'

Turning around, she felt the corner of her lips twitch. Was he going to suggest they try again? 'Yes?'

'You know I forgive you, don't you?'

'Huh?'

'You know I forgive you for finishing with me, don't you?' His brow was furrowed, his eyes dark, brooding. Her answer obviously meant a lot to him.

'Yes, I guess so.'

She hoped he'd forgiven her. She hadn't been sure though, not after their conversation at Harold's.

'Good. Because I do. I forgive you for ending things with me, and I understand why you did what you did. I understand you were trying to protect me.'

Meeting his eyes, she nodded.

'Good.' He uttered the word quietly, barely above a whisper, a whisper almost lost as a log caught fire and shifted.

'Shall we order that takeaway?' She fanned the takeaway leaflets in his direction.

'Absolutely.' Pushing himself to standing, he came to sit next to her and took a leaflet. 'This looks good.'

* * *

'Do you want the last spring roll?' Andy held it up and raised his eyebrow.

'Nope, you have it. I don't think I'll need to eat for days. I'm that full.'

'Okay. You don't have to say that twice.' Grinning, he stuffed the spring roll into his mouth.

'I can't believe you just ate that whole.' Sally slid her plate onto the coffee table and laughed.

'Can't you?'

'Well, now you mention it, it shouldn't have surprised me.' Shaking her head, she bundled up the takeaway tubs.

'I was going to wait until you told me but I'm getting the distinct feeling I'm going to be waiting forever at this rate – how did things go with your parents?' He stacked his plate on top of hers and sat back against the sofa cushions, looking at her.

Sighing, Sally shoved the empty tubs into a bag and looked over at him. She hadn't not told him intentionally; she'd just been tired and had been enjoying the evening with him.

'It was okay, actually. More than okay. Quite surprising, really.'

'Oh? In what way?'

'My mum is fine. Fit and well now and determined not to end up in hospital again. She's had her scare, and she doesn't want another.' Sally drew a cushion onto her lap. 'In fact, that's why she's not been in the office much. She's trying to take it easy. And of course, where she goes, my dad does too, so that explains why Linda's been left in charge.'

'That's a good thing, isn't it? Your parents taking a bit of time out for themselves? They've worked hard enough over the years.'

'Yes, it is. They devoted more time to that firm than they did to bringing me and Linda up.' She ran the pad of her index finger along the edge of the cushion.

'And Linda always wanted to run the family business...'

'She did. And she does.' Sally frowned. 'I think it's because she's devoted her whole life to getting where she is now, and she doesn't want to leave it in anyone's care while she's on maternity leave.'

'Apart from yours?'

'Yes, well, I'm sure that's only because she knows taking it over would be the last thing I'd want. It's not as though I'm even fully qualified. I'd only be finishing my training. She just wants someone to be there day to day to feed back to her what's going on.'

'Did she admit that?'

'Umm, kind of.' Watching the flames flicker up the glass door of the wood burner, Sally thought back to the conversation she'd had with Linda. She hadn't even asked her how she was, how her job at Wagging Tails was going. She'd just been intent on telling Sally exactly why she thought she should 'step up' and take her turn in the office. Of course Sally had reminded her that their career dreams were different, and that Linda had always wanted to run the company whereas the thought had always made Sally want to run at sixty miles per hour in the opposite direction.

'What do you mean, kind of?' Andy crossed his arms.

'I tried to get her to understand that if I were to join the company even just while she was on maternity leave, I'd lose the life I've made for myself down here. I think in the end she realised that what she was asking was a big deal and that she'd chosen the path she'd wanted to take.'

'That's good then.'

Sally glanced at him and blinked, all the feelings she'd been trying to squash today suddenly rushing to the surface.

'I just feel guilty. I feel guilty that I left. I feel guilty that they didn't tell me about Mum being ill. I feel guilty not being there for her, for Dad, for Linda. And I feel selfish for telling Linda that I don't want to move back.'

'You've nothing to feel guilty about.' Andy took her hands in his. 'Besides, they didn't tell you about your mum being ill. How were you supposed to know? You can't feel guilty for that.'

'I know.' She looked down at their hands, his fingers wrapped around hers. 'I asked my parents why they hadn't told me, and they promised it was because they hadn't wanted me to worry. Not that they didn't want me there.'

'Okay, that's a good thing. Isn't it?'

Sally shrugged. 'I guess. Still, I'd rather have known.'

'Hey, they just wanted the best for you. And you certainly shouldn't feel selfish for not jumping to Linda's demands. You're the least selfish person I know.' He smiled, a glint in his eye.

'Besides, can you imagine her cleaning out dog kennels if you asked her to?'

Sally laughed despite herself. 'No, no, I can't.'

'There you go then.'

She nodded slowly. She knew he was right. She knew Linda was being her usual self by expecting her to give up her life for her.

'I asked my parents if they thought I should go back and help Linda.'

'And what did they say?'

'They said no. They actually said that they're proud of me for quitting my training and instead doing something I wanted to do.'

'Wow.' Andy nodded. 'From your parents, that's high praise.'

'That's what I thought.' She smiled. That afternoon had probably been the longest conversation she'd ever had with her mum in her adult life and it had felt good.

'I'm glad.'

Sally looked down at their hands. Their fingers were interlaced now, and Andy was making no sign of pulling away anytime soon.

'Me too.'

Andy rubbed the pad of his thumb across her finger and looked into her eyes. 'Do you ever wonder what our lives would look like if we hadn't split up?'

Sally opened and closed her mouth. Had she thought about it? Of course she had. For the first few years after she'd moved back home, she'd thought about him every day, almost every minute of every day. She'd fantasized about what they'd be doing if they had still been together, whether they'd have got married yet, had children. Even since moving down here, she'd sometimes catch herself thinking about him and what their lives together would be like if she hadn't made the decision she had. Even without being there, he'd shaped her future. He was the reason her love life was so disastrous, the reason she couldn't get past the third date, however lovely and well suited her dates had been.

'I think about it,' he said, looking down at their hands.

He did? Sally kept her eyes focused on his, her answer caught in her throat.

'Do you think we'd have gone travelling again? Or still be travelling?'

She'd often wondered that. Did people tire of wanting to see the world? Of wanting to experience new things?

'I always thought we'd perhaps have travelled for another couple of years and then settled down. Maybe in a small village in the Scottish Highlands or somewhere.'

'Yes, the village we saw the Northern Lights,' he said, meeting her gaze again with a grin.

'Ha, yes. I could see us living there.'

'Bringing up our three kids, living on a smallholding...'

'Yes.' She froze as he inched closer. She could feel his breath against her skin. Her fingers tightened around his as she met him halfway, their lips touching, igniting a thousand memories. Leaning back, Sally looked at him closely. 'What does this mean?'

Was it a kiss-kiss? Just an in-the-moment quick touch of the lips? Or was it a kiss? A proper kiss? Did it mean something? It had to her. It had stirred up all the feelings she had tried so hard to bury, but did it mean anything to him?

She held her breath, waiting for his reply.

Glancing down at their hands, their fingers still gripping each other's tightly, he met her eyes. 'I've missed you. I'd like it to mean something. Going forward, I mean.'

'Really?'

He actually thought they stood a chance together? After everything?

Shifting position, Andy pulled his fingers slightly away and looked at her. 'If I'm honest, I've never gotten over you, over our relationship, and I don't know how you feel, but running into each other again... I'd like to give us another chance. Do you?'

Sally nodded. She did. Another chance at their relationship was all she'd ever wanted.

'Really?' He raised an eyebrow, waiting for confirmation.

'Really.' It was her turn to lean forward this time, her turn to reach around his neck and pull him closer.

18

'You sound happy. I can hear you singing from the courtyard.' Ginny kicked the reception door closed behind her, carrying a large bag of dog biscuits.

'I am happy.' Sally grinned as she clipped a lead to Cindy's collar.

'Your trip to London to see your family went well then?' Ginny lifted the bag to the counter and tore it open.

'It was okay, I guess. Not the best, but...' She shrugged.

Turning around with a scoop in her hand, Ginny leaned against the counter. 'Then there's something else.' She pointed the dog food scoop at Sally. 'Umm... now I wonder what that could be? Or more specifically, who that could be?'

Sally could feel the heat of embarrassment flush across her face as she picked up a handful of dog poop bags.

Ginny tapped the scoop against her chin, her eyes glinting. 'Your happy mood wouldn't have anything to do with a certain Andy by any chance, would it?'

Laughing, Sally held her hands up. 'Ha ha, yes. We've decided to try again.'

'You're dating him? Again. After what was it? Eight years?'

'Seven. And yes. As from about half past ten last night, we're dating again.' She couldn't help but grin.

'Aw, that's brilliant. No more comparing your dating app guys to Andy!'

'Ha, hopefully not!' Squishing the poop bags into her pocket, Sally grabbed a handful of treats, and slipped them on top.

'Sally, I thought I heard your voice.' Flora walked out from the kennels. 'Look what Helen has sent me.'

'Oh, about Eric?'

'Yes. Hold on, where did I put my mobile?' She patted down her fleece, searching her pockets.

'I'm sure I saw it…' Ginny rushed around behind the counter and pulled it from the shelf. 'Here you go.'

'Thanks, lovely.' After pulling her reading glasses from her head, Flora scrolled through her phone, her eyes lighting up. 'Yes, here, look at this.'

Sally took Flora's phone and looked at the screen. A photo of Helen cuddling Eric stared back at her.

'Aw, that's amazing. He looks so happy to be home. They both do.' The only way to describe how happy Eric looked was to say he was beaming, his mouth open, his tongue lolling to the side.

Ginny took the phone and stared at the screen. 'They do. That's a fab picture.'

'It really is.' Flora took her mobile back and smiled at the photo before returning it to the main screen.

'Darryl wants to write an article about them being reunited after all this time. Do you think Helen would agree?' Ginny looked at Flora.

'I don't see why not.' Flora pocketed her mobile. 'Give her a call. I'm sure she'd only be too happy to show people there's always hope, however long it's been.'

'Okay, I'll do that then and pass on Darryl's details. That way she can contact him if she wants to.'

'Good idea, lovely.'

'Right, I'm off to the top paddock to do some lead training with this gorgeous one.' Sally nodded towards Cindy, who was sitting comfortably at her feet, Cindy's long legs stretched out across the floor.

'Good luck.' Flora stepped forward and fussed Cindy whose tail was wagging from side to side. 'You're going to make someone a wonderful companion one day, aren't you?'

'I'll do some training on her anxiety too this afternoon.'

'Thanks, lovely.'

Sally smiled at Flora before calling Cindy, patting her side. 'Come on, let's go and have some fun.'

As soon as the door to the reception had clicked shut behind her, Sally pulled her mobile from her pocket and grinned. Andy had messaged.

Hope you have a great day. Can't wait to see you later xxx

'Sally, I wanted a quick word with you, if you've a moment?'

Looking up, Sally noticed Percy had approached. She'd reply to Andy later.

'Yes, of course. We're off up to the top paddock, if you want to join us?' She stopped, waiting for him to join them.

'I will.' Percy walked across to them, pausing to fuss over Cindy before they set off.

'What can I do for you?' Sally asked as she opened the gate to the bottom paddock.

'Well, it's Flora's birthday soon. And I'm getting myself in a state over what to buy her.'

'I'm sure she'll love whatever you get her.'

'Ah, but it's a special one, isn't it? Sixty-five. I want to give her something which shows how special she is, you know?'

'You've got a great eye for gifts. Look at that necklace you bought her for Christmas.' Sally glanced across at him; his face had reddened. 'Or whoever her Secret Santa was, I mean.'

'Ah no, you're right. It was me. Keep it between us though, please? I don't want everyone finding out. It'll... er... spoil the surprise of Secret Santa.'

'Of course. I won't say a word.' Trying desperately not to give away the fact that everyone already knew who had bought Flora's gift, Sally ran her index finger and thumb along her lips. 'My lips are sealed.'

'Thanks, love.'

'So, what have you thought of so far? For Flora's birthday gift?'

Pausing, Percy rummaged in his pocket and pulled out a piece of folded up paper. He leaned down and smoothed it against his knee before holding it up. 'That's the problem. I don't have many ideas. I have jewellery on the list, but, of course, I gave her the necklace for Christmas. Besides that, I've got a crystal vase. I thought I could get Wagging Tails engraved on it? And that's about it.'

'Umm...'

'You don't like it, do you?'

'I think it's a lovely idea and Flora does like her flowers, so maybe.'

'No, you're right. A vase isn't a great idea. She only has flowers out in the cottage if someone has given them to her. And she always says they're a waste as she's never home.' Percy stopped and pulled a pen from behind his ear before scribbling on the piece of paper.

'How about something more personal?' Sally leaned down and fussed over Cindy.

'Yes, something more personal.' Percy tapped the pen against his beard before tucking it back behind his ear. 'I'll have a think.'

Sally looked up and began walking again. 'I'll have a think too.'

'Ah, I've got it! How about a—' But Percy stopped speaking as they reached the gate into the top paddock. 'What on earth?'

Sally opened and closed her mouth. On the other side of the back fence stood a Portakabin, a huge Portakabin, right on the boundary line.

* * *

'I don't like this. Not one bit.' Flora leaned her elbows on the fence and stared at the grey prefab building in front of her.

'Nor me.' Percy shook his head, still a little out of breath from running to raise the alarm.

'Can they even do this? Put it right there?' Alex pointed to the Portakabin. 'It's so close I can touch it.'

'It's on their land. I'm assuming they can do what they want.' Susan shook her head.

'Well, that's ridiculous,' Alex complained. 'They've got acres and they choose to put this monstrosity right here. Why?'

'Because they're trying to intimidate us, that's why.' Flora turned around and began to search in the grass before picking up a rock. 'And I won't have it. I'm not going to stand by and let that daft Lyle man scare us or our dogs. I just won't.'

'Flora, what are you doing?' Percy looked at her, frowning.

'I'm going to show him what it feels like to be intimidated, that's what.'

Gripping the rock in her hand, she pulled her arm back, ready to throw.

'Oh no, don't do that, Flora. That's what he wants us to do.' Holding Flora's arm, Percy prised the rock from her fingers. 'It'll only be you getting in trouble. Not him.'

Dropping her arm to her side, Flora sighed. 'You're right. I know you are, Percy. It just all feels very unfair. This is our land and we've lived and worked here for over thirty-five years. How can they be allowed to do this to us? To try to force us out?'

'No one's forcing us out, love.' Percy hugged her.

'I'll speak to Darryl again,' Ginny said. 'I know he was trying to get some information from the council.' Turning, she pulled her mobile from her pocket and left.

'Let's get inside,' Percy said. 'Get a nice cuppa and have a think.' With his arm around her shoulder, he gently turned Flora around.

'That's right. Let's strategise,' Alex added. 'We need to bring that protest forward.' He held the gate open as everyone filed through.

'Protest?' Sally asked.

'Yes, it was decided at the meeting that we'll descend on the council offices in Trestow.'

'Oh, yes.'

Sally grimaced. How could she have forgotten? After leaving before the end of the meeting, Alex had given her a run-through of what she'd missed but she'd been so wrapped up in her mum and Linda and Andy, she obviously hadn't taken it all in.

Back at reception, Sally let everyone file through the reception door into the kitchen before bringing Cindy in.

'Sorry, girl. We'll go out and train later, okay, sweet one?'

Sally took her back to her makeshift kennel, fussing over her a lot before joining everyone in the kitchen, making sure to keep the kitchen door open wide so Cindy could hear them.

'This is terrible.' Susan placed a mug in front of Sally as soon as she'd sat down. 'How could he do this?'

Sally pulled the mug towards her, and took a deep breath, the aroma of coffee filling her lungs.

'It's scare tactics, I tell you it is.' Percy stroked his beard. 'He's trying to scare us into selling.'

'Well, it's not going to work.' Alex crossed his arms as a scowl crossed his face.

'No, no, it's not. But it does worry me as this Lyle is making it clear he's going to make things as difficult as he can for us.' Flora tapped the table with her fingers. 'We're not selling to him and he's still trying to push us out. I worry for our dogs.'

'I think we should all write to the local MP. State our concerns over how planning has been passed and about the Portakabin and Lyle harassing us.' Ginny grabbed a piece of paper from the work surface and began writing a list.

'Ha, as long as he's not corrupted too.' Alex shook his head.

'No, no, Graham is a good man. He'd be as fuming over this as we are.' Flora patted Ginny's hand. 'That's a good idea, lovely.'

'What else shall I pop on the list?' Ginny looked around the table. 'The protest outside the council offices. When shall we bring that forward to?'

'As soon as possible, I reckon. If we go knocking on doors this afternoon hopefully, we can arrange it for a few days' time.' Percy nodded.

'Great.' Ginny scribbled on the paper.

'I'll draw up some posters to stick around the village and further afield before I start on the placards.' Alex went to grab some paper and pens from the cupboard, ready to make a start.

'Oh, while I've got everyone here, some of you will remember the beautiful Bonnie?' Flora said. 'She was here five years ago.'

'Yes, I do.' Ginny looked up from her list. 'The gorgeous grey Staffie-cross?'

'I remember her too. She had a habit of carrying around that toy...' Percy clicked his fingers. 'I can't remember if it was a stuffed bird or what now, but she carried it everywhere.'

'It was a reindeer teddy I think.' Susan held her mug against her lips.

'Oh, she wouldn't let that toy out of her sight. She'd take it to the beach, to the vet's, everywhere with her.' Percy smiled.

'That's right. She was a real sweetie with a heart of gold.' Flora sat back in her chair. 'Well, she's coming back to us.'

'Oh, really? That surprises me – she and Jerry had such an instant connection when he came to visit her. They were the perfect match for each other.' Susan frowned.

'Yes, they were. They still are. Jerry is absolutely heartbroken about having to return her, but he's lost his job and his house and can't find anywhere to rent which will allow pets. It's a terrible situation.' Flora sighed.

'That's awful. He must be devastated, poor love.' Susan shook her head.

'He is. He's moving in three days and has said he's going to drop her off at the last possible moment as he just can't bear to be without her.' Flora wiped her eyes.

'Oh that's terrible.' Percy took a sip of his drink. 'Lovely little soul, is Bonnie.'

'Yes, hopefully she'll find a new home soon enough but my heart breaks for poor Jerry.' Flora sighed before picking up her mug. 'Right, I'll come with you, Percy, to walk around the village and sign people up for this protest. I need to do something to take my mind off all the worrying, to feel proactive.'

'Yes, okay.' Percy stood up and downed the dregs of his coffee before grabbing his cardigan from the back of the chair. 'Coming.'

The shrill ping of Sally's phone interrupted the chatter in the room and Sally pulled it out of her pocket, excitement fluttering in her stomach despite the worried atmosphere in the room.

Are you free for that day trip tomorrow? Andy xxx

'Everything okay?' Ginny looked up after she'd finished scribbling on the paper.

Sally smiled. 'Yes, it's Andy asking if I want to go out for a day trip with him tomorrow.'

'That's cool. Where are you going?'

'Oh, I'm not. I had yesterday off so I have to work tomorrow. Still, it feels good he's asked.'

Ginny stood up and grabbed the clipboard with the rota on. 'Yes, just as I thought. It's your day off tomorrow.'

'Yes, but I had yesterday off instead.'

'No, that was annual leave. You're still off tomorrow.' Ginny tapped the clipboard and grinned. 'You can go.'

'Aw, no, I'd feel bad taking the day off after I've just had one. Plus, with everything going on with the build next door, I should be here to help.' Sally bit at her thumbnail.

Ginny nudged her shoulder. 'Go. Have fun. What can we actually do here until the protest?'

'I guess you're right.' Sally looked down at the rota again. Tomorrow was definitely scheduled as her day off. 'I'll write the letter to the MP tonight.'

'Good idea, I'll do the same.' Ginny looked at her and raised her eyebrows. 'Back to you and Andy though. Where are you going on your day trip? You never did answer.'

'I don't know. He's only asked if I'm free, he's not mentioned if he has somewhere in mind.' Sally traced the pad of her index finger across her lips. She'd be happy wherever they ended up as long as she could spend some time with Andy.

19

'How do I look?' Sally grinned as she slipped on the bright yellow hard hat she'd been given.

'Stunning.' Andy chuckled as he pulled his hard hat on too. 'And just as though you're going to go and work down the mines.'

Leaning forward, Sally kissed him before straightening his hat. 'There you go.'

'Thank you.' Andy grinned.

'How did you find out about this place, anyway? I've been living down here for almost a year now and this is the first time I've heard about the Carnglaze Caverns.'

Andy shrugged. 'On my way down here, I spent a couple of days exploring near Bodmin Moor and a couple of hikers I ran into recommended visiting. This is my first time here too, though.'

Sally looked around the small group of people donning helmets and waiting for the short safety talk before being allowed into the old slate mine. When Andy had invited her on a day trip, she'd assumed he'd had a day of exploring planned, but even she hadn't guessed it would be something as unique as this.

A woman who had introduced herself as the current owner of the caverns made her way to the entrance and turned around to face everyone. 'I'd like to give you a warm welcome to Carnglaze Caverns, Cornwall's only slate mine.'

Sally smiled as she felt Andy stand behind her, wrapping his arms around her waist as they listened. Taking his hands in hers, she tried to focus on the woman speaking rather than the possibility that their relationship might work out this time. Why wouldn't it? It had been Sally herself who had done the breaking up. It was she who had ruined the best relationship she'd ever known.

'As you make your way around the three caverns, you'll find small plaques telling you about the history here.' The woman stood to the side and indicated the entrance. 'Enjoy.'

Waiting until the other visitors had made their way inside, Sally squeezed Andy's hand and followed. She could see the first cavern stretching out in front of her, bigger than she'd imagined it would be.

The air grew chillier as they made their way further inside and Sally pulled her cardigan tighter around her before pausing in front of one of the informative plaques.

'Oh look, this cavern is named the Rum Store because the Royal Navy kept their rum supply down here during World War Two.'

'Wow.' Andy looked around the vast cavern and raised his eyebrows. 'I wonder how full it was.'

'No idea.' Sally laughed and led the way deeper inside.

'Look, they hold concerts here.' Andy pointed to another information board before glancing around the large cavern. 'I bet it's amazing to attend one. Think of the acoustics.'

Sally nodded and read on. 'And they hold weddings too.'

As soon as she'd uttered the words, she felt the heat rise from her neck and flush across her face. Why had she said that? Yes, it was written on the sign, but why hadn't she continued along the theme of the concerts, left the wedding fact unspoken?

'Underground weddings and concerts? Who'd have thought?' Leaning forward, Andy kissed her on the forehead before taking her hand.

Sally nodded, relieved the awkward conversation had been avoided.

After perusing the collection of rocks and minerals on display, she followed Andy down the steps into the cavern below, pausing midway. She ran her hand over the wall of the cavern, lost in the thought of hundreds of boys and men working long hours to mine the slate. Maybe the slate on her cottage roof originated from here?

'You okay?' Andy squeezed her hand.

'Yes, I was just thinking what it must have been like to be down here for hours at a time.'

'It must have been tough. Really tough.' Andy frowned before ducking as something small and black flitted between them.

'What was that? A bat?'

'Yes, I think so. I read on one of the information boards that there used to be loads of bats in here before the Navy used it for storing their rum. Apparently, they didn't like the smell so moved out.' He chuckled. 'Now the rum's gone, the bats are back.'

Sally laughed. 'The Navy were lucky the bats didn't like the rum enough to try to drink it.'

'Exactly!'

Sally paused on the staircase and looked at the cavern beneath them. 'Wow!'

Hundreds of candles, probably battery operated for health and safety reasons, filled little ledges and grooves in the rock, illuminating the cavernous space.

'This must be what they call the Cathedral Chamber.'

'I can see why.' Andy stepped towards her as another couple passed them by.

'It's beautiful.'

With his lips millimetres from her ear, he whispered, 'Just like you.'

'Oh, ha ha. Come on, let's go and explore.' Shaking her head, she led him down the remaining stairs and into the huge cavern. Inside, Sally tilted her head back, looking up, trying, and failing, to make out where the walls ended and the ceiling began – the space really was incredible.

'Look, that must be the Baby Pool.' Andy pointed to a small pool to the edge of the cavern and walked towards the information point. 'The water drains from the fields above before draining out again.'

* * *

In the third cavern, staring at the impossibly blue water of the Mother Pool, Sally leaned against Andy as he wrapped his arm around her shoulders. Their trip around the caverns had been perfect, just like old times, exploring together.

She shuddered.

Shifting slightly, Andy looked at her. 'Everything okay?'

'I was just thinking that it was pure luck we met up again. We could have easily passed each other. I mean, what are the chances that the house you're renovating was down here, so close to where I'd moved? If you hadn't been staying at Harold's, if I hadn't popped in for lunch... I don't usually. It was only because I'd been into town to the pet shop.'

'I know. A very strange but wonderful twist of fate.' Andy hugged her tighter.

Sally looked across at the ledge beyond on the other side of the pool. What a beautiful place... That must be where they held the wedding ceremonies, and then the receptions would be up in the Cathedral Cavern. She shook her head. She'd only just met up with Andy again. She shouldn't be thinking of weddings already, thinking that far ahead.

She took a deep breath. There was a question she needed to know the answer to though, one that had been playing on her mind since they'd ran into each other again, particularly since the night after the phone call with Linda. One he'd answered already but one she needed to hear his answer to again. She needed to know he meant what he had said. For sure.

'Do you forgive me? For leaving you?' She bit down on her bottom lip before looking up at him again. 'I know you said you did, but do you mean it? I mean, I wasn't there for you when you'd needed me most. After your dad passed away. I should have been there. I would have been if I we hadn't broken up.'

Andy took a deep breath, his chest rising and falling beneath her head as she hugged him back.

'I was being honest the other night. I do. I forgive you now. Yes.'

'You didn't before?' Sally searched his face.

'Honestly? It took a long time and when we first ran into each other, it played on my mind. A lot. I know you had your reasons and I respect you for trying to do the right thing by me.'

'Even if it wasn't?'

He shrugged. 'Hey, we've both had some life experiences because of it.'

Was he talking about his marriage and subsequent divorce? It was strange to think he'd been married to someone else. Loved someone else fiercely enough to marry them, to want to spend the rest of his life with them. Growing up, she'd always assumed it would be her. That they'd be husband and wife. That she'd be his first and last love.

'Yes, I guess we have.'

'You're happy now, though, right? I know you had a few rough years of training and working at your parents' law firm, but since you decided to train dogs, you're happy, aren't you?'

'Yes, I am. I love the dogs' home, and I also like being able to be my own boss by running the training sessions in the evenings. It's the best of both worlds.' She smiled. 'The team at the dogs' home is just like I imagine a super close-knit family to be like. There's Flora, who founded it, then Percy, the caretaker, although we all think he's secretly in love with Flora.' She laughed. 'Well, not so secretly, really.'

'That sounds like a great place to work.'

'Oh, it really is. In fact, why don't you come and meet everyone? We're holding a birthday party for Flora, you'd be more than welcome.' Sally watched as his forehead creased into a frown. She knew she'd asked him to visit before and he clearly hadn't wanted to, but they were together now. They were trying again. Besides, there'd be loads of people at the party. It wouldn't be just him visiting.

'Maybe.' Andy shifted on his feet. 'Are there many dog homes around here? Well, not here, but Trestow way?'

Sally frowned. Maybe it was still too soon. She'd described the people she worked with as family, maybe he felt it was too much pressure meeting them. 'No, not that I know of. I mean there's the pound in Trestow town, but as for actual dogs' homes... I'm not sure. There might be one like an hour away or something.'

'Oh, right.' Looking away, his eyes focusing on something in the distance, Andy rubbed the back of his neck. 'And what did you say the one you work at is called?'

'Wagging Tails Dogs' Home.' Sally smiled, a warm glow filling her stomach. It was good to see that Andy's love of animals was just as strong as it was when they'd been together. 'Do you remember when we helped the lady in Athens who looked after and fed the stray dogs?'

Andy nodded slowly before clearing his throat, his voice hoarse. 'Yes, her name was Alexandra, wasn't it?'

'That's right, and she'd literally dedicated her life to rescuing as many of the stray dogs as she possibly could and feeding the ones she didn't have room for.'

'I remember.' He looked towards the large pool again.

Sally looked down and read the information sheet in front of them. 'Huh, it says those stalactites are a hundred and fifty years old. Wow, and they won't be fully grown...' She frowned, was grown the right word? 'Sorry, formed... until they reach thirty thousand years! Can you imagine that?'

'Uh no.' Andy turned. 'We'd best head back now.'

'Oh, right. Yes, of course.'

Turning away from the board, Sally knitted her eyebrows together. Was it something she'd said? She shouldn't have invited him to the party. He must be thinking she was moving too fast.

20

'Just in time for party talk?' Alex grinned as Sally walked into the kitchen.

'Great.' She slipped into the chair next to him and yawned. She wasn't sure if she'd be able to focus on the meeting ahead, let alone muster up the brain power to offer any ideas for Flora's party. Still, Alex had gone to the trouble of organising the meeting whilst Flora was out, the least she could do was to stay awake and try to contribute.

'Late night?' Ginny nudged her.

'Not really.'

It definitely hadn't been. In fact, as soon as they'd finished the tour of Carnglaze Caverns, Andy had dropped her at home and hadn't even accepted her invitation to pop in for a coffee. She'd assumed they'd have spent the whole day together. Looking down at the table, she straightened a pen, lining it up next to Flora's notebook and forced a smile. At least she'd been able to catch up on some household chores, as well as having a couple of hours to relax before bed. If going over every detail of the day trip and the conversations she and Andy had had was called relaxing. No. And then she'd spent the entire night tossing and turning wondering what exactly it had been that she'd said or done to make him want to cut short their day together and what it meant for the future of their relationship. If it could even be called that. Could it? After a few days?

'Oh. You'll have to tell me all about your trip later.' Ginny tilted her head towards Alex. 'I know he's itching to get the last-minute party preparation sorted.'

'That I am.' Alex twisted in his chair and looked back at the door as Susan and Percy walked in. 'Can you shut that, please? I don't want Flora to hear anything if she comes back from the supplier's early.'

'Hold on one moment then and I'll get Cindy,' Susan said. 'It's that or as soon as we shut that door and she can't hear us, she'll start crying.' She disappeared out into the reception area again before returning with Cindy.

'Right, is everybody ready now?' Alex shuffled papers in front of him.

'Yep. Think so.' Percy placed a tray of mugs in the centre of the table. 'Help yourselves, loves.'

'Thanks, Percy.' Sally took a mug. She needed to take her mind off of yesterday. She could wonder all day if she'd said something to put him off but she wasn't going to know for sure. Not without speaking to him. Had it been because she'd asked if he'd forgiven her? No, he'd been fine after that. Or had he?

'Earth to Sally.' Alex tapped his pen.

'Sorry. Sorry I was miles away.' Shaking her head, she wrapped her hands around her mug and focused on Alex.

Laughing, he scribbled on the paper. 'I was just asking if you'd heard from Wendy about Flora's birthday cake?'

'Right, yes. She messaged the finished design across, and Elsie will bring it just before the party.' Picking up her mobile, Sally scrolled through her messages before holding up the photo Wendy had sent her of the cake she'd designed. It really was amazing, and she actually couldn't wait to see the finished product.

'Fab.' Alex waited until Sally's phone had been passed around the table to exclamations of amazement before looking towards Susan and Ginny. 'And how about the guests? Any luck in reaching any of our previous residents? Please tell me at least some have agreed to come.'

'They have indeed.' Susan grinned and flipped through a small notebook in front of her. 'We've got at least twelve on the definite list already.'

'Ooh good! Please tell me gorgeous Cleo is coming?' Alex straightened his back. 'The cocker spaniel who was crazy about her ball?'

'Ah, yes. I don't know who would win the competition of fetching the ball the most if her and Tyler went head-to-head. Let me check...' Susan laughed and ran her finger down the list in front of her. 'Yes, Cleo is on the list. You spoke to her owners, didn't you, Ginny?'

'Yes, I did. They mentioned she's got something wrong with her eyesight, bless her.' Ginny nodded. 'I didn't get to ask much as they were rushing out of the door, so I'll have a good catch-up when they come.'

'And how about that beautiful Staffie-cross-Jack Russell? Umm, what was his name? A beautiful lad who came to us as shy as they come and then blossomed when his family adopted him.' Percy stroked his beard. 'A real transformation, that one.'

'Rex! Yes, he's coming.' Susan smiled.

'Yes, Rex, that was it!' Percy nodded. 'Good, good. I know it was a fair few years ago now that he was one of our residents, but I'll always have a special place in my heart for him. A lovely soul.'

'That was at least ten years ago now that he was here.' Susan shook her head and chuckled. 'It makes me feel old just thinking about all the dogs who have come through these doors.'

'How many dogs do you think Wagging Tails has helped?' Sally looked from Percy to Susan and back again.

'Since Flora and Arthur opened it? Gosh, I don't know.' Susan frowned. 'Fifteen kennels. Say if each dog is adopted within what a month, two months, then that's fifteen kennels times twelve months. Of course, there are our resident dogs like Ralph, or those who end up waiting to be adopted for months or years, so...' Susan shook her head. 'I've no idea but hundreds, thousands?'

'Yes, it must be. At least two or three thousand dogs.' Percy nodded in agreement. 'At least.'

'Wow, yes, it must be. Then there are all the puppies we've had through and multiple dogs from the same household who have shared kennels...' Ginny raised her eyebrows. 'Flora has really made a difference to all those lives, the dogs and all the people who have adopted them.'

'And their families and friends.' Sally blinked. 'That's crazy how many lives she's touched.'

'I'm just so proud to be a part of it. Of all of this.' Susan dabbed at her eyes and waved her hand around the kitchen, encompassing Wagging Tails.

Sally swallowed as a silence hung in the air. She knew they were all thinking the same. They were all wondering what would happen if Lyle and his company got their way and either bought them or forced them out. What would she do? What would any of them do?

Percy placed his hand in the middle of the table and nodded to Alex who placed his on top of Percy's. Percy then nodded to everyone in turn, each person placing their hands on top of each other's in a mound in the middle of the table. 'We're all in this together and we've got this. Wagging Tails will save another three thousand lives.'

Alex cleared his throat as they all raised their hands. 'Yes, we will.'

'It's just such a shame that awful Portakabin is visible from the top paddock where we'll be having the party.' Ginny shifted in her chair.

'Unless we keep the party in the bottom paddock and the courtyard?' Susan suggested.

'No, I think everyone coming needs to see it,' Percy said, sitting back in his chair. 'Be reminded of what we're all battling against. It'll raise awareness of what we and the local community are up against, if anything else.'

'You're right.' Sally picked up the pen. 'There'll be loads of people from West Par and the surrounding villages coming along and they'll all see how intimidating and uncaring he's being by placing the Portakabin so close to us. It's likely to only get us more supporters.'

There was no way Lyle and his disgusting company would win. No chance.

'Exactly, so is it agreed that we will use the top paddock for the party?' Alex said. 'And maybe we'll just have the cake and food stall in the bottom paddock away from the Portakabin. We want it to be visible but not to take all the focus of the party away from Flora.' Alex underlined something on his sheet of paper.

'Agreed.' Susan nodded.

Alex tilted his head to one side and stage-whispered, 'I think I've just heard Flora's car pull up. Quick, hide all evidence.'

Susan stood up. 'I'd better take Luke for a run around in the paddock.'

'Oh, can I just run up to the top paddock with Ralph before you get him, please?' Ginny downed the dregs of her coffee and placed her mug in the sink.

'Of course.' Susan looked down to Cindy and patted her thigh. 'Come on, let's get you back to your kennel.'

Percy pushed back his chair. 'Come on, Alex, let's go see if we can locate some trestle tables for the food and cake. I have a feeling one of them has a dodgy leg that needs fixing.'

Sally watched as everyone filed out of the door then pulled her mobile from her pocket. She just couldn't shake the feeling that she'd done something wrong with Andy, said something wrong, and the last thing she wanted after running into him again after all this time was for them to fall out over something daft. She quickly typed out a message and pressed send before she could change her mind.

Is everything okay between us? x

'Sally, are you free for a moment?' Flora peered through the kitchen door.

Slipping her phone back into her pocket, Sally looked up and nodded. 'Yep. What's up?'

Flora chuckled. 'Can you give me a hand with these boxes, please? I think I got carried away at the supplier's.'

'Yes, of course.' Sally followed Flora out to her car and laughed. Boxes, trays of dog food cans and large bags of biscuits filled the boot and back seat, not to mention the other bags crammed into the footwells. 'Were they having a sale or something?'

'The manager found me and offered us five per cent off today's shopping.' Flora pulled a face. 'I may have been a bit cheeky with his offer, but in my defence, he did say I could buy as much as I wanted.'

'Ha ha, that's brilliant.' Sally hefted two pallets of tins on top of each other and picked them up just as a car pulled up at the front gate.

'Oh, that'll be poor Jerry. Here, pop those back. We'll unload once he's been. I have a feeling this is going to be a difficult goodbye.' Flora's smile faded as they watched Jerry open the back door of his car and the Staffie-cross hop out.

Sally followed Flora across the courtyard before holding the gate open.

'Hello, Jerry, lovely.' Flora gave the man a quick hug before turning her attention to Bonnie, who, recognising her, wagged her tail energetically from side to side. In her mouth was a stuffed toy in the shape of a reindeer. 'And hello, Bonnie. You recognise me, don't you?'

'She sure does. Her tail was going as soon as we turned down the lane.' Jerry pulled a hankie from his pocket and dabbed his eyes.

'Oh, did you, sweetheart?' Flora picked up the stuffed toy as it fell from the dog's mouth. 'And I see you still have your reindeer.'

'Yes, it's a firm favourite of hers. It's a different one, mind you. The one she brought home with her from here got left up in Scotland a couple of years ago after a holiday.'

'Aw, you're a beauty, aren't you?' Letting the gate fall shut, Sally knelt down next to Bonnie and fussed her behind the ears.

'She sure is.' Jerry's voice cracked. 'I've got all her things in the boot. Her bed, her favourite blanket, the food she likes and the arthritis medication she's on.'

'I'll help you with those.' Sally held out her hand. 'I'm Sally, by the way.'

Taking her hand, Jerry nodded. 'Good to meet you, Sally.'

'Likewise.' Sally bundled a large dog bed in her arms and hooked the handles of a bag around her wrist before pushing the gate open again.

'Thank you, lovely. Come on, Bonnie, let's get you in and settled.' Flora waited for Jerry to pick up the rest of Bonnie's things before nodding to him to go ahead of her. 'You go through, and I'll shut the gate.'

Nodding his thanks, Jerry did as instructed and followed Sally inside the reception area before gently placing Bonnie's things on the counter.

'I don't know how I'm supposed to do this,' he said.

'Whichever way is best for you, Jerry.' Flora rubbed Jerry's arm. 'You can come and have a cuppa with us or make it a quick goodbye, whichever is less painful.'

Jerry wiped his eyes and sank to the floor, his arms wide open as Bonnie ran towards him. She snuggled her head against his chest.

Smothering kisses on her head, he returned the hug. 'I don't know how I'm ever going to get over losing you, Bonnie, my love, my best friend.'

Sally quietly lowered the bag and bed to the floor, blinking back tears. The love and connection between Jerry and Bonnie was clear. She couldn't imagine how he must be feeling. First to lose his job and his home and now to have to say goodbye to his best friend, the one constant who'd been by his side through everything.

Kneeling on the floor next to him, Flora rubbed his arm. 'Oh, lovely, I feel for you. I really do.'

Jerry nodded as Bonnie, still excited and energetic, oblivious to what was about to happen, wagged her tail and licked his arm.

'You've worked miracles with her. You really have. I remember when she was brought to us after that police raid. Do you remember, she'd been left alone in that house for days, weeks maybe, scavenging on what food she could drag out of cupboards and living in her own filth and that which those... humans...' Flora spat out the word '...had left her in.'

'I know. I know. She's been through so much.' Jerry wrapped his arms around the beautiful dog, tears running down his face, all self-will to keep his emotions in check long having disappeared.

'She has, but it's been you who has given her a second chance at life, you who taught her to trust again, you who offered her a safe space, a home.' Flora spoke quietly.

'And now I'm abandoning her. I'm leaving her all on her own again.' Jerry wiped his sleeve across his eyes.

'You're not abandoning her, lovely. You're doing what's best for her despite your own wants and needs. And I can see that. I can see your heart is breaking.' She rubbed his back.

Turning away, Sally let her own tears fall. She didn't think she'd ever seen such an emotional surrender before. Yes, they had people return the dogs they'd previously adopted, but it was usually after a few days, or a week, maybe slightly longer, and it usually turned out that the adopters just weren't ready for a dog, hadn't quite realised the reality of owning one. This was different. Bonnie was Jerry's family, and he was being forced to walk away from her. From everything Sally had heard about Bonnie – from Flora, Percy and Susan – Jerry really had transformed her life and was responsible for the confident, happy dog in front of them today.

'You've done everything for her. Just look at her, Jerry. This beautiful, well-rounded and healthy pup is down to you.' Flora smiled weakly. 'And I know it's probably hard to hear, but because of the love you have shown her she won't be here at Wagging Tails for long. She'll be offered a home by the first people who see her.'

'No, I want to hear that. I want her to be happy. That's all I want. All I've ever wanted.' Jerry planted a huge kiss on Bonnie's forehead and stood up. 'Please, please let me know when she's adopted.'

'I will, lovely. I will.' Standing up too, Flora held her free arm out, the other holding Bonnie's lead, and wrapped Jerry into a hug. 'You're a good man, Jerry. A very good man and I wish you all the best and when you're back on your feet and ready, please think about offering another dog a place in your heart.'

Nodding, Jerry turned and left.

Sally watched as he walked quickly and purposefully across the courtyard. It was obvious he was trying to hold it together as much as he could. Bonnie gave a slight whimper as the door closed behind her beloved human.

Kneeling down, Sally fussed over her. 'Oh, sweetheart, you're realising what's just happened, aren't you?'

'Well, I don't know about you, but I think I need a strong coffee and a chance to compose myself again.' Flora cleared her throat. 'I don't know what's worse sometimes – the plight of a dog who has found and lost their perfect loving home or a dog who has never known love in the first place.'

Stepping back, Flora grabbed a tissue from the counter and passed it to Sally before taking another and wiping her own eyes.

'Well, I do, but you know what I mean.'

'I do. I know what you mean.' Sally watched as Jerry's car pulled away.

'And I really do hope Jerry gets back on his feet.' Flora held a treat down next to Bonnie in an attempt to lure her away from the spot she was sitting in, her dark eyes still fixed on the closed door. 'Come on, sweetie, let's go into the kitchen and have some fusses.'

21

Sally looked down at her watch before glancing across the beach towards the cobbled pathway that led down to the cove. It was quarter past one now. Andy was late. She looked down at Bonnie, who had just brought a ball back to her and picked it up.

'He's late, isn't he?'

The beautiful Staffie-cross held her paw up, grains of sand falling from her fur and her tongue lolling to one side.

'You're tired out, aren't you?' Sally laughed. 'One more throw and we'll settle down for a treat, okay?'

'Okay.'

Spinning around, Sally smiled. 'Andy. I was starting to wonder if you'd stood me up.'

'Never. Who's this?' He bent down, placed the bag he was carrying on the sand, and fussed over Bonnie.

'This is Bonnie. Her owner has just had to surrender her back to us after five years.'

Sally bit down on her bottom lip as the image of Jerry leaving flashed into her mind. Poor Bonnie knew something was wrong and had been crying in her kennel, scratching the door to get out and find her owner, which was why Sally had asked Andy to meet her at the beach instead of at Harold's where they'd arranged.

'Oh, that's awful.' Andy frowned as he continued to fuss over the dog.

'It really was. He was devastated, but unfortunately a change of circumstances meant he was left with no choice.'

'That must have been difficult for him. She's gorgeous.'

'She really is, both inside and out. Aren't you, Bonnie?'

Andy chuckled as Bonnie stuck her nose in the bag Andy had brought. 'You've found our lunch, haven't you, girl? If I'd known you were coming, I'd have brought some chicken.'

Sally grinned. Andy had always loved dogs.

'It's okay. I've got a pocket overflowing with treats. I don't think she'll go hungry.' She patted her bulging pocket.

Standing back up, Andy turned slowly on the spot, looking around the cove. 'So, this is West Par then?'

'It sure is.' She followed his gaze. 'It's beautiful, isn't it?'

He cleared his throat. 'It looks idyllic.'

Sally threw the tennis ball and watched as Bonnie ran to catch it, leaving a pattern of paw prints in the sand.

'It's scary to think how much it could change,' she said.

'It is.'

Sally glanced across at him. Had she told him about the proposed development and Lyle trying to force Flora to buy? She didn't think she had.

'You heard about the development?'

Andy watched as Bonnie bounded back to them and dropped the ball at his feet. 'I remember reading something.'

'Of course. Darryl said he'd written a few pieces about the proposed development in the paper. He's been helping us drum up support. Flora's had so many emails and phone calls from people pledging their support and promising to join us at the protest. Plus, of course, the other West Par residents and those living close by.'

'Protest?' Andy rubbed the palm of his hand across his face before bending to pick up the ball again. 'But the development shouldn't affect

West Par. Apart from bringing in more business, which can only be a good thing, surely? Everywhere needs more housing.'

'It won't bring in more business though, not really. It'll be just as easy for people to drive to one of the supermarkets on the outskirts of Trestow. Besides, West Par will lose its charm, not to mention the strain on local amenities. Getting a doctor's appointment is rarer than winning the lottery at the moment, and where is the school supposed to put the extra pupils?'

Throwing the ball overarm, Andy waited until it had bounced and rolled to a stop before speaking again. 'Think of all the new people moving in, looking to settle down, there'll be an influx of people wanting to adopt your dogs.'

Sally scoffed. Andy had always been the optimistic one of them both, the one who could see the beauty in a rainstorm, the adventure in getting lost. 'That's if Wagging Tails survives.'

Andy turned to her, a frown on his face. 'What do you mean?'

'Didn't you read about it in the paper?' She shook her head. She'd not read any of the articles Darryl had written. She didn't like reading or watching the news if she could help it, but she'd assumed Darryl would have highlighted the danger to Wagging Tails. 'Lyle, the owner of the proposed development, has been trying to intimidate and force Flora to sell. We think he needs the land for access.'

Andy slowly bent down and picked up the ball Bonnie had retrieved, and turned it over in his hand before looking out to sea. 'I'm sure the planning permission wouldn't have been passed if they foresaw any access problems.'

'You'd think so, wouldn't you?' Sally shrugged. 'Keep it to yourself, but there's talk of corruption between that Lyle guy and the former planning officer.'

'Former?'

'I think that's what I heard. Apparently, he's been suspended. Of course it's all hush-hush. The council obviously doesn't want anything getting out.'

'Right.' Andy threw the ball again.

Taking a deep breath, Sally picked up the picnic rug Flora had lent her and threw it down. She smoothed its corners before sitting down.

'Anyway, let's talk about something positive and eat. I'm starving. What did you bring?'

* * *

Sally closed the gate behind her and fished another treat from her pocket.

'Here you go, sweetheart.' She passed Bonnie the treat, the lovely dog lapping it up immediately. 'I think you've made a lifelong friend in Andy, haven't you?'

She smiled. Andy had been besotted with her. After a bit of an awkward silence as they'd transitioned from the discussion about the proposed new development into something more positive, Andy had spent most of the time playing and fussing over Bonnie.

'And you seemed equally besotted with him.' Sally laughed. Not that she could blame Bonnie. Andy was pretty special. She was glad she'd taken the chance and messaged him earlier.

After securing Bonnie in her kennel, her beloved stuffed reindeer dangling from her mouth and all her home comforts surrounding her, Sally pulled open the door to the reception area.

'Hey, lovely.' Flora looked up from her notebook. 'Did you and Bonnie have fun at the beach?'

'Yes, thanks. I think Andy has made a firm friend in Bonnie.' Sally grinned as she shut the door behind her.

'Oh good. Thanks for taking her. Hopefully, she won't be here for long.' Flora scribbled something down. 'In fact, I'm just about to ring Darryl now. I'm hoping he can pop her adoption advert in tomorrow's paper. The sooner she can get settled into a proper home again, the better it will be for her.'

'Good idea.' As Flora picked up the phone, a slight tapping on the window behind her made Sally turn around. Alex's face bobbed quickly into view before disappearing beneath the window. What was he up to?

Sally frowned as he bobbed back up, this time indicating she join him outside. She glanced back at Flora, who was now speaking into the phone, seemingly oblivious to Alex's antics, and stepped outside.

'What—?'

'Shush. Close the door.' Alex stepped away from the window, his back against the wall.

Sally did as she was told and followed him as he led the way across the courtyard. 'What's going on?'

'We've started putting the decorations out in the top paddock. We're trying to get as much prep done as we can today to make it easier tomorrow.'

'Good idea.' Sally stopped as he pulled open the storage shed door.

'Here, take these, would you please?' He placed two large bundles of fabric in Sally's arms.

'What are they?' She looked down at the brightly coloured materials.

'Bunting. We're going to string them around the paddocks on the fences.' He glanced back in the direction of the reception area. 'We'll have to keep Flora away, but she's going down to Darryl's office in a bit to give him Bonnie's adoption advert.'

'Umm, she's on the phone to him now.' Sally grimaced.

'Oh no.' Alex hid his face in the palms of his hands.

'I'm afraid so.' Sally shifted the material in her arms. 'I'm sure we can think of something else to keep her occupied.'

'What about Bonnie's photo?' Alex picked up a huge bag and kicked the shed door closed. 'No, she'd have just sent it by email or on her phone.'

'We'll see if anyone has any other ideas,' Sally said. 'She'll likely hang around in the reception area for a while anyway because of Cindy, so we should have a few minutes to think of something at least.'

'That's true.' Alex held the gate into the bottom paddock open as Sally slipped through.

'I can't believe the party is tomorrow. It feels as though it's just crept up on us, doesn't it?'

'It sure does. And we've tonnes to do yet. Susan is going home early to bake snacks and I'm sure she said Malcolm is on sandwich-making duty.'

'He certainly is.' Susan rushed forward from where she'd been tying a birthday banner to the trestle tables and held the gate open for them into the top paddock.

'We'll get it done.' Using her elbow, Sally unhooked the gate to the top paddock and Percy, who had just jogged over, opened it for them.

'We've got a problem,' Alex said, filling him in on the news. 'Flora isn't going to the newspaper offices now. Sally's just heard her on the phone to Darryl.' He dumped the bag he'd been carrying on one of the three trestle tables set up against the fence.

'I'll take Flora out for a birthday tea – well, late lunch – in a few minutes and then drop her off at Poppy's school when school finishes.' Susan took the bundle of bunting from Sally. 'I've told her I'll take her somewhere nice for her birthday anyway and I know she wanted to take Poppy somewhere or other this evening, so I'll just make up some excuse why I can't drop her back here.'

'Are you sure?' Alex drew Susan in for a hug. 'You are a lifesaver. And we can bring Cindy up here with us so she's not left alone.'

'Ha ha, it's no problem. I get to eat cake with Flora rather than finish up here.' Susan patted Alex on the back and laughed.

'Still, thank you.' Alex shrugged and turned to Percy. 'It was a good idea of yours to pop the trestle tables here instead of the bottom paddock. I know we've got that monstrosity to look at…' He indicated the Portakabin overlooking the fence at the far end of the paddock. 'But at least we can set things up without worrying that Flora will see.'

'Oh, I do have some rare moments of being a genius.' Percy smiled and tapped the side of his head before helping Susan unravel the bunting. 'Now, these are going round the fences, right?'

Taking a length of bunting, Sally walked with Percy to the far end of the paddock and tied her end around a fence post before threading the rest around the other posts.

'Did you find a present for Flora in the end?' she asked.

'I did, yes.' Percy grinned and pulled out his phone. Holding it up, he tapped the screen. 'Look, I asked Chris down at Honeysuckle Sanctuary to paint me a montage of some of the dogs we've rescued.'

Taking the mobile from him, Sally squinted at the screen. The dogs in the painting looked almost lifelike.

'Wow, and that's a painting? Not a collection of photos?'

'Nope, it's a painting for sure.' Percy chuckled. 'He's a very talented lad, is Chris.'

'That's amazing.' Sally smiled and passed the phone back to him. 'She'll absolutely love that.'

'Yes, I think she will. Thank you for talking me out of buying that daft vase.' He slipped his phone back into his pocket and began to help with the bunting again.

'The vase wasn't daft. It was nice, but that painting is in a different league entirely.'

22

'Can you pass me that knife please, Sally?' Susan pointed at her.

Turning around, Sally put down the plastic cups she'd been stuffing into a bag and searched the work surface behind her before passing Susan the knife. The kitchen was heaving with volunteers, all there to get Wagging Tails ready for Flora's party, and an excited buzz filled the room.

'Thanks, love.' Taking the knife, Susan wrapped it in a tea towel and placed it in the bag Sally was packing. 'I think we're almost there.'

'Yes. I think I've got all the party cups and plates. Umm... cutlery, I've forgotten cutlery.' Standing on her tiptoes, Sally pulled the bundle of plastic cutlery from the cupboard. 'That's it. I'm done.'

'Great.' Susan turned around to face the kitchen and clapped her hands, getting the room's attention. 'Thank you so much, everyone, for coming early to help us get organised for Flora's party. I think we have about half an hour until she gets back. Is that right, Alex?'

Alex held up his mobile. 'Yes, about half an hour. Mack, the vet, has kept her and Luke waiting for as long as he can for Luke's vaccination appointment, so she'll be on her way back soon.'

'Great, thanks.' She turned back to address the group. 'As most of you know, everything is set up in the paddocks so it's just all of this...' she gestured to the table filled with plates and trays of food and jugs of squash '...that needs taking out and arranging on the trestle tables.'

'Here you go,' Sally said, passing plates to Mack's younger brothers who'd come to help. 'Are you okay taking these please?'

She moved on to the next volunteer, and shortly after, having passed the final tray of cupcakes out, she turned to pick up the bag of bits she'd packed earlier.

Outside, she found Alex running across the paddock. 'Let's start getting in the party mood!'

Tim, the college student who volunteered at Wagging Tails as part of his college course, followed behind, struggling with some speakers.

'Tim, do you need a hand?' Sally stepped towards him, the bag still in her grasp.

'No, it's cool, thanks. This is the last of them. I'll have them set up in just a few minutes.' He smiled. 'And this is Ava, from my college, who makes balloons.'

'Hi, Ava. Thanks so much for coming. The kids are going to love your balloon animals,' Sally said. This party was going to be great. Darryl had managed to talk one of the newspaper photographers to take photos too.

'Thanks for inviting me, I'm looking forward to it.' Ava hefted a large holdall further up her shoulders before pulling her dark hair caught beneath its strap.

'We'll go and get set up. See you in a min.' Tim nodded goodbye before he and Ava walked off towards the paddocks.

Just before she began following them, Sally glanced towards the gate and squinted. Was that Darryl and Luna walking across the courtyard? Yes, she was sure it was. She paused until they were closer.

'Luna! And Darryl, of course.' Waiting until they had stopped beside her, she lowered the bag to the ground before turning to Luna and fussing her behind the ears.

'I'm glad I'm not forgotten, even if my welcome was merely an afterthought.' Darryl chuckled as he shifted a brightly wrapped present to his other hand.

'Ha ha, what can I say? I have no excuses. I'm just one of those people who notices the dog before the owner.' Sally grinned as she stood up again.

'Yeah, I'm not sure that helps,' Alex said as he paused on his way to the paddocks, a large tray of cupcakes in his hands.

'Definitely not, I'm afraid. You're simply digging a deeper hole,' Darryl teased.

'What can I say? Dogs are more amazing than humans. Isn't that right, Luna?' Sally laughed as she gave Luna another quick fuss before standing and watching Ginny as she hurried across to them.

'Aw, hello, Luna,' Ginny greeted, fussing over Luna before pecking Darryl on the lips and grabbing his hand. 'You need to come and meet these dogs. And you two, Sally and Alex. We've had a really good turnout of dogs who Wagging Tails have rehomed.'

Darryl looked across at Sally and raised his eyebrow. 'Someone else who always greets the dogs first.'

'What?' Ginny looked at them, confused.

'Sally greeted Luna before saying hello to me.' Darryl shrugged.

'Oh, ha ha, all the best humans do that.' Ginny winked at Sally before turning and leading the way to the corner of the bottom paddock.

Sally nodded, trying to keep a straight face as Darryl opened and closed his mouth. Picking up the bag again, she grinned at Alex as they followed Ginny, Darryl and Luna through the gate to the bottom paddock.

The paddocks were filling up. She squinted at the crowds. All of the volunteers, both casual and permanent, had come along bringing their family and friends. People from West Par had turned out to wish Flora a happy birthday. There were also a lot of people Sally didn't recognise, but she knew Percy had invited some of Flora's friends and there would be people who had adopted from Wagging Tails before she'd arrived. It was amazing to think that Flora had touched the hearts of all of these people. And the dogs! There were so many!

'Alex, you'll recognise these gorgeous pups, but, Sally and Darryl, I'd like to introduce you to a few of the dogs who have come through Wagging Tails.' Ginny knelt down and held her arms out as a tiny apricot curly-haired dog ran towards her. 'Here, we have the beautiful Taffi. Look how tiny she is! And this is Nia, her owner.'

'Aw, she's gorgeous.' Kneeling down next to Ginny, Sally held out her hand as Taffi sniffed her.

'Don't be fooled by the size of her. She has a personality to match a Great Dane!' Nia laughed.

'Ha ha, I can well imagine that. Especially after little Puddles, sorry, Eric, the dachshund we had in recently. He definitely thought he was a few feet taller than he actually was.' Sally grinned as she fussed over the tiny Taffi. 'What breed is she? I can see the poodle in her.'

'She's a cavapoochon, so part Cavalier, part poodle and part bichon frise.'

'Oh yes.' Sally gently stroked Taffi's ears. 'I can see that now.'

'And...' Ginny looked around the group. 'Where's Archie gone?'

'If Archie's a Lab, Luna has found him.' Darryl chuckled and turned towards Luna, who was greeting a beautiful black Labrador.

'Aw, they've made friends already.' Sally smiled as she watched the two Labs twist and sniff around each other.

'That's our Archie. He'll make friends with anyone.' A couple stepped forward, the woman holding the end of a brown lead. 'I'm Helen and this is Andy, by the way. I remember you, Ginny. It was you who first introduced us to Archie.'

'Yes, that's right. He was just a little pup, wasn't he? Full of energy?' Ginny fussed over the two of them.

'That's right, six months old, he was.'

'I can't believe he's what, four already?' Ginny looked across at Helen.

'No, he's five now.' Andy grinned.

'No way! Wow, it only feels like yesterday when he arrived.' Leaning down, Ginny kissed Archie on the head.

Standing up, Ginny left Luna and Archie to play and turned to a small Jack Russell. 'And this is Maisie.'

'Oh, I remember you, don't I, girl?' Having just returned from placing the cupcakes on the trestle tables, Alex knelt down on the grass as the small black, brown and white Jack Russell swung her tail from side to side as she bounded across to him, pulling her lead taut. 'You were rescued by a local farmer who found you with your head stuck down a rabbit hole. That's right, isn't it? And you're Meg, aren't you?'

'Yes, that's right.' Meg smiled. 'And unfortunately, Maisie still likes to search for rabbits, given half a chance.'

'Oh, you cheeky pup.' Alex grinned as he fussed Maisie behind the ears. 'Cheeky, but beautiful with it.'

'Oh, you really are beautiful.' Sally fussed over Maisie too. 'Flora's going to be so shocked to see you all here today.'

'She really is, isn't she?' Ginny turned towards the courtyard. 'Talking of which, I think she's just arrived!'

'Oh, she has! Where's Poppy?' Alex looked around.

'There.' Sally waved frantically across to Poppy, Flora's niece, who was chatting with a group of people in the middle of the paddock. Poppy waved back and ran across to them.

'Is she here?' Standing on her tiptoes, Poppy looked across to the courtyard. 'I can't wait to see her reaction.'

At that moment, Alex stuck his fingers in his mouth and whistled, waiting for a hush to descend and for the crowds to face him. Cupping his hands around his mouth, he shouted, 'Flora's here. Everyone gather together.'

As people and dogs alike surged forward to surround the gate, Sally watched as Flora stepped out of her car, walking around to the other side to get Luke out before noticing them all.

Flora raised her hand to her mouth as she looked at the large group waiting for her. Even from as far away as she was, Sally could see realisation flood across Flora's face as she broke into a huge grin.

When she arrived at the gate, loud cheers of 'Happy Birthday, Flora' and 'Surprise' swept through the crowd, followed by a huge round of applause.

Rushing forward, Alex tried to usher her through the gate, but Flora, seemingly frozen to the spot with shock, shook her head, tears of surprise and happiness flooding across her cheeks.

Excited by the welcome, the tall greyhound at her feet jumped, bobbing up and down on his legs and barked.

'Thank you, Luke. I think I needed that to bring me back to my senses.' Flora fussed over him before letting Alex lead her through the gate and turning to the group of people in front of her. 'I don't know what to say. This is just such a shock.'

'A nice shock, I hope?' someone in the crowd, a previous adopter, Sally thought, called out.

'Yes, yes, a nice shock. A wonderful shock. A wonderful surprise. I didn't expect anything... anything like this.' Flora stepped forward and squinted, looking at the woman who had shouted out. 'Oh my, that's not you, is it, Jenna? And, no, that can't be little Roxy?'

'It sure is.' Jenna grinned.

Holding her hands over her mouth, Flora bent down as the small bichon frise ran towards her. 'Do you remember me, Roxy?'

'It looks like it.' Jenna followed, Roxy's lead in her hand.

'Aw, Roxy, you always were such a sweetheart.' Flora fussed over her as Luke stood watching. 'How long ago was it you adopted her? Six years? She was an older dog then. How old is she now?'

'She's thirteen now.'

'Thirteen, and just as lively as she was back then.' Flora straightened her back as Roxy trotted back to Jenna. 'Thank you so much for coming.' She glanced around the crowd and pointed at numerous dogs. 'Oh, I can spot more of our old residents. You've all come here for me?'

'Of course.' Jenna laughed as she and Roxy rejoined the group of gathered people.

'I don't know what to say. I really don't.' Flora pointed towards Alex, Sally, Percy, Ginny, Poppy and Susan. 'You lot! This is your doing, isn't it?'

Sally laughed as she wiped happy tears from her eyes. All the planning had been worth it.

Percy stepped forward and took Luke's lead before linking arms with Flora. 'Come on, love. Come and see everyone. Enjoy your day.'

'Oh, I'm sure I will, lovely. Thank you.' Patting Percy on the arm, Flora grinned as they walked into the crowds, pointing this way and that way as she noticed more and more dogs and people she recognised.

23

'You're so lovely, Tyler. And you too, Fluffles.' Sally turned her attention from the spaniel to the poodle she'd worked with before the Smiths had adopted her. 'And how is she getting on with the lead walking?'

'Great. She's being a little star, believe it or not.' Mrs Smith, their owner, grinned. 'I think she's actually helping Tyler calm down a little on walks, too. He doesn't pull on the lead as much as he used to.'

'Wow, that's fantastic to hear.' Standing up, Sally noticed a woman alone at the top of the paddock by the fence. 'It's been so lovely to catch up with you all. I'll see you in a bit.'

'Lovely to catch up with you, too.' Mr Smith nodded. 'The dogs always get so excited when they see anyone they remember from Wagging Tails around the bay.'

Smiling, Sally began to walk towards the woman by the fence. Was she okay? She didn't have a dog with her, so she probably wasn't the owner of a previous resident of theirs. Unless she'd chosen not to bring them.

'It's a bit of an eyesore, isn't it?' she said once she'd reached her, gesturing to the Portakabin on the other side of the fence.

'Sorry?' The woman turned and looked at her quickly before returning her attention to the Portakabin.

'The Portakabin, it's a bit of an eyesore and so close, too.' Sally shifted on her feet.

Who was this woman?

'Yes, yes, it is.' The woman nodded, her eyes still fixed on the dark grey interruption to their view.

'Do you want to come and get some food? Susan and Malcolm have created quite the spread.' Sally glanced towards the trestle tables behind them.

The woman shook her head, and then looked at Sally as if only really realising she was there.

'No, thank you. I'd better get going.'

'Oh, are you sure?'

'Yes. Thank you.' Giving Sally a tight quick smile, the woman stepped away, heading back down the paddock where she disappeared into the crowds of people.

Sally sighed. Had she said something to upset the woman or was it the sight of the Portakabin and the realisation that West Par might be transformed forever that had driven her to leave? That was if she was from West Par, anyway. Sally was certain she'd never seen her before.

And where was Andy? He'd said he could make the party in the end.

She pulled her mobile from her pocket and frowned. There was no message or missed call. Straining her neck, she searched the paddocks again. She couldn't see him. She had told him the right time, hadn't she? She was sure she had. She'd asked him again when she'd met him on the beach with Bonnie and he'd even noted the details in his phone.

She watched as Flora and Poppy came towards her.

'Sally, come with me. I'd like to introduce you to a few of our previous residents and their families. You too, Poppy. In fact, you might just remember one of them.' Flora linked arms with them both and led them towards a group of people and their dogs in the corner of the top paddock, who were relaxing and chatting on camping chairs.

'Really?' Poppy glanced back towards Mack to make sure he was looking after Dougal before turning and looking back at her aunt.

'Oh yes, you might.' As they reached the group, Flora dropped their arms and began to fuss over the dogs. 'Hello, everyone. I've brought Sally and my niece, Poppy, to meet you.'

'Happy birthday, Flora. It's so lovely to come back here to where our journey with this little one all began.' A woman stood up from her chair and hugged Flora.

'Thank you for coming, Wendy. Hello, Douglas too.' Flora grinned and turned back towards Poppy and Sally and indicated a small black and white Parson Russell terrier at Wendy's feet. 'This is Dora. Do you recognise her, Poppy?'

'Aw, yes. I'm sure I do.' Poppy knelt on the grass and fussed over the dog. 'Hello, Dora. I do remember you. Wow, she must have come in a while back?'

'Nine or ten years ago, I think, wasn't it, Wendy?' Flora looked across to the woman.

'Nine years we've had her, and she was at Wagging Tails for three months before we adopted her.'

'That's right.' Flora fussed over the small dog. 'Am I right in thinking she was about six when she was brought to us?'

'Yes, she reached the grand age of fifteen three days ago.' Wendy grinned.

'Fifteen.' Flora shook her head as she fussed Dora behind the ears. 'You must share this party with me then, Dora.'

At that moment, Sally could feel another dog nudging into the back of her knees. Twisting around, she laughed as she saw a large ginger vizsla plonking themself down at her feet.

'I know you, Jolene. You still demand your fusses, hey? I see you haven't changed one little bit.'

'Oh, she definitely hasn't. Five months on from when we adopted her, and she's still just as strong-willed!' Rosie, Jolene's owner, laughed. 'Ben nicknamed her Jolly, which has kind of stuck.'

'I can see why, what with her tail wagging at that speed.' Flora chuckled. 'And what does this beautiful bandana say?'

'Read it.'

Stepping forward, Rosie straightened the pale pink bandana crumpled around Jolly's neck, so the glittery gold words were visible.

'"Happy Birthday, Flora",' she read. 'Oh, that's so lovely.'

'Well, we thought it was fitting for such a special occasion.' Rosie gestured to Ben, who nodded.

'Well, this day has certainly been full of surprises. Thank you.' Flora straightened her back.

'Look, that's Scooby too!' Sally pointed towards a small black and white jackapoodle who was straining on his lead towards Jolly. 'They must remember each other. They had kennels next to each other, didn't they?'

'Yes, yes, they did. We moved Scooby next to Jolly after we noticed they were playing so nicely together in the paddock. They loved walking and playing together.'

Flora and Sally watched as Scooby nudged Jolly, wanting to play.

'That's right, I remember. The age difference seemed to help. Scooby calmed Jolly down,' Flora said as she fussed over the small dog.

'They were so cute together.' Sally smiled. 'And they remember each other!'

'Ha ha, we might have to start going on walks together.' Rosie looked towards Scooby's family, Hamish and Hector. 'What do you think? Keep their friendship going?'

'I think that's a great idea.' Hamish grinned.

'That's so lovely, and it's so wonderful to see all of our old residents looking so happy and healthy after coming to us the ways they did.' Flora fussed the three dogs in front of her.

'Hey, Sally, can you help me with the cake, please?' Alex cupped her elbow and whispered in her ear.

'Yes, of course.'

Sally waved her goodbyes before linking arms with Alex, and they made their way through the paddocks, weaving between clusters of people and dogs, chatting and enjoying the party.

'It looks as though Flora is having a good time.' Alex nodded back towards Flora.

'Aw, it does. It looks as though everyone is. It was definitely a good idea to throw a party for her.'

'Wasn't it just?' Alex grinned as he held the door open to the reception area.

'I'm guessing the cake is in the kitchen?'

'Yep, Elsie brought it over with her. I can't wait to see it. I hid the candles in the cupboard earlier.'

'Okay, brill.' Sally followed Alex through and carefully lifted the lid on a large box. 'Wow, have you seen this?'

'Not yet. Let's see.' Alex carefully lowered the sides of the cake box, revealing a large rectangular cake. Wendy had not only recreated a number of the Wagging Tails dogs on the actual cake but had also moulded little dog figures using royal icing around the sides.

'It's perfect. Look, you can literally tell which dogs Wendy modelled them on. Look, here's Ralph.' Sally pointed to a perfect miniature replica of Ralph relaxing on the silver cake board, a tiny yellow tennis ball held in his mouth.

'I don't know how she does it.' Alex shook his head.

'I know. I'd love to be half as talented as she is.' Sally pulled open the cupboard door and took out the candles.

Alex paused as he picked up the cake from the box and tilted his head. 'Do you hear that knocking?'

'I doubt it. Why would someone knock when they could see a party going on?'

But as she placed the candles on the work surface, she could hear it too. Sally frowned. Alex was right. There was knocking.

'Hello?'

Sally grinned. 'It's Andy.'

'Ooh, isn't he the one you've been pining over for years? Your ex, right? I've heard so much about him. I feel as though I know him already.'

Laughing, Sally headed out of the kitchen before calling over her shoulder, 'Don't you dare tell him that!'

'I won't.'

She pulled the door open and stood to the side, ushering Andy into the reception area. 'Hey, you managed to come.'

'Hi, yes. Sorry I'm so late, I got held up.' He leaned forward and kissed her on the cheek before stepping back and looking around. 'I saw you come in here, so I thought I'd follow.'

'Don't worry. You're just in time to sing "Happy Birthday". We're just taking the cake out.'

'Is this where you keep the dogs?' He pivoted on his feet, looking around the reception area.

'They're through there. Apart from Cindy; Susan brought Cindy to the party because she can't be left alone, but the others are in the kennels. I'll show you around in a bit, if you like? After we've done the cake?'

Andy nodded.

'Here it is.' Pushing open the kitchen door with the cake in his hands, Alex looked across at Andy. 'So, here he is, then?'

Swallowing, Sally could feel the rush of heat flushing across her face.

'Alex meet Andy, Andy meet Alex.'

'Great to meet you, Andy. I'd greet you properly and shake hands but...' Alex nodded towards the cake and laughed.

'Here, let me get the door.' Holding the door to the courtyard open, Andy let Alex and Sally through before falling into step with Sally. 'That looks like a great cake.'

'It's amazing, isn't it? Wendy from the bakery in Penworth Bay made it.' Sally slipped her hand into Andy's as they made their way across the courtyard.

'Well, she must be very talented.' He squeezed her hand.

'Oh, she is. You should see some of the other cakes she makes.' Sally pulled open the gate to the bottom paddock. 'Are we taking it to the trestle tables, Alex? In the top paddock?'

'That's the plan. Sorry, can you just...?' He looked towards the cake as it began to tilt in his grasp.

'Yep.' Pausing, Sally helped straighten the cake board in Alex's arms. As they began walking again, she noticed guests had begun to follow, realising they had the cake. 'Ha ha, we don't need to shout to get people to gather round. People are following already.'

Alex grinned as they walked towards the trestle table and when they got there, Andy stepped forward to help Sally shift bowls of crisps and platters of sandwiches to the sides to make room for the cake.

Sally scanned the gathering crowds. 'Where's Flora?'

'Umm...' Standing on his tiptoes, Alex pointed. 'Over there talking to the Smiths.'

'I'll go and get her.'

'No, don't worry. She's spotted something's going on and Percy is bringing her over.'

'Great.' Sally pulled the matches from her pocket and began to light the two numbered candles and the three small sparklers. As the flames flickered to life and the sparklers' sparkles began cascading, Sally stood back to make a pathway for Flora and Percy.

Led by Alex, the guests began singing. 'Happy birthday to you...'

Flora stood in front of the cake, her hands to her cheeks, grinning.

Sally looked around the vast group in front of them, all here to celebrate Flora's birthday, all here, in one way or another, to pay their thanks to her. This was what had drawn her to living down here, in West Par, and to apply for the job at Wagging Tails. She'd been welcomed with open arms.

Feeling Andy's fingers interlace with hers, she glanced across at him as the song came to an end and Alex called for 'three cheers' for Flora. She didn't even want to think about Andy going home. She knew the time would come. She knew that when he'd finished renovating his house he'd have to move on to the next project, but, for now, she was determined to make the most of having all the people she so cared about in the same place.

'And one for luck. Hip, hip, hooray!'

A loud applause rang through the paddock.

'I guess I'd better blow out the candles before the wax ruins this amazing cake.'

After wiping happy tears from her cheeks, Flora tucked a loose strand of hair behind her ear and blew out the candles. Then she waited for the applause to die down before taking a deep breath.

'I just want to say a few words, if I may? I know I've already thanked you all but, honestly, this has all been such a wonderful surprise. And this cake...' She looked around the crowd in front of her and pointed to Wendy, who was standing next to Elsie. 'I'm assuming this has something to do with you?'

Wendy looked down at the floor, a soft blush flushing across her cheeks as Elsie nudged her.

'It has everything to do with her, designed, baked and decorated.' Elsie grinned.

'I thought so. Well, it's fabulous. Thank you! And I can spot some of our current residents as well as previous ones.' Flora studied the group of adopters and friends in front of her until pointing towards the back of the group. 'This little dog on the cake is the spitting image of you, our darling Scooby, and there's Ralph and Dougal, too. Thank you so much, Wendy.'

'You're welcome.' Wendy smiled, the flush of heat still visible across her cheeks.

'Right, back to the party! Let's enjoy ourselves!' Flora nodded to Tim to turn the music up, and the crowd dispersed.

Sally turned to Andy and frowned. He was looking around the paddock, his expression anything but happy, sad almost. He must be feeling the pressure of meeting the people she cared about. Still, it was a party and she wanted him to enjoy himself. Maybe he just needed a bit of time away from everyone to relax before getting into the party spirit. 'Come on, I'll introduce you to the dogs we have in our care now, if you like?'

Slipping her hand into his, she led the way back across the paddocks towards the reception area.

24

'Just to warn you, they might get a little excited as you're new to them.' Sally pushed open the door to the kennels and sure enough, Nala began pawing at her kennel door and barking excitedly, starting a chorus of barking and whining. Laughing, Sally plunged her hand into her pocket, drew out a selection of treats and offered them to Andy. 'Here, do you want some?'

'Thank you.' He took some and knelt down next to Nala's kennel, reading the small chalkboard hanging from her kennel door. 'So, you're Nala then? Aren't you a lovely one?'

'She sure is.' With her foot flat against the wall opposite the kennels, Sally smiled as she watched him work his way down the kennels.

'It looks a lovely place here. For the dogs and for you, I mean.' Andy slipped Nala another treat before standing up and pausing in front of Sally.

'Oh, it is. I love working here, not that it feels like work. Which probably sounds daft...'

'No, it doesn't.' Andy shook his head. 'Once I'd taken over my dad's business and began renovating houses, I used to feel as though I was cheating the system, you know? How could I earn money by simply doing something I enjoyed? Seeing the project through from start to finish. Stepping inside a time capsule of a building, or even worse, a house someone had begun to "renovate"—' he hooked his forefingers around the word '— and by doing so they'd pretty much ripped out the heart of the property, all the features that made the house a home, leaving nothing to salvage and restore. And then, at the end of the project, seeing the new owners walk through the door for the first time, ready to enjoy what I created.'

'Aw, I can imagine you being able to see the potential in even the most derelict properties. You were always really creative.' Sally reached out and took hold of his hands, careful not to squash the dog treats he was holding. 'It's good that we've both found jobs we're passionate about and actually enjoy. When I thought I'd have to be working at my parents' firm for the rest of my life...' She shuddered. Part of her would have liked to have enjoyed it, but it just wasn't for her, law or working in such close proximity to her family.

'Yes, well, things change and have done more than a little recently.' He held her hands a little tighter and looked down at the floor before fixing his eyes on hers. 'My dad's business, sorry, my business...' He shook his head. 'It still feels strange to call it mine. That's silly, isn't it?'

'Not at all.'

'Well, I've taken a bit of a different direction with my business this year and I'm having more than a few doubts that I've made the right decision.' He bit down on his nail, the dog treats in the other hand.

Sally frowned. As far as she knew, he hadn't done that in years. Or at least he'd stopped after their exams at school and hadn't started again whilst they'd been together. She remembered before their English exam, she'd painted his nails with a nail varnish she'd found that was supposed to taste so disgusting it removed all temptation to bite your nails. It hadn't worked. He'd simply sat there in the exam room and gnawed on his cuticles instead. This change in the direction of his business was clearly worrying him.

'I'm sure it is. You've always been very good at looking at all of the options available and working out which one is best.'

'I'm not so sure this time.' Andy glanced behind him at the dogs.

'Hey, is it something you can change?'

'Possibly but not easily and not without loss.'

'Okay, but you must have chosen to go down the route you have for a reason?' She rubbed his arm.

'Yes, yes, I did.'

'Then maybe it's a good thing.' She smiled. 'Maybe you're just worried about it because this new step is changing how your dad ran the business? What is it you've done differently on this project?'

'I...' Andy looked behind him as Bonnie began to whine, her cries growing louder and echoing down the corridor.

'Oh, Bonnie, sweetheart. It's okay.' Sally walked towards her kennel and opened it, watching as Bonnie walked out straight towards her. Sally looked across at Andy. 'I don't think she fully understands that Jerry isn't coming back for her, but she knows something is wrong.'

Andy frowned and knelt down next to her, holding out a treat. As soon as she'd walked across to him and eaten the treat, he fussed her, her whole body swinging from side to side in excitement.

'She likes you.' Sally grinned.

'Well, I like you too, Bonnie.' Andy smiled.

'Sorry, you were talking about your business?' Sally closed Bonnie's kennel door quietly and clipped a lead to her collar. They could walk her around the paddocks for a bit; mingling with the other dogs and the guests would do her good and hopefully take her mind off things.

'I don't really know where to start.' Andy stepped towards her. 'You know how much I care for you, don't you? I've enjoyed these last couple of weeks so much, running into you again. What we have at the moment just feels so natural, doesn't it?'

'Yes, it does.' Sally nodded. It really did. 'It almost feels as though we've started back where we'd finished.'

'Before the ending of the relationship part, I hope?' Andy raised his eyebrows.

'Ha ha, of course. But it does, doesn't it?'

It wasn't just her, was it? He must feel it too.

'Yes, it really does.'

'But what has this got to do with your business?' Her heart sank. He was leaving, wasn't he? That's what he was trying to tell her. He'd found a property to renovate elsewhere.

'Because—'

'Sally, quick! You'll never guess what's happening.' The kennel door was thrown open and Ginny peered in, her face ashen and her eyes wide.

'Oh no, what's happened?' Wrapping Bonnie's lead around her wrist, Sally hurried outside. From the courtyard, she could see the bottom paddock had emptied. Where had everyone gone? Had they left? 'Where is everyone?'

'Up in the top paddock.' Picking up the pace, Ginny led the way to the top paddock, Sally and Andy running behind her.

There was a noise, a low rumbling sound, vibrating through the ground beneath her feet. What was that? As they neared the entrance to the top paddock, Sally could see the party guests. This was where everyone was then, gathering together by the top fence, their attention fixed to whatever was happening in front of them. What was going on?

Squeezing through the tight crowd, being careful to make sure Bonnie stayed close by her heel, Sally followed Ginny to the front, and they came to a halt beside Flora, Percy, Susan and Alex.

'It started...' Ginny's voice was lost as the rumbling grew louder, closer.

Sally dropped Bonnie's lead and scrambled quickly to pick it up as she watched a huge yellow excavator inch closer to the fence. Eventually, it stopped – precariously close to the Portakabin – and lowered its arm. The teeth of the large metal bucket sliced through the earth with ease. Sally watched as the bucket swung higher again, dirt spilling down its sides and falling to the ground as it turned before dispelling its load into a heap.

Were they really doing this? Now? It was the weekend. What kind of man was Lyle? What kind of company did he run? Sally looked around; everyone's faces were fixed on the excavator as its jaws cut through the earth again.

Lyle knew what he was doing. He was making a point.

Percy wrapped his arm around Flora and gently turned her before walking slowly away. And one by one, the partygoers dispersed. The party was over.

Sally looked to her side, expecting to see Andy standing there, but he wasn't. Had he left? Without saying goodbye? She frowned as she searched the thinning crowd. Had he run up here with her and Ginny? She thought he had but she'd been in such a rush she might not have noticed him slip away before making it to the top paddock. Maybe he'd assumed Ginny had wanted to talk to her privately or something when she'd told Sally to follow her? She should have told him to come along.

With a shudder, the excavator came to a stop and Sally watched as the operator jumped from the cab and walked across the field.

'Is he leaving that there?'

'It looks like it.' Ginny spoke quietly.

'Why?' Alex walked towards the fence and peered down into the hole closest to them. 'What's the point of digging a couple of holes and then leaving them?'

'Intimidation.' Darryl placed his arm around Ginny's waist. 'They're just intimidating us.'

'Huh, trying to scare Flora into selling, no doubt.' Alex glared at the excavator. 'Well, it won't work. The Portakabin didn't and neither will this.'

'No, but what are we going to do? If they're going to be building that close to our fence, we're not going to be able to use the top paddock to exercise or train the dogs any more. Not with all the noise, strange sights and smells, not to mention the people.' Susan frowned.

'Did Flora and Percy go back towards the kennels?' Ginny glanced towards Wagging Tails. 'If not, I'll go and check on the dogs now, see if the noise has disturbed them.'

'Yes.' Susan nodded. 'They went that way.'

'Let's get inside.' Darryl spoke quietly to Ginny. 'We can see how Flora's doing.'

'Good idea.' Ginny nodded and they began walking back.

'I'll come with you.' Alex ran to catch them up.

'We will too. I'll get that kettle on.' Susan took Malcolm's hand,

Cindy's lead still in her other. 'We'll all need a good cuppa after this. Are you coming, Sally, love?'

Sally glanced towards Wagging Tails before looking back at the excavator. 'No, I think I'll let Bonnie off the lead for a bit of a run around first. If you run into Andy though, can you tell him where I am, please?' She assumed he'd gone home being as he hadn't followed her and Ginny, but he might still be hanging around the reception area.

'Okay, love. I'll get you a cuppa for when you come back.' Susan rubbed her arm and turned away.

'I'll keep an eye out for Andy.' Ginny called over her shoulder as she and Darryl walked across the paddock.

'And I'll make sure to shut the gate on our way out so Bonnie here can't escape.'

'Thanks, Malcolm.'

Sally watched them make their way back, and once Malcolm had shut the gate, she reached down to unclip Bonnie's lead.

'There you go, sweetheart. You go and explore.'

As Bonnie beelined for the trestle tables still laden with half empty bowls of crisps and a few abandoned sandwiches, Sally turned back to the excavator. It was even more of an eerie sight with the paddock empty. Was this what their new reality would be? Huge machinery ripping up their view until new builds loomed above the fence? Could they really stay with all of this disruption? What about the dogs?

Feeling her mobile vibrate in her pocket, she pulled it out and answered it. It would be Andy explaining why he'd left or where he was.

'Andy?'

'Err, no. That name is a blast from the past, isn't it?' Linda's voice was as clipped as it normally was. Possibly more so. Maybe she hadn't built as many bridges as Sally had hoped when she'd visited London.

'Linda, hi.' Sally sank to ground and crossed her legs, readying herself to have to justify her decision not to move back to the city. Again. If their parents understood, why couldn't Linda?

'How is everything down in Devon?'

'Cornwall. I live in Cornwall.' Tucking the phone between her shoulder and her ear, she picked up a discarded red napkin and began folding it, trying to avoid looking at the Portakabin and the excavator next to it. 'Good, thanks. How's the pregnancy going?'

'Fine. Not long now.'

Sally took a deep breath. It was coming, the guilt trip.

'I'm ringing to let you know that Dad is going to step back into the office whilst I'm on maternity leave, so we don't need to inconvenience you any longer.'

Sally looked up, the bright yellow of the excavator an eyesore even in the dimming light of early evening. She was grateful Linda was letting her know she no longer had to feel guilty about refusing to leave her life here, but did she have to make out that she was doing her a favour by getting their dad to return to work?

'That's good then.'

'Yes, it is. Well, I'd better run. Bye.'

'Bye.' Sally spoke into the silence, Linda already having hung up.

Shaking her head, she tried to clear her thoughts. What with everything going on here, she hadn't given much more thought to Linda's request, but now... now all she felt were stirrings of guilt at the thought of her dad being forced to break his retirement. It wasn't really down to her though, was it?

'Oh, hello, Bonnie.' Sally grinned as Bonnie nudged her from her thoughts and laid her head on her knee. 'Have you had enough running about for the evening? Shall we go back and have that cuppa Susan was talking about?'

25

Sally leaned her placard up against the wall next to the others and followed Flora, Percy, Ginny, Susan and Alex into Wagging Tails. Since Flora's party and the huge excavator turning up, the few days had been overtaken with letter writing, another village meeting and preparing for today's protest. Sally followed everyone through to the kitchen and slumped into a chair. Everyone looked exhausted. Beaten.

She hadn't even had the chance to meet up with Andy. Not that she was sure he'd have wanted to anyway. After the party he'd messaged to apologise for running off. He'd said something had come up with work and whatever the problem was had been taking up his time since the party. Sally frowned. Or at least he'd said it was. She was beginning to wonder if this whole work thing was just an excuse he was using not to see her. Maybe he was beginning to feel they'd made a mistake getting back together? She pinched the bridge of her nose.

'I'll pop the kettle on.' Flora turned the tap on.

'You go and sit down, love. I'll make the drinks.' Percy took the kettle from Flora's hand and rubbed her arm.

'Thanks.' Sinking into her chair, Flora leaned back. 'Well, I'm not sure what, if anything, we gained from standing outside the council offices with our placards. I don't think even one of them looked up and read what was actually written on them when they pushed through us.'

'Nope. Not one. They didn't seem to care at all.' Alex slumped his shoulders.

'Let's not give up. One of them might have been paying attention and speak about us at one of their fancy meetings.' Percy placed the mugs on the table. 'Besides, it got everyone talking and brought together the West Par residents.'

'Yes, it did. And there were a fair few of us there. At least thirty people showed up to join in.' Susan pulled her mug towards her.

'And Darryl is going to cover our campaign on the front page of the *Trestow Telegraph* tomorrow,' Ginny said. 'That can only bring in more support.'

'Yes, you're right. It's not over until it's over,' Flora said, slapping her palm down on the table. 'And we're still standing, so it's not over yet.'

'That's the spirit.' Percy grinned as he slipped into his chair.

'Oh, I don't know.' Flora pinched the bridge of her nose. 'It feels as though it's been one thing after the other over the past couple of years. We always seem to be fighting to survive. I just hope we can pull through this time.'

'We will. We will.' Percy stroked his beard, thinking. 'Wagging Tails has been here for thirty-five, almost thirty-six years, it's not going anywhere now. These developers will get their comeuppance. Just wait and see.'

'But how? Planning permission has been granted already and whether that was done through the proper channels or as a result of corruption, it's still been put through.' Flora shook her head.

'That's the problem, isn't it? If the council admits to the corruption, then I'm guessing they'll have to look into all the other permissions that Trevor Watson oversaw. That would not only make them look terrible but also cost them thousands, if not more.' Ginny tapped her fingers against the table. 'If we just had the evidence to prove the permission was given illegally, then we'd be able to go public and force the council into doing something.'

'But we're not going to get proof, are we? There isn't any. All tracks will have been covered. These people aren't stupid. That's why they get away with it.' Flora held up her mobile. 'I had another phone call from that Lyle again. That's one call each day now.'

'You never said.' Ginny leaned forward and rubbed Flora's arm. 'Why didn't you tell us?'

'Oh, you know, I didn't want you to worry.' She shifted in her seat. 'I'm guessing he really needs this place to put in a good access route to his development.'

'Umm, I bet. I still don't know how they got that excavator down the narrow lane on the other side of the fields.' Sally shook her head. The number of times she'd walked the dogs that way, behind Wagging Tails, and she'd only ever seen the odd car and that had looked a squeeze.

Alex shrugged. 'In that case, then surely we just have to sit tight, and the houses won't get built? If they can't get the lorries to the fields, then what else can they do?'

'I don't know, lovely,' Flora said. 'Try to wear us down, I guess.'

'We just need to stay strong, then. Lyle and his crew will eventually realise they'll get nowhere and move on.'

'It won't be as easy as that, lad.' Percy sighed. 'He would have paid a lot of money for that land; he's not going to walk away now, not from the potential profit.'

'I guess.' Alex leaned back in his chair.

'Right now there's nothing we can do about it apart from to keep writing to the MP, Graham, and hope for a breakthrough, so let's try to focus on what we can control. That's all we can do.' Flora smiled. 'And thank you again, all of you, for my surprise. It really was a wonderful party. I know it was a few days ago now but since then everything's been such a blur. Thank you.'

'Talking of which…' Standing up, Percy slid his chair across to the counter and clambered up on it, from where he pulled a large brightly wrapped flat rectangular present down from the top of the cupboards.

'Careful.' Flora stood up.

'I've got this.' Stepping down from his chair, he passed Flora the present. 'I'm sorry I didn't get a chance to give this to you before now.'

'Oh, that's okay. Thank you. I'm guessing it's a picture frame?' Flora pushed her mug away and placed the large present on the table, carefully pulling the sticky tape off before folding down the paper.

'Oops, I always do that. Wrap it up the wrong way so the back of the present is shown first when the paper is taken off.' Percy chuckled.

Flora turned over the large picture frame as her eyes lit up and gasped.

Percy grinned. 'I commissioned Chris to draw it.'

'Oh, thank you so much, Percy. It's absolutely stunning.' Turning it around, Flora held the painting up to show everyone. 'Look, I can see Ralph, Dougal, Cleo and Rex and so many more. This means so much to me, Percy.'

'You're very welcome. I'm glad you like it.' Percy stroked his beard, his cheeks reddening.

'Like it? I love it!' Standing up, Flora crossed the room and drew him into a hug. 'Thank you.'

'I thought Rex and Cleo were supposed to be coming to the party?' Susan frowned. 'I didn't see them there. Did anyone else?'

'No. They couldn't make it. They were travelling together, and the car broke down.' Ginny grimaced. 'They sent me a message to say they would try and pop by another time, though.'

'Aw, that's lovely of Caroline and the Wilsons.'

'I can't get over how you remember all the dogs' names, let alone the people who adopt them.' Sally shook her head. She was shocking with names.

Flora chuckled. 'I'm as terrible as the next person at remembering names usually, but when they're one of ours, they somehow stick.' Flora tapped the side of her head. 'Now, I think I'm going to go and tap a nail in behind the counter to display this beautiful picture. I spend far more of my time over here than I do back at the cottage, so it seems a waste to hang it at home.'

'I'll go and get the hammer.' Percy followed Flora out of the room.

Sally pulled her phone from her pocket and looked at the screen. There was a message from Andy.

Are you free to meet for lunch? If so do you want to meet me at Harold's?
Andy xxx

'Everything okay?' Ginny nodded towards Sally's phone.

Sally smiled. 'Yes, I'm going to go over to Trestow to meet Andy for lunch.'

Finally, he was free to meet her. Had she been worrying over nothing or had he really been avoiding her? She frowned. She supposed she'd soon find out.

'I can give you a lift if you like? I'm meeting Darryl in Trestow anyway, so it seems a shame to use two cars.'

'That'd be great. Thanks.' Sally pushed her chair under the table before raking her fingers through her hair. It was quite windy outside, and what with standing in front of the council offices for three hours, she was sure her hair must resemble a bird's nest. Never mind, on their travels, Andy had seen her looking far worse.

* * *

Sally pushed open the door to Harold's Café and stepped around the small queue of customers waiting to be served, searching the faces of the people sitting at the tables. She couldn't see Andy anywhere.

Harold passed by with a tray full of food. 'Sally, love, Andy said to go right up to the flat.'

'Great, thank you.'

Slipping behind the counter, she went through the door leading up to the flat above. Pausing at the top of the stairs, she pulled her hair back, fluffing it up with her fingers before knocking. She really should have taken the time to run a brush through it before they'd left for Trestow.

Andy opened the door and pointed at the mobile in his hand before indicating her to come inside. 'Sorry.'

'Don't worry,' she mouthed back as she slipped through the door. She held her hand up to her mouth, mimicking a cup shape to ask if he wanted a drink.

He nodded and leaned forward to peck her on the cheek before going through to the living room to finish his call.

Sally smiled, relief flooding through her body. They were okay. Things between them were okay. He must have been telling the truth when he'd said he was busy with work.

In the kitchen, Sally switched the kettle on and leaned against the counter. She closed her eyes for a moment, thoughts of this morning's protest and the conversation with the Wagging Tails team whirring in her mind. What would actually be the outcome of it all?

Hearing the kettle click, she opened her eyes and turned back. What other outcome could there be apart from the eventual sale of Wagging Tails? These developers always got what they wanted, eventually. The very fact they'd got planning consent in the first place was evident of that. What would Flora do? Wagging Tails would have to relocate. The cottage would go too. Would they find somewhere as perfect as their little piece of paradise just outside West Par?

She poured the boiling water, watching the granules dissolve, and stirred the coffees. She couldn't imagine anywhere being as perfect as where they were now. And what would they do whilst they relocated? Yes, they could wind down for a while, refuse to take on any new dogs, but the dogs in their care – what would that mean for them?

She picked up Andy's mug and walked towards the door. She'd pass him his before giving him the space to finish his phone conversation. Ouch. It was hot. She should have picked it up by the handle instead of wrapping her hand around it. As she lowered it to the table, the cup tilted, spilling a small pool of coffee onto the tabletop. After steadying the mug, she reached for the tea towel hanging on the cupboard handle beneath the sink and began wiping up the spilt coffee from the table, careful not to disturb the papers stacked carefully.

Phew! At least she hadn't ruined any of Andy's paperwork. Turning back around, she felt the tea towel catch on something and froze, watching as a folder fell to the floor, spilling papers across the tiles. She rolled her eyes. So much for not ruining or disturbing anything.

Throwing the tea towel in the direction of the work surface, Sally then knelt and began to shift the papers into a pile. She reached for a number of papers that had settled against the wall. As she picked one up, something caught her eye; it was a technical drawing of a house. A five-bedroomed detached house. She picked up another. It was another drawing, another house – the designs to a semi-detached three-bedroom this time. Huh, Andy's dad had always renovated and restored old properties, not knocked them down to start over again. Is this what Andy had been talking about when he'd said his business was beginning to take on a different direction?

'You didn't fancy sitting on one of the chairs?' Andy stood in the doorway and chuckled.

Twisting as she heard him, Sally knocked her head on the tabletop. 'Ouch!' She rubbed the back of her head. It hurt. 'I spilt some coffee on the table so was cleaning it up when I somehow managed to knock these papers down.'

Andy frowned and crouched down to help her.

'I've got it. I'll just finish bundling these up.'

'Don't worry. I can do that.' He held his hand out towards her.

Quickly retrieving the last of the papers, Sally placed her other hand in Andy's. 'It's okay, I've got them now.'

'Thank you.'

Standing up, she passed the pile across to him.

Andy put the papers back on the table, pushing them to the back before reaching out and gently touching the back of her head. 'Are you okay?'

'I'll survive.' She grinned as she took his hand in hers and stood on her tiptoes to kiss him. 'I made coffee before the whole chucking papers on the floor incident.'

Andy chuckled. 'Thanks. And thanks too for coming over at such late notice. I just wanted to apologise for disappearing at the party and being busy since.' He indicated his phone on the table. 'I had a work emergency.'

'That's okay. It was probably a good thing. The party pretty much ended as soon as you'd left, anyway.' Sally sighed. 'That's what a huge excavator does to the party mood.'

Andy stepped away, his Adam's apple bobbing up and down as he swallowed. 'I can imagine.'

Sally passed him his mug before taking a sip from her own. 'Is this what you meant when you said your business was taking a different direction?' She indicated the papers.

'Umm, yes.' Leaning across, he pushed the pile of drawings further towards the back of the table.

'You're demolishing old properties to build new ones?' She leaned against the work surface, her mug in her hand. 'I thought you enjoyed the whole creative process of renovating?'

'I do. This is something I...' He stared at the papers before shaking his head and looking across at her. 'Do you fancy getting out of here and doing something?'

'Sure. Why not?' Sally grinned. 'I don't have long, though.'

'No worries. I know just the place we can go.' He took her mug, placed it on the table next to his and reached out for her hand.

26

'Are you sure we're actually allowed to just let ourselves in?' Sally glanced up and down the street. Mature oak trees lined the paths, their roots pushing up through the tarmac.

'What are you expecting? Police officers to jump out from behind the trees and parked cars?' Andy chuckled and carefully lifted the gate to one side, the hinges worn and broken years ago.

'Umm, I'm not sure, but I'm sure we can't just go around breaking into people's houses.' She began making her way through the overgrown front garden towards the front door, or where she'd imagine the front door to be if she could see through the dense bushes and brambles obscuring her view.

'It's abandoned and, besides, it's for a good reason: I'm trying to track the owner down so I can put in an offer.' Andy indicated for her to go in front of him.

'Oh great, so it's my job to go first and ward off any guard dogs?' Sally raised her eyebrows at him.

'As if I'd ever put you in any danger.' Andy shook his head, grinning. 'I've been here before and there are definitely no guard dogs. I can't promise there won't be the odd mouse or rat, but I can assure you the chances of them being the human-eating variety is relatively low.'

'Oh ha ha.' She pushed aside a branch as she waded through the weeds.

'Careful, I'll get that.' He held back a bramble branch.

'Thanks.' She could actually see the house now. It was a large Victorian style detached house. She could imagine that the front door, although now a washed-out pink, had once been a magnificent deep red, and with its patterned brick archway feature and the two large bay windows on either side, the house must have once been someone's dream home. 'Wow, it's stunning.'

'It could be, yes.' Andy grinned, the familiar flicker of excitement reaching his eyes. Leaning around her, he pushed against the front door.

It swung open with ease, revealing a small porch-way. Stepping inside, she glanced back towards the overgrown front garden. Nobody had noticed them coming in.

'This one's a bit stiffer,' Andy said, indicating the main door. 'There's a pile of old post on the other side. I'd meant to kick it out of the way when I visited last, but I left the back way.'

He shouldered the door open, the peeling black paint of this door leaving a dusting down his jumper.

She squeezed through the narrow opening and stepped into the hallway. Two doorways stood either side of them, another one a little further back, and another at the end of the long hallway. In front of them, a staircase rose towards the first floor.

Sally looked up at the high ceilings: intricate cornicing wound around the room and a cracked glass lampshade hung from a delicate ceiling rose.

'It has the old features,' she said.

'Yes, and check this out.' He scraped his trainer against the floor, lifting what must have been at least twenty years of dust and dirt to reveal the original black and white tiled flooring.

'Wow, I can imagine it was once beautiful.'

'Absolutely, and it can be again. So easily.' He grinned and held out his hand, taking hers in his. 'Come with me, this is really exciting.'

Sally smiled as she followed him down the hallway. This was how she remembered him – happy, passionate, excited – and she suddenly felt part of it. She felt the bubbles of excitement in her belly, the passion in her heart. It felt just like old times. They were just exploring a derelict house this time instead of an island or a village in the middle of nowhere.

'Here.' Andy led her into what she assumed would have been the kitchen, only there weren't any cupboards or work surfaces, just a rickety gate-legged table thick with dust, with a lone sun-bleached yellow phone book, its corners curling, sitting in the centre.

Sally ran her fingers across a series of doors cut into a cupboard next to the table. 'Is this the larder?'

'Yep. And even better, come this way.'

She followed him to the other side of the kitchen, pausing to look out of the cracked panes of glass in the side door. It looked as though a path ran down the side of the house, a wall stood opposite the side door. Perhaps the garage? She stepped through an archway into a smaller room and twisted around on the spot. This room had cupboards, waist-high, with a series of shelves above and a sink under another window.

'Ooh, so you could knock through and make a large kitchen/diner?'

'Or even better, keep it separate, the scullery and the kitchen.' Andy's eyes glistened. 'I can almost see it now. All the original features could be kept – the tiles, the larder, the scullery, ceiling roses, cornicing.' He ticked them off on his fingers. 'With a lot of restoration and cleaning, it would be magnificent once again.'

'I love it when you get like this.' Sally grinned and stepped towards him, taking his hands in hers, not caring that he had a couple of decades' worth of grime sticking to his skin.

'You love it?' He grinned back.

'I do. You're so passionate, so excited for the next adventure. Just like you were back when we were travelling. The adventures are a bit different, but it doesn't matter. I can see that houses like this spark something in you.' Standing on her tiptoes, she leaned across to him, her lips touching his first as she felt his arms wrap around her and draw her closer. With her hands gently cupping his cheeks, she leaned back a little. 'Please, let's not let anything come between us again.'

Andy glanced towards the side door and stepped back. 'Do you want to look at the outside toilet? This place actually still has one. Most in a house of this age have been converted into some fancy outside office space or downgraded to garden storage.'

Letting her arms fall to her sides, Sally watched as Andy fiddled with the side door before pushing it open. Had he even heard what she'd said or, throughout their kiss and exchange, had the subject of outside toilets been on his mind? 'Andy, wait.'

A scraping noise sounded from outside.

Stepping down the steps and onto the concrete pathway that led down the side of the house, she followed Andy to the outhouse where he held open a wooden door. Again, the paint was peeling here, great swatches of sunshine yellow revealing a layer of white paint beneath. She glanced inside. Sure enough, it was an outside toilet. With the cistern positioned high on the wall above the bowl, she took a guess that it might just be a really old one, too.

'Hey, what was that about?' she asked.

Andy shut the door with a creak behind him and rubbed his hand over his face. 'What do you mean?'

'You know what I mean.' She frowned. He must know. Surely he did? 'I was telling you that I hoped nothing would come between us again and then you started talking about toilets.'

'Oh, that.' He looked behind him, towards the overgrown back garden, which may just have been worse than the front.

'Yes, that.' Sally shoved her hands in her pockets. 'What's going on? Something's wrong.'

Bringing his thumb towards his mouth, Andy looked at his hand before thinking twice about chewing the nail. Instead, he copied Sally and shoved his hands in his pockets.

'Well,' she continued, 'you're either going to finish with me or you really are more excited about outside loos than our relationship.'

Should she have said that? What if he told her she was right, that he did want to finish things, that he'd tried and he simply didn't like her as he once had?

Andy looked at her, his face ashen.

'You are, aren't you? You're going to finish things.' She swallowed, a lump suddenly forming in her throat. 'You don't want me.'

Meeting her gaze, Andy shook his head. 'I do want you. You're the only person I've ever wanted.' He held his palm against his chest. 'You're the only one I've ever loved. Properly.'

'Then what? What's going on?' She frowned. She could feel her mouth tugging down at the corners, her eyes filling with tears.

'There's something I need to tell you.' He took a deep breath. 'And I can't keep it from you any longer.'

Sally opened and closed her mouth. What was he talking about? It was obviously something serious, or he'd have just blurted it out. 'You're not still married, are you?'

'What? No! Of course not.' He held out his hand. 'Will you come and sit with me?'

She shrugged and took his hand before glancing around. Where? Everywhere was either filthy or overgrown.

Andy turned the corner of the house as they stepped through to the back garden.

With her hand in his, Sally followed. A patio area opened out in front of them, and beyond, the garden sloping downwards. At least she thought it did. It was difficult to tell as the grass and weeds were so tall, but she could just about make out some stairs to the right.

'We can perch on these steps.' Andy held a bramble branch aside.

Stepping through, she paused. The patio area here was cleared, and the brambles and weeds had been pulled up and thrown in a heap at the side, the three wide stairs leading up to patio doors clear of debris.

'How many times have you been here?'

Andy shrugged. 'It's a good place to think.'

She followed him up the steps, turning around and facing the garden before sitting down next to him. From here she could see that the house was situated on the side of a hill and from their vantage point they could see the houses stretching out below them before the edge of Trestow morphed into fields. 'It's beautiful up here.'

'It is.' Andy's voice was quiet, sadness seeping into his words. He twisted his leg beneath him so he was looking at Sally. 'I need to tell you something, but before I do, I need to know that you trust me and will believe what I tell you?'

Sally nodded. Of course she trusted him. In fact, besides the Wagging Tails team, he was the only other person she'd ever trusted.

'Good, because it breaks my heart to think what I have to tell you might come between us.' His voice cracked. 'I need to know that it won't.'

Sally looked at him, her forehead creasing with worry. 'Please, Andy, just tell me.'

'Okay. Well, you remember I said I'd taken my business in a different direction?'

'Yes.'

'Well—'

'You're leaving, aren't you? This is what it's about. The property you were going to renovate has fallen through and you've got to move on to the next one.' She swiped at her eyes and looked around, using her arms to encompass the house they were sitting outside of. 'But what about this one? Like you said, it's the perfect project.'

Andy rubbed the back of his neck. 'I don't own this one yet.'

Please don't leave. Please don't.

'Right.'

'It's not that anyway. I'm not telling you I'm leaving.' Placing his elbows on his knees, he stared at the view in front of them.

Relief flooded Sally's body. He wasn't leaving. Anything else they could deal with. He wasn't still married, he still cared for her, and he wasn't leaving. Nothing else mattered.

'Then why so serious?'

'Because I need to tell you something about my business. I've got myself in a bit of a sticky situation and I'm not sure how to correct it. If I can correct it.' Straightening his back, he took her hands in his.

'Okay.' She frowned. His hands were clammy. Through the dirt and grime, they were clammy. Whatever was going on was obviously affecting him, and she'd been so worried about him leaving her, imagining all sorts of things. Whatever had happened with his business was clearly worrying him, and yet she'd been so focused on her own feelings that she'd failed to see it. She squeezed his hands. 'What's happened?'

'I—' The loud tring of a mobile cut through his words and he stood, patting down his pockets before pulling his phone out. Looking at the screen, he frowned. 'I'm so sorry. I'm going to have to take this.'

Sally nodded and watched as he made his way back down the side of the house. Turning back to the view ahead, she bit down on her bottom lip. Whatever was happening with Andy, she hoped it wouldn't lead him to lose his business. Even just stepping into this house had given her the chance to see how much renovating houses meant to him, how much he loved his job.

'Sally, I've got to run.' Walking hurriedly back around the wall of the house, Andy held up his mobile.

'Oh, really?'

'Yes. Sorry. I can give you a lift and drop you off at Harold's?'

She looked at the lines creasing his forehead and the way his jaw was set. The phone call had only added to his worries. She could see that.

'No, don't worry. I'll get Ginny to pick me up from here. You get going.'

'Are you sure?'

'Yes.' Standing up, she walked across to him and wrapped her arms around his waist. 'I'm sure that whatever is happening with your business will work itself out.'

'Umm, I'm not so sure. Sorry, I feel awful bailing on you and leaving you here. Are you going to be okay before Ginny comes?'

'Absolutely. I have this view. What's not okay about that?' She smiled softly and looked out across the garden again.

Andy nodded slowly before shifting on the spot and tucking his finger beneath her chin, gently encouraging her to look up at him. 'I love you, Sally. I always have. I want you to know that.'

Did he just tell her he loved her? Opening and closing her mouth, not quite knowing what to say, she blinked.

After a quick peck on the lips, he turned and hurried away.

Sally faintly heard the creak of the side door as Andy let himself back into the house. After that, all was silent. She looked out across the garden towards the outskirts of Trestow below, the fields beyond. Apart from the sound of a robin making its way from branch to branch in the trees lining the garden, she felt as though she could be the only one around for miles.

Lowering herself back down on the steps, she hugged her middle and smiled. He loved her. He still loved her.

27

'Come on, Nala. Let's get you back to your kennel.' Sally yawned. She'd spent another night tossing and turning, Andy's words whirring in her mind. He loved her. He loved her! But what had he wanted to tell her? What had he been about to say before he had to rush off?

Sally stooped to pick up Nala's favourite toy. The collie-cross had carried the soggy blue teddy out to the paddock but, excited after her agility session, she'd walked straight past it on the way back. 'You had a great session, didn't you, Nala? Even the new seesaw didn't faze you.'

Nala had taken to the new equipment like a pro. Sally was sure that if Nala's forever family, once they were found, continued with Nala's training, she might just give the other dogs in the group a run for their money.

Swapping the teddy to the hand holding the lead, she pulled open the door to the reception area.

'This way, sweetheart.' Leading Nala through, she glanced towards the kitchen door. It was closed and Cindy's kennel was empty, so either someone had taken her on a walk or she was in the kitchen, but she could hear voices she didn't recognise. She couldn't hear what was being said, just mumbles of a conversation coming from the kitchen. Had Flora found a prospective adopter for Cindy?

After shutting Nala's kennel door, Sally pulled a treat from her pocket and pushed it towards Nala's nose, who was waiting expectantly at the bars. 'Good girl, Nala.'

As Sally made her way back into the reception area, she pulled her mobile from her pocket and called Andy. Leaning against the reception counter, she waited for it to ring through to the answerphone. Again.

'Hey, Andy, it's Sally.' She pushed herself away from the counter and walked across to the window. 'I know you must be busy and are probably completely sick of having to listen to my voicemails.' She frowned. 'That is, if you have been listening to them at all. But anyway, I just wanted to check you were okay after yesterday. I know you wanted to tell me something.'

She wiped a line of condensation from the bottom of the window-pane. 'Well, give me a call and maybe we can meet up and talk properly.'

Sally ended the call. That was all she could do. Just ring him and let him know she was there for him. Short of going round to Harold's and trying his door, which she'd do after work, all she could do was let him know she was thinking of him. She just hoped that whatever was happening with his business got sorted out quickly.

'Sally, I thought I heard you out here.' Flora peered out from the kitchen. 'Have you got a few minutes?'

'Yes, of course.' Sally smiled.

'There're some people and dogs I'd like you to meet.' She held the kitchen door open for her and ushered her through.

Pausing in the doorway, Sally looked around the room. Percy and Susan were sitting at the table chatting with people Sally didn't recognise, and Cindy was sprawled out by Susan's feet. A tan Staffie-cross-Jack-Russell by the washing machine stretched and walked across to her.

'Oh, you're lovely, aren't you?'

'He sure is.' Percy beamed as he stroked the dog. 'This is Rex. He was found scavenging in a skip in Trestow. What, eleven years ago now?'

'That's right.' Flora flicked the kettle on. 'Sally, meet the Wilsons, Rex's family. And somewhere under the table is Cleo, and this is Caroline.' Flora indicated the people sitting around the bale.

'Hi, lovely to meet you all.' Sally laughed as Rex pawed at her leg, his nose resting on her, pointing at her pocket. 'You can smell the treats I have in here, can't you, Rex?'

'Oh, he can sniff a treat out half a mile away, given the chance.' Rex's owner chuckled.

'Ha ha, I'd better give you one then, hadn't I, sweetheart?' Pulling a treat from her pocket, Sally gave it to him. 'If he came here eleven years ago, how old is he now?'

'Fifteen, believe it or not.' Percy took his mug from Flora. 'He was such a frightened little thing when he came but as soon as he met the Wilsons it was as though he knew they would be his forever family and his confidence seemed to grow overnight, didn't it?'

'I remember.' Flora passed mugs of steaming coffee around the table. 'Thank you again for popping by today. Such a lovely surprise.'

'You're very welcome. I'm just sorry we couldn't make it to your party.' Caroline took a sip of her coffee.

'Don't worry, lovely,' Flora said. 'These things happen. Besides, the party didn't end on a good note, so it's lovely to have a little pick-me-up seeing these two gorgeous ones today.'

'Oh no, what happened?'

While Flora and Percy told them all about the excavator turning up, Sally bent down and fussed Rex behind the ears. 'You like that, don't you?'

Rex twisted around, nudging her pocket for another treat.

Laughing, Sally gave him one before holding another towards the black and white cocker spaniel curled under Caroline's chair. 'Here, do you want one?'

The cocker spaniel stirred and stretched.

'Oh, she probably will. Thank you.' Caroline looked towards Sally. 'This is Cleo. Unfortunately, her eyesight is failing her, but her sense of smell definitely isn't.'

'Aw, hello, Cleo.' Sally held out her hand, the treat in her palm as Cleo sniffed around her. 'That's it. You've found it. You're a beauty, aren't you?'

The kitchen door opened, and Ginny hurried in. 'Sally, can I borrow you please?'

'Yes, sure.' Sally gave Cindy a treat before joined Ginny.

'Is everything okay, Ginny?' Flora called from the table.

'That dog that keeps being sighted around Trestow has been seen down the canal path, so we'll go and take a look.' Ginny grabbed the van keys from the work surface.

'The German shepherd? Oh, that's great news. I was worried that we hadn't had any sightings for a few days.' Flora walked towards them. 'I'll get a kennel set up for her.'

'I'll do that.' Susan stood up. 'You have your cuppa and chat.'

'Thanks, lovely.'

* * *

'Down here?' Sally pointed down the towpath.

'That's right. She looks frightfully skinny.' A man in a flap cap hung over his boat and pointed down the towpath. 'I did try to lure her onto the boat with some chicken, but she just scarpered.'

'Great. Thanks.' Sally waved and ran down the narrow path beside the canal. Brightly painted canal boats bobbed up and down on the water to her right and trees and shrubbery clung to the slope to her left.

'Hold on, what's that?' Ginny called from behind her.

Stopping, Sally retreated back to Ginny and followed her gaze into the shrubbery.

'Did you hear that?' Ginny tilted her head.

Sally parted some tall weeds that were growing close to the path as a slight movement caught her eye a little further up the slope. 'Yes, there's something there.'

'Look, those plants are moving.' Ginny pointed.

Pulling her sleeves down to protect her arms from the stinging nettles, Sally made her way up the slope, parting the weeds and branches as she did so. She slowed down as she came close to where the movement was, inching forward until she was close enough to reach out. She slowly used her left hand to separate the plants, keeping her right ready to grab the dog if possible.

As soon as Sally had disturbed the shrubbery, a pigeon flew up towards the branches above. Sighing, she turned and called down to Ginny, 'It was a pigeon.'

'Aw, no.' Ginny shook her head as she held out her hand, ready to steady Sally as she made her way back down to the towpath.

'Thanks.'

'If you're looking for a stray dog, it's just run into the tunnel,' a woman shouted from the other side of the canal, pointing behind her.

'Thanks,' Ginny called across before running down towards where the woman had pointed.

Sally ran after Ginny, quickly approaching the tunnel. She matched Ginny's pace as the towpath narrowed further and the sides of the old brick-built tunnel surrounded them, the air around them turning damp and musty.

Holding her hand up, Ginny signalled Sally to stop and pulled a bag of treats from her pocket.

There she was, crouching down near the wall of the bridge. The man had been right. Sally could see from here how malnourished the German shepherd was. Sally readied the catch pole in her hand, ready to slip the collar part over the dog's head as soon as the dog had either approached them or they were able to get closer.

Ginny threw a treat close to the dog, waiting until the German shepherd ate it hungrily before throwing another, slightly closer this time.

'That's it, girl. You're safe now.'

Sally held her breath as the dog inched nearer, until she was close enough for the pole to reach. It was now or never. If she waited a few more seconds, they might miss the opportunity. She glanced up the towpath behind the dog. A couple were approaching with a small Jack Russell. Yep, she needed to act now. Stepping forward, in one flush movement, she looped the collar at the end of the catch pole over the dog's head, securing her.

'That's it. You've got her.' Ginny's voice was quiet so as not to startle the dog.

Sally gripped hold of the pole tighter as the dog tried to back away and then pawed at the stick, realising that she was caught.

'It's okay. We'll keep you safe,' Sally said, glancing up at the couple approaching them. She nodded thanks as they paused after seeing what they were trying to do.

Stepping towards the dog slowly, Ginny threw down another treat, which again disappeared in milliseconds. She took another treat from her pocket and this time instead of throwing it, she held her hand out, palm flat, the treat in the centre.

Sally watched as the dog tentatively took the treat and Ginny was able to throw a slip lead over her head before removing the collar of the catch pole. Pulling the catch pole back, she waited until Ginny had the dog secure before waving at the couple further ahead.

'That's it, sweetheart. You come with us and we'll get you some proper food.' Ginny smiled at the dog which was now walking beside her.

'She looks so malnourished. She must have been loose for weeks.'

Sally frowned as they turned and made their way back up the towpath towards the van. The calls they'd had telling them of sightings had all been over the past few days, but looking at the dog's condition, it was obvious she'd been a stray far longer than that.

'Yes, she must have been.'

The way the dog hung slightly back, the lead taut as she slowly followed them, suggested she was nervous.

'I wonder if she's been mistreated or if she's just in flight mode, which is why she's so nervy of humans.'

'I'm not sure. I'll scan her as soon as we're back and see if she's chipped.' Ginny glanced up and down the canal. 'It could be she's from a canal boat and has just been following the water trying to find her way home.'

Sally nodded and swallowed, hoping if that was the case, they'd be able to locate the owners, as they had with Puddles.

28

The van lurched to a stop as the car in front had suddenly braked.

'What on earth?' Ginny scowled and flashed the headlights as the car in front decided now to put their indicators on, signalling they'd pulled over. 'A bit late, thanks.'

Sally twisted around and looked through to the back of the van. The German shepherd was still sitting crouched at the back of the crate. 'She's fine. Still shaking, but I think that's from nerves rather than the sudden stop.'

'Oh, poor little thing. Let's hope after some quiet time in her kennel she'll start to come round to us.' Ginny slowed down as the traffic lights turned to red.

'I'm sure she will.' That was one thing that had shocked her since working at Wagging Tails. Yes, some of the dogs may come to them nervous and shy but it rarely took more than a few days for them to realise they were safe and to gain in confidence. It was true that dogs could pick up on the subtle differences in body language and knew innately who would treat them kindly and who would not.

Ginny glanced at Sally. 'Can you think of any names?'

'Umm, how about Brooke? I know we found her at the canal, but they're kind of related.' Sally shrugged.

'Yes! Brooke's a lovely name.' Ginny grinned as she put the van into first gear and pulled away. 'Brooke. I really like that.'

Sally smiled. So did she. Turning to look out of the window, she had to do a double take. That wasn't Andy, was it? It looked like him.

'These traffic lights.' Ginny rolled her eyes as she pulled the handbrake up again. 'I swear if you hit one red one, then all the others on the journey are destined to turn to red as soon as you approach them.'

'You could be onto something there,' Sally muttered as she squinted her eyes. It was him. Now he'd walked along the path a little more and was closer to them, she could see that. But who was he with? She shifted in her seat to get a better view. Where did she recognise that woman he was walking with from?

'Ginny?' she asked.

'Yep?'

'Do you recognise that woman?'

'Which one?' Ginny turned to look out of the passenger window. 'Is that Andy?'

'Yes. Do you recognise her?' Sally tapped on the glass, indicating the woman with the dark hair.

'I don't think so.' Ginny frowned.

'I do. I'm sure I do.' Sally watched as Andy held the door to a café open for the woman. What was he doing having lunch with another woman when he couldn't spare the time to ring her back? Huh, she knew where she recognised the woman from, but why was Andy with her? 'I know. She was at Flora's party.'

'Was she?'

'Yes, I'm certain it was her. Before we cut the cake, she was just stood in the top paddock by the fence looking at the Portakabin. I'm a hundred per cent sure it was her. I thought it was strange as she didn't have a dog with her and wasn't chatting to anyone, so she kind of stuck in my mind.'

'Is she someone from West Par, then? She might live there and just decided to wander down? Although I must admit I haven't seen her around.'

'No, well, maybe, but I'd never seen her before either. And as soon as I went over to speak to her, she made an excuse and left.' Sally bit down on her bottom lip. What was that woman doing with Andy? She'd definitely left the party before Andy had arrived, so they hadn't crossed paths. He'd been late and came whilst she and Alex had been getting Flora's cake ready. She remembered.

'Oh, that is odd. I wonder what she's doing with Andy?'

'I don't know.' Sally watched as the café door closed behind them and glanced at the clock on the dashboard. It was half twelve – lunchtime.

'Could it be business? He renovates houses, doesn't he? Could she be a seller? Or a contractor, maybe?' Ginny lifted the handbrake, and the van set off again.

'She must be.' Sally turned back to the front. There would be a logical explanation. He wasn't the kind of man to cheat. She was certain of that. She took out her mobile. Still no call, no message. Nothing. How long would it have taken to type a quick 'Sorry I missed your call, will ring later' message whilst he was waiting for his coffee to be made?

'Are you okay?' Ginny glanced across to her quickly.

'Yes.' Sally gave a quick, short smile. 'I don't know. I don't know what's going on with me and Andy, to be completely honest. Yesterday lunchtime he told me he loved me and yet today he hasn't answered my calls though he does have time to go out for lunch.' She shrugged.

'I'm sure it'll be okay.' Ginny touched her on the forearm before changing gears. 'You've got a lot of history and you know him. He's probably busy with work and this is a working lunch.'

'Maybe.' Sally nodded.

The van pulled away from yet another set of traffic lights as they travelled out of town.

'Not long now, Brooke,' Ginny called back to the dog they'd just rescued. 'We're almost at your new home.'

Closing her eyes, Sally pushed all thoughts of Andy and the mysterious woman to the back of her mind. She needed to focus on Brooke and the other dogs now. She twisted in her seat. Brooke was still crouched as far back in the crate as she could. She'd tucked her head beneath the blanket in there now, too.

'You won't need to scavenge for food any more and you'll be nice and warm too. Safe.'

Ginny pulled the van to a stop in the courtyard before turning to face Sally. 'Ready?'

'Yep.' She was. She was ready to settle Brooke. After that, she had Luke and Annie down on her list to do training. All thoughts of Andy could wait until that evening. Besides, he'd probably get in touch before the day was out. She watched as Flora hurried out to them. She must have been waiting at the window to see the van turn in.

* * *

'She is absolutely gorgeous, isn't she?' Flora fussed Brooke before standing up.

'She sure is. She's wolfed down that food though, so she's definitely been on the loose for a while.' Sally shut the kennel door as Flora stepped out.

'I'll ring Mack, see if we can get her in later for a quick vet check. Make sure there isn't anything else going on with her.' Flora turned back and looked at Brooke through the bars. 'See you later, sweetheart.'

Sally held the door into reception open for Flora.

'Oh, it looks as though Darryl is here. He said he had some news about the development – something one of his reporters unearthed.' Flora pushed the kitchen door open.

'Let's hope it's good news.' They needed some good news after the last few weeks.

'Fingers crossed.' Flora held her hand up, crossing her index and middle fingers.

Taking the door from Flora, Sally stepped into the kitchen and a hushed silence fell over the room. Darryl, Ginny, Percy, Susan and Alex all looked down at the table. Frowning, she watched as Ginny, who had let Flora and Sally settle Brooke, quickly turned over a piece of paper and turned to them.

'What's going on?' Walking over to the table, Flora placed her hands on the back of a chair. 'I'm hoping you've had a breakthrough, Darryl, lovely?'

Shifting on his feet, Darryl looked from the papers to Sally to Ginny. 'A little.'

'Well, go on then. Give it to us.' Flora rubbed her hands together.

'Right, yes.' Darryl cleared his throat. 'We've found some documents to suggest Lyle has been involved in some pretty dicey deals before. And, although Fresh Image Housing is a brand-new company, it seems his tactics aren't.'

'What do you mean "dicey deals"?' Flora clasped her hands together, still leaning over the back of the chair.

'We've found articles which imply developments he's been involved in have only been passed after a sum of money was donated by his old company to the local council.' Darryl glanced down at the papers on the table.

'So, he's been paying people off? Paying the planning officers to get his way?' Flora shook her head.

'Well, possibly. We don't have any evidence of any money passing between him and any individuals, but we do have evidence of money being donated to the council before his planning was accepted.'

'Ha, so he has been paying off the council. How can he get away with that? If it's public knowledge?' Sally indicated the papers.

Darryl glanced towards Ginny before looking back at Sally and shrugging. 'Councils are always short of money, and I guess they weigh up the benefits of the donation against the proposed development. The money was donated to build infrastructure, things such as street lighting and recreational facilities.'

'I don't understand. How can they get away with it?' Flora gripped the back of the chair. 'And what about here – in our case, there isn't even proper access to the site. I can't imagine the council or this Fresh Image Housing being able to cut through farmland and completely change the existing road layout in order to build the houses.'

'No. We have no hard evidence but I'm guessing that Lyle didn't just give a donation to the council to get the planning passed this time.'

'So that Trevor was paid off then.' It was a statement, not a question. 'I know we'll probably never know for sure, but now we have evidence of these "donations"...' Flora curled her index fingers around the word.

'I still don't understand how permission could have been given without a clear access point.' Percy stroked his beard. 'Yes, I understand that the council was paid off and the planning officer likely was too, but surely there would have had to have been access? For it to even look as though it had been pushed through legitimately?'

Darryl looked at his shoes. 'Normally, yes, but...'

'He was counting on us selling?' Flora shook her head.

'Exactly. Trevor probably told him it would be easy to gain access through this site.'

'And he wouldn't have cared if Flora sold or not.' Ginny looked around the room. 'He had his money.'

'I see.' Flora stepped forward and reached for the papers. 'Let's see these then.'

Ginny grabbed the papers off Flora before she'd had the chance to look. 'I... umm...'

'What's going on, lovely?' Flora crossed her arms. 'You two are hiding something from us, aren't you?'

'No... we...' Ginny looked around the room. Percy, Susan, and Alex avoided her gaze.

'I should get going.' Alex stood up, his chair scraping against the kitchen floor. 'I need to get Ralph up to the top paddock before Susan takes Nala out.'

'Yep, I really should get Nala ready for her exercising.' Standing up, Susan placed her hand on first Flora's arm and then Sally's as she walked past.

Sally watched them leave, the kitchen door shutting quietly behind them. What was going on? Was there something that Darryl and Ginny wanted to talk to Flora about in private? She indicated towards the door. 'I should go and get on with some training.'

'No, Sally. Wait. There's something you should see.' Ginny looked from Sally to Flora and back. 'Something you should both see.'

'Oh, okay.' Sally nodded. Why had everyone else left then? She'd been there the least time out of all of them. What could affect her more than Susan, Alex, and Percy?

'Come and sit down. Both of you.' Darryl pulled out a chair for Flora.

'Now you're worrying me. That monster hasn't somehow got a purchase order on Wagging Tails, or something has he?'

'No, no, nothing like that.' Ginny indicated Sally to sit down too. 'But there is something that... umm...'

Sitting down, Sally looked from Ginny to Darryl and back. They both looked uneasy, as though they were about to deliver some bad news. But what?

'I think it's best if we just show you.' Darryl passed them both a sheet of paper.

Taking it, Flora skimmed it quickly before holding it in the air. 'It's just the company details. What's so important about that? It doesn't matter who we're dealing with, surely? They're all the same, these big developers. They think they can wade in and build where they want, no respect for wildlife or the local community.'

Sally blinked, the black ink dancing on the white paper. She couldn't focus. She cleared her throat, her voice barely a whisper. 'Andy is Lyle's partner.'

'Your Andy?' Flora lowered the piece of paper onto the table.

Looking up at Darryl, Sally said, 'That's right, isn't it?'

Darryl nodded and sat down.

Sally let the paper fall from her hands. Darryl didn't need to say anything else. Thoughts whirred through her mind, Flora, Ginny and Darryl's conversation a blur as she fought to make sense of it all. All the talk about his business taking a different direction. Questions about her work and whether there were other dogs' homes local to them. In the garden yesterday, had he been going to say something? Had he been trying to be honest? Him saying he hoped nothing would come between them...

'I think I'm going to be sick.'

She stood up and ran from the room.

29

Sally looked out towards the ocean and rubbed the sleeve of her jumper across her eyes. Not that there were any fresh tears. They'd dried up long ago. After collecting Bonnie, she'd ran down here straight from the meeting with Darryl, Ginny and Flora. She hadn't waited around to hear the inevitable. She hadn't been able to stay and listen to the words she knew Flora would be forced to utter to her. She knew she had to leave. She knew she would no longer have her job. Her dream job. It was clear there was no way forward from this. There couldn't be.

No, but she'd just needed one last walk to the cove with Bonnie. She needed to process what had happened.

She tilted her head and listened to the footsteps coming towards her, soft against the sand, and kept her eyes fixed on the ocean, the gentle roll of the waves as the tide pushed the water further up the beach. She wasn't sure how long she'd been sitting there. It must have been a while though, as Bonnie had tired long ago from chasing the waves and was now sitting with her chin on Sally's leg, the warmth of drool seeping through her jeans.

'Here you are. I've been looking all over.' Flora lowered herself to the sand.

'It's okay. I'll bring her back before I collect my things.' Her voice cracked. She knew what was coming. She expected it.

Andy had lost her everything. She'd been so worried about Linda jeopardising her life down here that it hadn't once occurred to her that she was worrying about the wrong person. Andy. The man who she had loved since school, the man who had told her he loved her. That must have all been lies too, then. That and everything else. It didn't matter if he'd been going to tell her, had tried to, or not, he'd lied simply by omitting the truth. He'd taken her for a fool.

'There's no need to collect your things, love. No need at all. You're not going anywhere.'

Sally felt Flora's arm wrap around her shoulder and let herself be pulled in for a hug. 'Why? How can you not want me to leave?'

'Sally, lovely, it's Andy's name on the company details, not yours, and by your reaction, you were as much in the dark from the whole thing as the rest of us.' She spoke quietly but firmly, her breath warm against Sally's hair.

'Everyone must hate me.' Sally closed her eyes. She'd finally found a place she could call home, colleagues she knew as family, and now...

'Nobody hates you. Quite the opposite. We're all here for you.' Flora pulled away slightly. 'Sally, look at me.'

Wiping her eyes, Sally looked at her.

'Nobody blames you. You are not Andy. Besides, I think you need to talk to him to get his side of the story.'

'Huh, I don't think there's any point in that.'

Why did she need to? It would literally be a waste of time. That, and it would only upset her further. She'd known him years, since school, and he'd thought so little of her to lie. For all she knew, he'd simply used her to try to get his hands on Wagging Tails. She looked out to sea. Would he really do that? She'd liked to think he wouldn't. Certainly the old Andy, the one she knew – or the one she thought she'd known – wouldn't, but then they hadn't seen each other in seven years. She was a different person to who she was back then. He was too.

'Even if it's just to find closure in the whole situation, you should.' Flora held her hands up. 'But you know him best, lovely.'

'I don't feel as though I know him at all. Not any more.' Sally gently fussed behind Bonnie's ears, her dark eyes flitting open ever so slightly before closing again, lost in the world of sleep once more. These past few days had been hard on her, too. She'd not settled. Whenever anyone walked into the kennels, she was there, alert, standing beside her kennel door, forever eagerly waiting for Jerry's return.

'I think that might just be more reason to talk to him then. When you're ready, of course.'

Sally shook her head, still focusing her attention on Bonnie. 'How can you be so forgiving?'

Flora chuckled. 'Oh, I'm not, believe me. Especially when someone tries to harm my dogs, and my humans.' Flora gave her a quick squeeze around the shoulders. 'But I also know that not everything in life is straightforward. Life by its very nature is complicated and until you speak to him, you don't know his side.'

'Umm.' She really couldn't begin to imagine what he could say to make her feel any better about what he'd done.

'I'll let you think about it. See you back at Wagging Tails in a bit, okay?' Flora stood up and retreated back up the beach.

Sally nodded and watched as Flora headed back up the beach. Should she speak to him? Listen to his side of the story? She pulled her mobile from her pocket. There was still no message, no missed call from him. Maybe she really had just been a pawn in his great plan. Maybe he knew she'd found out the truth and discarded her, knowing he could no longer use her the way he'd planned.

And the woman. What had that been about? She'd been at Flora's party, and then Sally had spotted her with Andy. What was her part in all of this?

She tapped her mobile against her knee.

'What do you think, Bonnie? Do you think Flora is right? That I should speak to him. Let him tell me his story from his perspective? Or do you think I should thank my lucky stars I've found out his game now rather than later?'

Andy had always been there for her. He'd been her constant, the person she'd wanted to spend her whole life with for such a long time now. Maybe he did deserve to be listened to?

She scrolled through to his name, her finger hovering over the 'call' button.

No. She turned her phone off, laying it by her side, face down on the sand. She didn't think she could. Not yet anyway. Everything just felt surreal at the moment. It was almost as though she'd come into work happy, her life normal, and now suddenly everything was plummeting in a completely different direction. She was trying to walk through quicksand, trying to make sense of her new world, her new circumstances. And she couldn't. How could she? The man she loved, had always loved, had betrayed her. Worse than that, he'd told her he'd loved her back and then proceeded to stab her in the back.

'Right, I suppose we'd best get you back, Bonnie. And I'd best face everyone.' She took a deep breath before standing up. She knew Flora had told her no one blamed her, but she still couldn't help that heavy feeling in the pit of her stomach. What if she was to blame? Not for the development, of course, but she should have spotted the signs that Andy was involved. If she had, maybe, just maybe, she could have talked him out of it before everything had got this far.

'Oops, we'd better remember your reindeer, hadn't we?' Stooping down, Sally picked up Bonnie's beloved toy before walking up the beach, the sand shifting slightly under her trainers.

The signs had been there. She saw that now. And there'd been enough of them – the 'change of direction' in his business he kept talking about, him being late and leaving early for Flora's party, and the housing plans. How had she not put two and two together? It had all been so clear. They'd all been there – right in front of her eyes.

Walking up the lane towards Wagging Tails, Sally could see a car parked in the lay-by outside the gate. It was a silver BMW, just as shiny as it had been the first day Lyle had turned up.

Pausing, she looked back down the lane. More than anything, she wanted to turn and sprint back down to the beach and hide there until he'd gone, but that wouldn't be fair on Flora or the rest of the team. No, she was more to blame than anyone else for this mess. She'd have to face him.

'Let's do this, Bonnie.'

As she approached, she slowed her pace across the courtyard and gripped Bonnie's lead tighter. Feeling her apprehension, Bonnie walked close beside her, the Staffie-cross's head close to the back of her knee.

Forcing herself not to pause, Sally pushed the door open and closed it quickly behind her. Lyle was inside and even from where she was standing, she could see he wasn't happy. A red flush had crept up the back of his neck, seeping out from the collar of his dark grey suit jacket and the tension in the air was palpable.

'I've told you time and time again, you're not welcome here. Now please leave.' Flora's tone was clipped, her arms crossed, and a deep crease had formed across her forehead, but she was standing strong. Flora behind the counter and Lyle standing opposite.

'Welcome or not, I can assure you this will not be the last you'll hear from me.' And with that, spinning around on his feet, Lyle stormed towards the door.

Stepping aside, Sally barely avoided him colliding with her as he strode out, the door shaking in its frame as he swung it shut behind him.

'What's happened?' she asked.

Flora wiped her brow with the cuff of her sleeve before rolling her shoulders back. 'Sorry, that man really does get to me. I don't know what's led to it, but he's just stormed in here demanding we sell to him. I know he's asked again and again, but this time felt different.'

'What did he say?'

'He offered more money. Or said he did. I ripped up the cheque again. I'm sure you probably saw his reaction.' Flora picked up a pen from the counter and put in back in its pot.

Looking up from Bonnie, Sally nodded. She had. She'd seen the way he'd become flustered, a stark contrast to the confident and self-assured businessman who had been round before.

'He did seem different.'

'Yes. He's obviously getting desperate. I just hope we don't have any more of his intimidation tricks.'

'No, hopefully not.' Sally sighed.

He was going to win, wasn't he? She bit down on her bottom lip. She couldn't say that to Flora, but that was what was going to happen. The houses would be built, and they'd be forced to relocate due to the stress it would all cause the dogs.

Flora leaned down and fussed over Bonnie. 'I'm sure it will work itself out, hey, Bonnie?'

Sally nodded. What was she supposed to say?

At that moment, Ginny stepped inside, Cindy's lead in her hand.

'This one has just rolled in something.' She looked down at Cindy and raised her eyebrows. 'Although I'm guessing you can smell it already.'

Sally scrunched up her nose. 'I can definitely smell it.'

'Oh, Cindy. What have you been up to?' Flora leaned over the counter and shook her head at the dog.

'The daft thing was she was on her lead when she did it. I ran into Mr Euston and Gray and got chatting and all of a sudden I felt her almost jerk the lead out of my hand and, yep, there she was lying on the grass covering herself in... umm... something.'

'Oh, they do like to keep us on our toes, don't they?' Flora chuckled.

'I'll pop Bonnie into her kennel and grab you a towel.' Sally looked down at the Staffie-cross. 'Come on, let's get you settled.'

'Thanks,' Ginny called over her shoulder as she headed out of the reception area.

Pushing the door to the kennels open, Sally led Bonnie through.

'Flora, is that you?' Susan's voice filtered down the narrow corridor.

'No, it's Sally. You okay?' She let Bonnie into her kennel before giving her a treat.

'I'm not sure. Annie isn't eating her food and you know what she's normally like. She normally scoffs it down, but she's just not interested this evening.'

In front of Annie's kennel, Sally knelt down, pulling a treat from her pocket. 'Annie, what's this? I know you like these ones.'

Annie clambered up from her bed and sniffed the treat. But, turning away, she walked back.

'See? That's not like her.'

'No, it's not.' Sally frowned.

'I'll go and speak to Flora.'

Leaving Annie's full food bowl on the floor of her kennel, Susan shut the door before heading back to the reception area.

'Aren't you feeling too well, Annie?' Sally lowered herself to the floor outside the dog's kennel.

Pulling her mobile from her pocket, she frowned. She had two missed calls and a message from Andy. Huh, about time.

Sorry I missed your calls. Are you free to meet this evening? Andy xxx

Should she meet him? Did she want to? She gripped her phone in her hand. Part of her wanted to, desperately wanted to. There wasn't anything she wanted more than to melt into one of his hugs, to have him tell her that everything was going to be okay. To promise that there had been some sort of mix-up and he actually had nothing to do with the development and had no idea who Lyle was.

She tapped her phone against her chin. That wasn't going to happen, though, was it? His name had been on the documents. There in black and white. There was no going back after seeing that, no carrying on with the relationship as though she didn't know.

Slipping her phone into her pocket, she stood up. She'd go and help Ginny. Give herself some time to try to decide what to do.

30

Sally slipped out of her coat and carefully hung it up. Flora had taken Annie to the vet's to be checked over; Ginny had said Mr Euston's dog had been off his food a few days ago, so they were all hopeful it was just a bug she'd picked up on a walk.

Sally stepped into the living room, letting the hall door swing shut behind her and headed towards the sofa. She felt as though she'd be asleep in five minutes. The day had been long and emotionally draining.

She picked up a cushion and hugged it to her chest before turning and picking up a takeaway carton that had been hiding behind it. Holding it in her hand, she stared at it. How could things between her and Andy have changed so drastically so quickly? They'd been enjoying a takeaway and a chat just days before and now she felt as though he was a stranger. The Andy she knew – had known – wouldn't be partnering up with the likes of Lyle and certainly wouldn't be trying to push for Flora to sell up. No, Andy cared about animals, cared about people. It would never have crossed his mind to even think about doing what he was doing now.

The ping of a message broke the silence in the room, and Sally pulled her phone from her pocket. It was Andy. Again.

Sally, are you home? Can I pop round? This is important. Andy xxx

What did she have to lose? Maybe Flora was right? Maybe she should just hear him out? At least if she did meet him she could quiz him, find out what had possessed him to try to push a rescue centre out of its home. She knew she wouldn't be able to change his mind. She didn't know him any more, but even if she could plant a niggle of regret, it might make him think twice about doing something so callous again in the future.

She didn't want him here, though. This was her sanctuary.

Not here. I'll meet you at The Unicorn. Sally

There she'd done it. She'd agreed to meet him. Standing up, she headed back to the hall and pulled her coat on again. She stood in front of the mirror in the hall. Her hair was limp and her skin pale. She felt as though she hadn't slept in days and although she had last night, the bags under her eyes suggested otherwise. Had one day's events really had such an impact?

She raked her fingers through her hair before pulling the door shut behind her. It wasn't as though she cared about what he thought of her any more.

* * *

As soon as she pushed the heavy wooden pub door open, the familiar aroma of stale beer hit her. She looked around. It was busy for a weekday evening. Groups of people were clustered around tables, some enjoying the pub grub, whilst others chatted over drinks. Stepping aside, she watched as another group entered, immediately heading for the bar.

Had she done the right thing in coming? In agreeing to meet Andy? She wasn't sure. Flora's words stuck in her mind, telling her to give him a chance to explain, but would any explanation excuse his actions? It wouldn't, so was there even much point in listening?

She took a deep breath; she was here now.

Walking further into the pub, she looked around. She spotted him sitting in the corner to her right, but he wasn't alone.

Who was he with?

Sally paused, her eyes fixed on Andy and the woman sitting at the table with him. The same woman who had been at Flora's party. The same woman who he'd been going into a café with at lunchtime. He'd been with her and yet he hadn't had time to answer Sally's calls or send her a text. And now he was here with her when he was supposed to be meeting Sally. Had he forgotten? In this short time? Or was this his way of showing her his feelings had changed without having to tell her?

She narrowed her eyes. She couldn't do this. She'd seen a completely different side to him thanks to the information Darryl had unearthed. Then she'd forced herself to come here, to give him a chance to explain and this was how he repaid her, by bringing her along.

Pinching the bridge of her nose, she twisted around and pulled the pub door open again. She couldn't think straight. She hadn't wanted to believe that he was cheating on her. She'd made excuse after excuse for him in her head, trying to make sense of everything, and now she had no more excuses left.

She walked back towards her car, picking up her pace as she got closer. She needed to get as far away from him as possible. She pulled her key fob from her jeans pocket and pointed it at her car, her finger slipping as she tried to unlock it.

'Sally?'

At the sound of his voice, she spun around and watched as Andy walked towards her.

'I got you an orange juice.' He paused. 'Are you leaving?'

Sally looked down at her car keys. 'Yes.'

'Why? I thought we'd agreed to meet.' He frowned.

Sally watched as her keys slipped through her fingers. He didn't have a clue, did he? He didn't realise that she knew what he'd done, what he was trying to do to Wagging Tails. But he must know she would have seen he was sitting with that woman. Bending, she picked up her keys, this time succeeding in clicking the car doors unlocked.

'What's happened? Why are you going?'

She looked at him as confusion swept across his face. She'd have to say something.

'I know what you're up to. I know you're working with Lyle to try to shut down Wagging Tails.'

'You know? Wait, no—'

She didn't give him time to explain, time to think up a feeble excuse as to why he was doing what he was. There was no point. It would all be lies. He'd been lying to her since that first time she'd run into him at Harold's. She saw that now. She pulled open the car door and slipped inside.

After starting the car, she drove slowly out of the car park, trying to focus on the road in front of her rather than the sight of him in her rear-view mirror, standing there watching her leave. She shouldn't have listened to Flora. She shouldn't have tried to give him a chance to explain.

Shaking her head, she turned onto the main road and accelerated. No, it wasn't Flora's fault. She'd probably have agreed to meet him, anyway. And if he hadn't been sitting with another woman, she would have likely listened to his feeble explanation. Not that it would have changed anything, but it might have given her some form of closure. It might have made her realise he truly wasn't the man she thought she'd known. That he had changed.

She drove straight through West Par, past the turning to her little street. She didn't want to go home. The last thing she needed now was to spend the evening sitting alone. No, she'd go to Wagging Tails. Flora would probably be back from the vet's and might be about for a chat. If not, then at least she'd have the company of the dogs to distract her mind.

Pulling into the car park, she realised that the van wasn't there. Flora must still be at the vet's with Annie. She gripped the steering wheel tighter as she backed into a space. Hopefully, that was a good sign rather than a bad one.

Sally stepped out of the car and crossed the courtyard, trying to focus on putting one step in front of the other rather than the thoughts whirring in her mind. Before she'd even reached the door, she could hear a dog whining.

Who was that? Cindy would be over at the cottage for the night and, even though Flora was out, Poppy would be home, so it couldn't be Cindy.

She unlocked the door and stepped inside. Now she could hear them properly, she realised it was Bonnie – her unmistakable cry as she called for her previous owner, Jerry.

'Hey, Bonnie, it's okay.' After letting herself into Bonnie's kennel, she lowered herself down onto the duvet and patted her knee. 'Come on, come over here.'

Bonnie walked across to her before lowering herself down, her head dropping to Sally's knee.

'That's it. You settle here.' Leaning her head against the concrete wall, Sally wiped her eyes with her sleeve. 'I think we're both missing somebody tonight.'

She closed her eyes. Were she and Andy really over? Was this really it? Even seven years ago when she'd finished the relationship, there had always been that tug in the back of her mind, that feeling that they were meant to be together.

Huh, she'd got that wrong. So wrong. She felt as though she didn't even know him any more. No, that wasn't right. She *knew* she didn't know him any more. It wasn't a feeling. It was fact.

She looked down at Bonnie. 'How can someone we love and trust so much betray us?'

Bonnie looked up at her, a deep sadness in her dark eyes.

'Oh, I'm sorry, Bonnie. I don't mean Jerry. Jerry loves you so much and it broke his heart to leave you here. No, the person I'm talking about pretended to love me. That's completely different.'

Bonnie shifted her weight on Sally's knee.

'No, Andy lied about everything. He even told me he loved me.' She shook her head. 'Can you imagine that? Why would he have told me that when he was trying to destroy the very place I love and work at?'

Bonnie walked slowly towards the door to her kennel and put her feet on the bars.

'You want to go out?' Sally shrugged and pushed herself to standing. 'That's probably a good idea. I think we both need a distraction, hey?'

Sally opened the kennel and let Bonnie go through to the reception area. 'Let's just get you a lead, and how about a ball? You like playing fetch, don't you?'

At the mention of the 'b' word, Bonnie was at Sally's heels waiting for her ball.

'There you go. This is the one you like, isn't it? The purple tennis ball.'

Stepping back into the dark night, Sally made sure to lock the door behind them before pulling out her mobile and turning the torch app on. She loved this place. It was so peaceful and being as it was set a little way outside the village, the sky was empty of any light pollution, so the stars glistened in the sky in a way she never really noticed elsewhere.

She took a deep breath in. She wasn't sure how she was going to get over Andy's betrayal, but one thing she knew was that she had the Wagging Tails team to support her. Them and the dogs in their care.

'I'm still thinking about him, aren't I?' She rolled her eyes at herself. Coming out here was supposed to be a distraction. She needed to think of something else. 'Come on, let's go into the bottom paddock. At least we won't have the Portakabin staring right at us then.'

'Good girl.' Holding the gate to the paddock open, Sally made sure Bonnie was in before shutting it and unclipping the lead. She picked up the ball and threw it. Her mobile vibrated in her hand. It was Andy ringing her. She shook her head and ended the call. There was nothing he could say. Nothing was going to change her mind about him.

Bonnie pawed at her trainers.

'Oh, sorry, sweetheart. Do you want me to throw it again?' Sally picked up the ball, drew her arm back and threw it through the night air. As she was lowering her arm, her mobile pinged again.

Please. Let me explain. I'm on my way to yours. We need to talk. Andy xxx

Sally looked up at the stars, memories of the evening they'd spent in the nature reserve resurfacing. Focusing her eyes on her mobile again, she began typing a message back before deleting it. It didn't matter. Let him go to her cottage. He'd soon realise she wasn't there, and that she didn't want to speak to him.

31

Bonnie had been a long time fetching that ball. She must have got distracted by something. Holding her mobile up, Sally scanned the paddock, the torchlight illuminating the agility equipment she'd left out from earlier. Where had she gone?

Ahh, the gate into the top paddock had been left open. Bonnie had probably run into there. Pushing herself away from the fence, Sally made her way across the paddock and through the gate.

'Bonnie, bring it back and then I can throw it again.'

Waiting in the open gateway, Sally called her again. 'Bonnie, fetch.'

Still no sign of her. Where had she gone?

Sally walked across to the large log which sat in the middle of the paddock and shone her torch behind it. No sign of Bonnie.

'Bonnie, fetch!' she called a little louder. Thanks to Jerry, Bonnie usually had fantastic recall, so why wasn't she coming back now? Unless she'd ran back through to the bottom paddock.

Retracing her steps, Sally walked the perimeter of the bottom paddock, shining the torch across the agility equipment and making sure to double-check the tunnel. Bonnie definitely wasn't in there. Back at the top paddock, she did the same, walking along the fence and shining the torch into the middle.

'Bonnie?'

Nothing. Sally shook her head. Bonnie couldn't have disappeared. Dogs didn't just disappear into thin air. She lapped the fence again. As she walked past the hulk of the Portakabin, something caught her eye and she shone the torch around. The fence had been broken, the wooden rail along the bottom had splintered in and the wire pulled up.

'Bonnie! Bonnie, come!' Had she gone through the gap? She wasn't anywhere else. 'Come. Bonnie, come!'

Sally tilted her head. Had she heard something?

'Bonnie?'

There it was again. The faintest of a whimper.

'Bonnie, where are you?'

Pulling back the wire to make the gap bigger, Sally kneeled down and crawled through to the field. She swung the torchlight around, a lump forming in her throat. The field beyond was empty, untouched. The Portakabin and the holes dug by the excavator near the paddock were the only scars on the horizon. No other work had been started. Lyle had literally only done it to intimidate Flora and the rest of them. She looked around again. Even the excavator had been removed.

She closed her eyes and swallowed. It wasn't just Lyle, was it? It was Andy too. He'd been responsible for this as well.

She called again, the words barely a whisper. 'Bonnie! Here!'

Holding the torchlight up, she squinted into the horizon. Bonnie could be anywhere. Yes, this field was enclosed, but it had been agricultural land, so the fences wouldn't keep a stray dog out. And even though she was well trained and had good recall, if she'd been chasing a rabbit or a mouse or even just heard a strange noise she wanted to investigate, she might have strayed too far to hear Sally or even to find her way back again.

'Bonnie!' Sally stopped and pivoted on the spot, straining her eyes and her ears.

There it was again. That quiet, muffled whimper. But where was it coming from? She tilted her head; she could still hear her.

Following the sound, she carefully walked around the first hole dug by the excavator until she came to the second one.

Shining the light into it, she peered down. 'Bonnie, are you down there?'

The whimper echoed around the hole, muffled by the earth.

'Oh, Bonnie.'

Kneeling down in the mud, Sally inched forward towards the edge of the hole. Sure enough, Bonnie was there at the bottom of the two-metre drop.

'Oh, sweetheart. Are you hurt?'

The grey Staffie-cross shifted a little in the hole, pawing at the side.

'Okay, you look as though you're all right. Hold on.' Standing up, Sally looked around. She needed to get down there to rescue Bonnie, but she also needed to be able to climb back out. There was nothing about.

The torchlight illuminated the Portakabin. There might be something in there. That or she ran back to Wagging Tails to see if they had some rope or something, but now Bonnie had seen her, the dog's whimpers were growing louder. Besides, Sally couldn't remember ever seeing any rope or anything. Would there be any in the Portakabin?

There was only one way to find out. Trying to block out Bonnie's ever-increasing whimpers, Sally tried the door and rolled her eyes. Of course it would be locked. Glancing around, she located a large rock, picked it up and hit it against the metal handle.

Nothing. She tried again, relieved that the handle seemed to budge under the weight of the rock. Again and again she hit it, the clang of rock against metal drowning out Bonnie's cries. On the fourth go, the handle loosened, and she flung the rock down, pulling the door open.

She looked around the cabin. It seemed a lot smaller inside than it had looked outside. There was a desk, a chair, and not much else. Why had she assumed there'd be a rope? Why would they need a rope in a Portakabin? Especially one that had only really been placed there to annoy and intimidate?

What was she going to do now? Bonnie's whimpers had turned into proper howls now. She knew there was a ladder in the shed back at Wagging Tails, but she wasn't sure where Percy kept the key.

Sally turned around, searching for something, anything, that could help her rescue Bonnie. There was literally nothing. Unless...

She strode across to the desk and picked up the chair. Could she use that? No, the hole probably wouldn't be big enough for the chair, her and Bonnie. Besides, it might hit Bonnie as she dropped it. She was clutching at straws. There was nothing here.

With Bonnie's howls becoming increasingly louder and more desperate, Sally placed her palms on the table, taking deep breath after deep breath. What was she supposed to do?

She'd just have to ring for help and stay with Bonnie until backup arrived. Yes, that could work. It would work. There was no other choice.

Looking up, she froze. The Portakabin wasn't that empty then. There was a folder on the desk. Without thinking, she picked it up and watched as the papers scattered onto the surface. She picked one up. It was a house design, an architect's drawing. She recognised it. It was the same as the one in Andy's kitchen. Exactly the same. She picked another one up and another one. They were all the same.

Bonnie's howls changed pitch, and Sally blinked. It didn't matter. She'd known Andy was involved, anyway. Letting the plans fall back to the desk, she rushed towards the door, pausing as she spotted two thick green fabric tape things hanging from a hook on the door. They could work.

'Shhhh, Bonnie. It's okay. I'm coming down to get you.'

Sitting on the edge of the hole with her legs dangling down, she positioned her phone against a clump of dirt, the light shining onto the tapes as she knotted them together.

She attached one end to the handle of the now shut Portakabin door and lowered herself down into the hole.

'Mind out of the way, Bonnie. I don't want to fall on you.'

As soon as her feet landed on the mud below, Bonnie's howling ceased.

Bringing her into her side, Sally hugged the frightened dog, feeling her legs over. 'Are you okay? You're not hurt, are you?'

Bonnie nudged Sally.

'Okay, so you're not hurt. That's good.' Sally squinted in the dim light. 'Now, how are we going to do this?'

She looked from Bonnie to the tape and back again. She hadn't quite thought this through. Without another person at the top of the hole to pull the dog up, she'd have to hold her under one arm while pulling herself up with the other. Would she be able to do that?

Kneeling down, she hooked her arm around Bonnie and picked her up, holding her for a millisecond before lowering her to the ground again. It wasn't going to work. Why hadn't she thought it through? Lowering herself again, she fussed over Bonnie's ears.

'You're going to have to be a brave girl while I climb out and call for help, okay? I won't be long.'

Bonnie sat down next to her.

'Good girl.'

Standing back up, Sally gripped the tape and began to pull herself up, her trainers flat against the side of the hole as she did so.

Great, she was halfway now. Just a few feet left to go. Moving her hand up, she gripped hold of the fabric tape again, but just as she did so, it shifted and she fell back, the tape landing on top of her.

'Ouch.'

Sitting up, she looked at the green tape in her hands. The knot must have shifted off the door handle. She looked at Bonnie, who was sitting against the dirt wall of the hole.

'Don't worry, Bonnie, I'll just pull myself up.'

Stretching above her head, Sally dug her fingers into the dirt before lifting one of her feet gingerly. As soon as she did, the dirt came away in her fingers. It was no good. She wasn't going to be climbing out, that was for sure. She looked down at Bonnie, whose big dark eyes were looking up at her expectantly, so sure that Sally could rescue her.

Sally wiped her hands down her jeans and bit down on her bottom lip. They were stuck. Well and truly stuck. Why had she left her phone up there? She should have tried to hold on to it as she'd lowered herself down, or just popped it in her pocket and attempted the feat in the dark. Anything but leave it up there.

Sinking to the dirt, Sally gently pulled Bonnie towards her, wrapping her arms around the beautiful dog.

'Don't worry. Flora will be back with Annie from the vet's soon. When we hear them, I'll shout, and they'll come and get us.'

Bonnie settled next to Sally, her muddy paws resting on her legs.

Fussing her behind the ears, Sally nodded. At least Bonnie believed what she was saying. She wasn't so sure she did herself. There were two paddocks between them and Wagging Tails. She wasn't even sure she'd be able to hear Flora drive up, let alone be able to shout loud enough to draw any attention to their plight.

She twisted the bracelet her nan had given her around her wrist. The last few weeks had been full of ups and down, of emotion after emotion. Why had she let herself believe she and Andy would finally get their happy-ever-after? How could she have been so naive? How could she have even let herself imagine that after seven years apart, they could have picked up right where they'd left off?

Leaning her head back against the earth behind her, she closed her eyes. She and Andy were over. She would never be getting her happy-ever-after with him.

Wiping the tears falling across her cheeks, she shuddered. They might well be stuck in here until morning, unless Flora noticed Bonnie was missing from her kennel, but then Mack might keep Annie in for observation. If he did that, she wouldn't need to go into that part of the building and there'd be no chance anyone would realise they were missing until the morning.

She wiped fresh tears from her eyes.

32

'Sally?'

Gently moving Bonnie from her resting place on her knee, Sally jumped up and listened. Had she heard someone?

'Sally?'

'Andy?' Cupping her hands around her mouth, Sally shouted as loud as she could. 'Over here.'

She didn't even care that it was Andy rescuing them, just as long as they got out of this hole.

'Andy, we're down here. Follow the light from my phone.'

Silence.

Rubbing her hands over her face, Sally tilted her head. Had she imagined his voice? Was that what being stuck down here had done to her? Was she so desperate to get out that she'd imagined his voice? She looked down at Bonnie, who was now standing next to her, the ball in her mouth ready to get out too. She hadn't imagined it then.

'Andy?'

A light shone in the hole, illuminating them.

'Andy? Is that you?'

'Yes, what are doing down there?' His voice changed, became muffled as the light swung away. 'One minute.'

Sally waited until his hand appeared over the side of the hole and then his head and chest were also visible. 'Can you lift the dog up to me?'

'Umm…' Sally turned around and hefted Bonnie into her arms. 'Yes, careful though, she's heavy.'

'I'll manage.'

Inching a little further towards them, Andy clasped Bonnie around the middle before shuffling backwards, pulling her free.

Chewing her bottom lip, Sally waited until Andy reappeared, this time holding his outstretched hand towards her. 'Take my hand.'

Doing as he instructed, she gripped hold of his hand, his grasp tightening around hers as he began to pull her up. Pushing her feet against the side of the wall, Sally tried to help as much as she could, and eventually reached the top, pulling herself out. Standing up, she mumbled, 'Thanks.'

'What…? How did you end up down there? When you weren't at yours, I knew you'd be here.' Andy shook his head. 'Not down a hole but at Wagging Tails, I mean.'

She shrugged. What was she supposed to say? She used the sleeve of her jumper to wipe her face, feeling the residue of yet more dirt streaking across her skin.

'Here.' Reaching out, Andy used the bottom of his top to wipe her face.

Sally leaned down and clipped Bonnie's lead to her collar. There was no chance she was going to risk her jumping into a hole again.

'I need to get Bonnie back to her kennel,' she said, and pushing past him, climbed back through the gap in the fence. None of this would have happened if it hadn't been for him and Lyle. She didn't owe him any more than a mumbled thanks.

'Hold on.' Andy's voice was flat.

Pausing, she kept her eyes still fixed ahead of her.

'I can explain. It's not what it seems.'

She could hear him catching up with her, but she didn't need to hear his feeble excuses. She didn't need to hear anything else from him.

'Please, Sally. I didn't know.'

Feeling a surge of heat from the pit of her stomach, she turned to face him.

'It doesn't matter if you knew I worked here or not. It doesn't matter if you didn't realise Wagging Tails was the dogs' home I worked at. You were still prepared to do all you could to get a dogs' home closed down.'

'No, I...'

Sally spun back around, quickening her pace, Bonnie jogging beside her. As they reached the door to Wagging Tails, Sally plunged her hands into her pockets ready to pull out the key. Where was it? Where was the key?

'Okay?'

'No!' She turned around and began to retrace her steps. 'I've lost the key.'

'I'll go. You wait here.'

Sally slumped her shoulders and sank to the steps outside the door. He could go. At least that would give her some peace. Some space. Some time to think. She watched as he hurried back through the courtyard before crossing her arms and ducking her head into the small dark space she'd created.

A brilliant light swung into the courtyard and Sally lifted her head to see the Wagging Tails' van pull to a stop in front of her. Within seconds, Flora had jumped out and was running towards her.

'Sally, what's happened to you?'

Standing up, Sally shrugged. 'There's a gap in the fence and Bonnie managed to get through into one of the holes the developers dug.' She spat the word 'developers'.

'Oh, lovely. Are you okay? You're not hurt, are you?' Cupping Sally by the elbows, Flora looked her up and down.

'No, we're both fine. Andy pulled us out.'

'Andy?' Flora frowned before shaking her head. 'Let's get you both inside.'

'How's Annie?' Sally looked towards the van seeing no sign of her. That couldn't be good news, not with Flora being at the vet's for so long.

'Annie's fine, lovely. Mack says she's just got a bit of a stomach bug. He's given her an anti-sickness injection and she should be fine. I'll get her in now.' Flora hurried back to the van and let Annie out before leading her back towards Sally and Bonnie.

'When you didn't come back, I thought the worst had happened.' Sally waited at the door.

'Ah, no, we were waiting a fair while. Mack had an emergency in.' Flora unlocked the door and stood back to let Sally and Bonnie through first. 'Go on through and have a sit down. I'll pop Annie back in her kennel just in case she's contagious. Although, let's be honest, if she is, they'll all catch it, anyway.'

Sally went through to the kitchen. She unclipped Bonnie's lead and slumping into the chair closest to the door, she watched Bonnie settle down by her feet.

'All done.' Flora closed the kitchen door and walked across to the sink. She ran a tea towel under the tap before passing it to Sally. 'Here, lovely, wipe away some of that mud.'

'Thanks.' Sally scrubbed at her face.

'I'll stick the kettle on and then you can tell me what happened.'

Nodding, Sally folded the tea towel over and laid it on the table just as a knock sounded from the reception area.

'Now, who could that be at this time?' Flora glanced at the clock on the wall and frowned.

'It's probably Andy. I lost my key, and he went to get it.' Sally shrugged, making no move to get up. He could stay out there. She didn't want to see him.

'Ah, I'll go and see.'

'No, I—'

Too late – Flora had already closed the door behind her. Sinking her forehead to the table, Sally relished the coolness penetrating her skin and closed her eyes. She listened as the kitchen door closed again and the kettle was poured.

'Try to get that down you.'

That wasn't Flora's voice.

Bolting upright, Sally opened her eyes. 'Andy.'

'Sorry, Flora said to come through.' He stood awkwardly by the kettle, another mug in his hands.

'Where is she?' Sally glanced towards the kitchen door, half expecting Flora to appear.

'She said to tell you she's gone to check on Annie and then she's going over to the cottage.'

'Oh.'

Clearing his throat, Andy indicated the chair opposite. 'May I?'

Sally nodded. What was the point in saying no? He was here now; besides, he had rescued her and Bonnie.

'I know you know about me being part of the development team.' He lowered his mug carefully onto the table before sitting down.

'I do.'

'I met Lyle when I was with my ex-wife. He was a family friend of hers. We got to know each other and, being as we were both into property development, we always said that one day we'd work on a project together.'

'This is the first time you've worked with him?'

Andy nodded. 'He always came across as the nice guy. You know, the one person who seemed to help everyone out?'

Sally picked up the tea towel and scrubbed at some mud on the back of her hand. 'He doesn't seem the nice guy.'

'No, no, he doesn't.' Andy shifted in his chair, leaning forward a little. 'But to me he was and to everyone I knew he was. It was who I thought he was. I trusted him.'

'So, you went into business with him?'

'Exactly. The agreement was he'd take care of the planning permission, the logistics of it all and I'd plan the site, organise things with the architects. That sort of stuff.'

Sally looked up at him, tea towel still in hand. 'Are you trying to tell me you had no idea what he was doing? The corruption? The intimidation?'

'No, I didn't. Like I said, that wasn't my area of expertise. The first I heard about there being access issues and that he'd been trying to buy out some land a dogs' home was on was the morning of our trip to the caverns.'

Sally bit down on her lip. That was why he'd cut their day together short then. She remembered their conversation about where she worked.

'His partner – well, ex-partner I should say, as she's recently left him – realised what games he was playing and we've been working together to try to find a solution.'

'The woman who came to Flora's party?'

'Sorry?'

'The woman you were in the pub with earlier today, she came to Flora's party and just stood there looking at the Portakabin.'

'Ah, yes, that's right. She said she'd been at the party before I got there. She wanted to find out what had been happening for herself, if Lyle had been as... umm... immoral as we suspected.'

Sally looked across at him, meeting his gaze for the first time that night. Was he telling the truth? Had he really not realised what Lyle had been up to?

'So, what now?'

'Now, I stop working with him. I withdraw my promise of investment.'

'Can you do that? Don't you have a contract?'

Andy swallowed. 'I do, but the contract is only valid if the development goes ahead, and without the correct planning permission, it won't.'

Sally took a sip of her coffee, grateful he'd remembered the two sugars.

'But he has planning permission.'

Andy shook his head. 'Despite what he's told you, the planning permission he's secured is dependent on an access agreement. It's just outline planning permission. I'm assuming Flora hasn't agreed to sell her land to him, so the planning permission will be void.'

'So did he really bribe the planning officer?'

'I'm not sure. He's not admitted to that yet. What he has told me and Megan, his ex-partner, is likely to be very different to what has really happened. We're still trying to break everything down and look into it all. She was the one who told me what Lyle had been up to.'

'Which is why you've been spending time with her?' She twisted her mug in her hands. The last few days were beginning to make sense.

'Exactly.'

'Why didn't you tell me what was happening earlier? When you found out?' Pulling her mug closer, she focused on the warmth of the ceramic against her skin.

Andy swallowed. 'Honestly? Because I'm a coward. I wanted to have a solution before I told you what I was involved in. I was going to tell you when we were at the house yesterday but then Megan called and I had to rush off.'

'I wondered if you were going to.'

Looking at the table, Andy took a deep breath before looking her in the eye. 'You know I would never have done anything to put this place in jeopardy. And I would never ever do anything to hurt you. You know that, don't you?'

Sally sighed and looked across at him. 'For a while I thought you had. I thought that I didn't know you at all.'

Andy looked up and met her eye. 'Exactly. You know I wouldn't then, right?'

She shrugged. She believed him. She believed that he hadn't known what Lyle had been doing. It made more sense that he hadn't than for him to have changed so much.

'I do.'

'I love you, Sally, and I'd never do anything to hurt you.' He stood up and walked around the table towards her. 'And I will fix this. I promise you.'

'Okay.' Standing up, Sally let herself be drawn into a hug. She loved him, she'd always loved him and knowing that he hadn't been involved in Lyle's games and corruptions was all she'd needed to hear. 'I love you too.'

33

Sally laughed as she watched Andy playing with Bonnie in the ocean. She knew what was coming.

'Ha ha, no.' Andy jumped back as Bonnie jumped into the water before shaking herself, a fine spray of seawater quickly covering Andy as he tried, and failed, to jump out of the way.

She lowered herself to the sand and began taking the picnic food out of the wicker basket. She may have forgotten the picnic rug, but at least she'd remembered to grab the basket before she'd left with Bonnie to meet Andy at the cove. For someone who had once avoided West Par and Wagging Tails, he seemed to be making up for the lost time now. He spent almost as much time there as she did now, helping out with the dogs and fixing a few things around the home that Susan or Percy hadn't yet gotten around to doing.

'Have you seen what she's done to me?' Andy called from where he was still standing knee deep in the water, watching Bonnie circle him, her tongue lolling to one side as happy as she could be.

'Oh yes! I saw!' Sally grinned. Of course, she knew why Andy was spending so much time at Wagging Tails. She knew it was because he still felt guilty about his part in the development, but Flora had assured him no end he had nothing to feel guilty about. Still, she had to admit, it was nice to be able to spend so much time with him.

Andy strode up the beach towards her before wiping his face with the bottom of his jumper. 'You saw that coming, didn't you? You knew what she was going to do?'

'Umm... maybe.' Sally laughed. 'But only because she's done the same to me on numerous occasions.'

Andy chuckled and lowered himself to the sand. Leaning across the basket, he kissed her before calling across to Bonnie, who bounded towards them.

'You've got a firm friend in her.' Sally smiled. Whenever Andy was around, Bonnie was beyond excited.

'Aw, I'm glad. I've got a real soft spot for her.' Andy fussed Bonnie behind the ears.

'Don't let Flora hear you say that. She'll be suggesting you adopt her if she hears you.' Sally smiled as she passed him a sandwich.

'Thanks.' Taking the sandwich, Andy's face lit up, the dimple on his left cheek appearing. 'She's already spoken to me about adopting her.'

'Oh, really?' Sally raised her eyebrows. 'You two make the perfect pair. She absolutely dotes on you. What did you say?'

'I said I'd think about it. I need to find somewhere to live first. I don't think Harold would appreciate sharing his flat above his café with both me and Bonnie.'

'Umm, that's true. Aw, it would be perfect, though. If you adopt her, I mean, not her living above the café. Although I'm sure she'd think it was perfect, what with Harold's cooking.' She laughed.

'Ha, she definitely would.' He turned to Bonnie. 'I can't imagine you'd turn down a piece of Harold's crispy bacon, would you?'

'Careful, you'll go giving her ideas.' Sally placed her sandwich down and reached over to fuss the beautiful Staffie-cross.

'I think she might just deserve a slice or two of bacon once in a while.'

'Oh yes, Flora is right, you two are a perfect match. She has you wrapped around her paw already.' Sally laughed as the shrill tring of her mobile disturbed the peace of the cove. Picking it up, she frowned. 'Oh, it's Linda. Sorry, I'd better get it.'

Andy nodded at her and gave her a quick smile.

Sally stood up and walked towards the ocean, holding her mobile to her ear. 'Linda, hi.'

'Sally. Have I caught you at a bad time? Have you got time to talk?'

Sally glanced back at Andy and watched as he gave Bonnie some chicken. 'No, I've got time.'

'Good.'

'Is everything okay with you and the baby? You must be due soon?'

'Not long. A few more weeks. Yes, we're both well. Thank you.'

'That's good news then.' Sally nodded into the silence. 'What is it I can help you with?'

'Oh, I don't need your help. I'm ringing for a chat.' Linda sounded unsure.

'Great.' A chat? They never chatted. Linda only ever rang when she wanted something, and Sally didn't. She didn't ring. She couldn't remember when the last time had been that they'd chatted. Even when they'd worked together, they'd spoken about the business but not anything else, not any everyday chatting.

Linda sighed down the phone. 'I've rung to apologise. I shouldn't have expected you to give everything up to come and help with the firm. You'd made it clear law wasn't your chosen career and I should have respected that.'

Sally opened and closed her mouth. Had Linda ever apologised to her before? She certainly couldn't remember when if she had.

'And I know Dad has told you he's stepping back in whilst I'm on maternity leave, so you needn't worry about that.'

'Yes, he had told me.' Sally dipped the toe of her trainer into the water. She didn't want to hear the answer to the question she felt she had to ask. She took a deep breath. She knew she had to ask. She knew she needed to know whether she still had to feel guilty or not. 'What if you go part-time? Do you know what will happen then?'

'Yes, yes. Do you remember Rachel?'

'Rachel?' She closed her eyes, trying to picture the people who worked at the firm. 'I think so. Did she always wear her hair in a bob and set of pearls round her neck?'

'Yes, she's the one. She's asked to go part-time to look after her grand-kids. She's going to wait until I get back off maternity leave and then we'll job-share.' Linda laughed, a strange strangled noise. 'I never once imagined I'd ever utter those words, "job-share", when it came to my own career, but I trust her. Mum and Dad trust her too.'

'Wow, that's perfect then.' Sally grinned as the tugging doubt of guilt vanished.

'It pretty much is.'

Sally cleared her throat. She knew it was her turn to apologise now. 'I'm sorry I spoke to you the way I did at Mum and Dad's. I shouldn't have.'

'Ha, I deserved it. I should never have expected you to give up everything you've worked for down there. You'd never ask me to, and I shouldn't have you. You were right. This is what I wanted, what I've worked my whole career towards, running the family firm. You didn't, and that was your choice.'

'Thank you.'

'Anyway, I'd better dash. You'll come back to London to meet your nephew when he arrives, won't you?'

'My nephew? You found out you're having a boy?' Sally grinned.

'Yes. We found out.'

'Aw, I'm so excited for you. I'm so excited to be an auntie.' Sally glanced towards Andy and Bonnie. Bonnie was now lying on her back, enjoying belly rubs. 'Look, while you're on maternity leave, why don't you, Pearce and my new nephew come down for a holiday?'

'To West Par?'

Sally raised her eyebrows. She hadn't even realised Linda knew where she lived. Of course, Sally had told her, but she just never thought Linda had taken much notice. 'Yes, to West Par.'

'Okay. why not?' Linda's voice became muffled as she spoke to someone at her end before returning her attention to Sally. 'Sorry, must dash.'

'Bye.' Sally ended the call and slipped her phone in her pocket. Things were working out for the both of them.

EPILOGUE

TWO MONTHS LATER

'Andy, hi. I didn't know you were coming here?' Sally looked down at her mud-stained jeans and grimaced.

Closing the door to Wagging Tails behind him, Andy chuckled. 'I wanted to surprise you.'

'Well, you certainly did that.' Sally laughed as she wiped her hands down her jeans, adding even more mud to the engrained dirt before swiping her hair out of her eyes.

'You've just got a little bit...' Stepping forward, Andy wiped her forehead with his thumb.

'Ha ha, I think I'm a lost cause, to be honest. I slipped while trying to retrieve Bonnie's ball.'

'I thought the dog was supposed to do the retrieving?' Andy grinned.

'Yes, well, apparently it was too muddy for her.' Sally looked down at Bonnie who was sitting panting at her feet, the rescued ball in her mouth.

'Oh, is this your fault, Bonnie?' Bending down, Andy patted his knees as Bonnie ran towards him, placing her paws on his jeans, the ball now forgotten on the floor.

'Ah, afternoon, Andy. I thought I heard your voice.' Flora walked through from the kitchen and nodded towards Bonnie. 'You really do have a friend for life in that one.'

'I hope so. You certainly are a gorgeous pup, aren't you, Bonnie?' Andy fussed her behind the ears before standing up. The grey Staffie-cross stood on her hind legs, resting her paws against his legs still eager for attention.

'Right, what are you two waiting for then?' Flora looked from Sally to Andy.

'What do you mean?' Sally stooped and picked up the now abandoned ball.

'Go on, tell her.' Stepping forward, Flora rubbed Andy's forearm.

'You've got the afternoon off work and I have a surprise for you.' Andy smiled, a slight pink hue flushing across his face.

'A surprise?' Sally tilted her head.

'That's right. Happy three-month anniversary!' Stepping forward, Andy pecked her on the cheek.

'Oh, it is, isn't it? I can't believe it's been a whole three months since we ran into each other at Harold's Café.' Sally clasped her hands over her cheeks. 'You haven't got me something, have you? I didn't think... I'm so sorry!'

'Ha, don't be. It's you who deserves to be treated today.' Andy leaned down and fussed Bonnie as she pawed at him again. 'And you, of course.'

'Are you sure I can have the afternoon off, Flora?' Sally looked across at her.

'Of course I am. You two lovelies go and enjoy yourselves.' Flora smiled before indicating Bonnie. 'Andy, have you had any more thoughts about my suggestion?'

'About adopting Bonnie?' Andy grinned as he stood up. 'I have, yes. I'd love to. She can come to work with me every day and we can keep each other company.'

'Oh good, I'm glad. You two, three, are a fantastic fit for each other.' Flora smiled. 'Ever since you rescued her from that darn hole, she's been besotted with you.'

'And I've been besotted with you too, haven't I, Bonnie?' Andy glanced down at her. 'In fact, can we take her with us today?'

'Of course you can. Now off with the three of you and have a lovely afternoon.' Flora held the door open for them and they stepped out into the courtyard.

'What plans have you made for this afternoon?' Sally asked as she slipped her hand into Andy's.

'Ah, now that would be telling.' Pausing beside his car, he looked at her and brought his hand to the back of her neck, gently inching her towards him until their lips met. 'I'm hoping you'll like it though.'

* * *

'Can't you just tell me where we're going?' Sally turned in the passenger seat to look at Andy.

'Nope.' He glanced at her before flicking the indicator on. 'Although, I think you might just guess in a moment.'

Sally scrunched up her nose and looked back out of the window. They were in Trestow and going somewhere special – somewhere, according to Andy, they'd been before.

Ha, she knew! It was their three-month anniversary, and they were heading into Trestow. The perfect place to celebrate would be where they'd run into each other.

'I know!'

'You do?' Andy raised his eyebrows as he slowed to a stop at a red light.

'Yep, you're taking me to Harold's Café. You've arranged for an anniversary lunch there or something.'

'Because we met there? This time around, I mean?' Andy nodded slowly. 'Now, that would have been a sweet idea, but—'

'We're not going to Harold's.'

'Nope.' Andy chuckled and touched her forearm gently. 'Close your eyes and all will be revealed.'

'Seriously?' Sally closed her eyes, keeping her left eye ever so slightly open.

'And put your hands over them. I know what you're like, remember?'

'Okay, okay.' Laughing, Sally did as she was asked and cupped her hands over her eyes, resisting the urge to ask if they were there yet.

'It's just down here.'

She felt the car turn to the left before slowing down and stopping. 'Can I open them now?'

'Ha ha, yes. We're here.'

Hearing the quiet whir as the engine shut off, Sally moved her hands and opened her eyes. Looking up the street, she frowned. She did recognise it.

'Look.' Taking Sally's hand, Andy nodded towards the passenger window.

Sally smiled as she realised where they were. They were at the house. The house that Andy had fallen in love with. The house they'd both fallen in love with. The house where he'd told her he still loved her.

'Have you bought it?'

Grinning, Andy nodded. 'The deeds were exchanged this morning.'

'So, you'll be hanging around to restore it, then?'

This is what she'd wanted, to give them a real chance to establish their newly rekindled relationship before he'd have to move on to the next project.

Andy pulled a face and shrugged his shoulders. 'I didn't buy it to sell on.'

'You're staying? You're moving here?' Turning, she cupped his face in her hands and kissed him. He was staying!

Pulling slightly away, he took her hands in his and looked into her eyes. 'I had rather hoped we could live here together. Not immediately, but after a while, I mean.'

'Well, I guess it does need a lot of work.' She shook her head and looked back out of the passenger side window. They could live here. Together.

'So, what do you say?'

Twisting in her seat to face him again, Sally beamed. 'Do you really need to ask?'

WELLINGBOROUGH DOG WELFARE (WELLIDOGS)

I'd like to take this opportunity to give a huge shout-out to Wellidogs, a no-kill shelter based in Grendon, Northamptonshire. The dedicated team rescue dogs from the pound and those abandoned or handed in to them. They work tirelessly to provide the gorgeous dogs in their care a safe home, full bellies and, above all, love and kindness.

At Wellidogs, dogs are given a second chance. They are shown patience, training and affection. The wonderful dogs are assessed, trained and given the opportunity to find their forever home, the home they deserve.

As with Ralph at Wagging Tails, they have resident dogs who, for various reasons, have made their home at Wellidogs. These beautiful dogs will spend the rest of their days secure in the knowledge they will forever be loved and cared for at Wellidogs.

Please, if you are considering rehoming a dog, then check out the deserving dogs at Wellidogs, waiting hopefully to be welcomed into a home just like yours. https://wellidog.org/

As a local charity they rely on the generosity of their supporters and the general public to continue rescuing and rehoming the dogs so if you can support them by liking their Facebook page, joining their group, or liking and sharing their posts, or donating, I know they'd be ever so grateful. Facebook page: https://www.facebook.com/wellidogs

Facebook group: https://www.facebook.com/groups/wellingborough dogwelfare

ACKNOWLEDGEMENTS

Thank you, readers, so much for reading *A Fresh Start at Wagging Tails Dogs' Home*. I hope you've enjoyed returning to West Par and the Wagging Tails family as well as catching up with Sally as her ex, Andy, reappears in her life. I know I have enjoyed writing about the wonderful dogs at Wagging Tails as well as Flora and the rest of the team.

A huge thank you to my wonderful children, Ciara and Leon, who motivate me to keep writing and working towards 'changing our stars' each and every day. Also thank you to my lovely family for always being there, through the good times and the trickier ones.

I'd like to thank Vicki and Lynn at Wellidogs (Wellingborough Dog Welfare – www.wellidog.org) for welcoming me into the home to meet the wonderful dogs they have at Wellidogs and for letting me volunteer. Thank you to Jasmine, Aidan, Amy and Ash for giving me more of an insight to volunteering at a dogs' home.

I'd also like to take this opportunity to say a huge thank you to each and every person who works or volunteers at a dogs' home or rescue centre. Thank you for caring for the dogs in your care, and for relentlessly fighting for their future and happiness. You are wonderful beyond words.

And a massive thank you to my amazing editor, Emily Yau, who reached out and believed in me – thank you. Thank you also to Sandra Ferguson for copy editing, and Shirley Khan for proofreading. And, of course, Clare Stacey for creating the beautiful cover. Thank you to all at Team Boldwood!

ABOUT THE AUTHOR

Sarah Hope is the author of many successful romance novels, including the bestselling Cornish Bakery series. She lives in Central England with her two children and an array of pets, and enjoys escaping to the seaside at any opportunity.

Sign up to Sarah Hope's mailing list for news, competitions and updates on future books.

Follow Sarah on social media here:

- facebook.com/HappinessHopeDreams
- x.com/sarahhope35
- instagram.com/sarah_hope_writes
- bookbub.com/authors/sarah-hope

ALSO BY SARAH HOPE

The Wagging Tails Dogs' Home Series

The Wagging Tails Dogs' Home

Chasing Dreams at Wagging Tails Dogs' Home

A Fresh Start at Wagging Tails Dogs' Home

Escape to... Series

The Seaside Ice-Cream Parlour

The Little Beach Café

Christmas at Corner Cottage

Milton Keynes UK
Ingram Content Group UK Ltd.
UKHW041128100324
439161UK00002B/8

9 781805 490692